RECIPE FOR A NATION
by
James Vasey

RECIPE FOR A NATION
Take One Chef,
Add A Winemaker
& Stir Gently

Book 3
in the
Seborga Series
by
James Vasey

RECIPE FOR A NATION
Take One Chef, Add A Winemaker & Stir Gently
© James Vasey 2021
All rights reserved

Softcover ISBN: 9798501506312
Hardcover ISBN: 9798515344856

The image on the cover was hand-crafted
by Mike Brough of Fresh Creative.

The line drawings contained in this book
are reproduced with the kind permission of the
artist Linda McCluskey
but remain her copyright material.
http://lindamccluskey.com

The author acknowledges the trademarks of the
Slow Food Organization, Carrefour, Michelin, and Fiat.

The characters in this work of fiction are invented
and any resemblance to anyone living or dead
is purely coincidental

*Like many hilltop village communities in Italy,
Seborga is at a fork in the road created
by the challenges of globalisation.
The route taken forward will depend on
the ability of its citizens and leaders to envisage
a bold new reality and make it happen. ~James Vasey*

Table of Contents

1. CAPRA ARROSTO 1
2. BISCOTTI QUARESIMALI 13
3. SARDENARA 19
4. PANSOTTI CON SALSA NOCCI 31
5. FRISCEU DI BACCALA... 41
6. ARANCINI AL RAGU 49
7. OYSTERS AT BENTLEY'S 65
8. CACCIATORE 69
9. PANINO CON VERDURE ARROSTA 79
10. BAGNA CÀUDA.. 83
11. CARDI ARROSTA.. 91
12. LINGUINE AL RAGU DI COZZE 101
13. SCIUMETTE.. 107
14. SARDE A BECCAFICO 113
15. BASTONICI DI POLENTA 119
16. GENOESE RAVIOLI 129
17. PICAGGE VERDI 137
18. TAGLIOLINI CON TALEGGIO & TARTUFO 145
19. TORTA DE CARCIOFI 157
20. PORCINI 165
21. RAVIORE... 171
22. RAVIOLI DI CARCIOFI 175
23. AZZIMINU 183

24. TOAST DI FICHE E RICOTTA..193
25. TORTA PASQUALINA 203
26. PINTXOS GILDA 209
27. AGNELLO AL PESTO DI FAVA...217
28. TURLE...225
29. FARINATA 239
30. CAVAGNETTI..245
31. LOUP DE MER A LA MENTON...251
32. PORCHETTA...259
33. FOCACCIA..271
RECIPES FOR DISHES FEATURED IN THIS BOOK.........................291

**An old Ape, like Vincenzo's,
at the annual Vallebona Ape & Flower Festival.**
Drawing by Linda McCluskey

1. CAPRA ARROSTO

Rare on this Earth are places where one can witness such extremes from a single vantage point. Opulence usually likes to keep a safe distance from impoverishment. Beaches and snow-capped peaks are seldom comfortable bedfellows. Domestication is tetchy with wild nature. And yet, from Seborga it is possible to watch a farmer toil all day to harvest olives worth less than a tip given to a valet parker a couple of dozen miles away in Monaco. Pampered pooches sit on their own chairs at restaurant tables, while wild boar that could fell a man forage in forests nearby. Although contradictory and irreconcilable, here it is—a ninth-century anomaly, persevering against all odds into the twenty-first century. Perhaps Seborga is the yin that gives yang a point of reference?

Seborga teeters precariously upon a mountain top, where ancient stone buildings cling to the terrain like swallows' nests. Rather than battle against nature, homes absorb the rocky terrain. They hug the topography of the mountain like children hugging the mother that nourishes them.

Houses appear stacked upon one another with their staggered roof lines. A labyrinth of ancient alleyways snakes by houses on various levels, each home uniquely fitted with windows of oak and doors of chestnut to fit the architecture of the terrain. Buildings of rough stone are rendered and painted from a palette of autumn leaves.

The concept of town planning is as foreign to the Italians as American fast food. Like their cuisine, homes are shaped by their locations, using only materials readily to hand. Any perceived aesthetic value which emerges from this chaos is nothing more than a fortunate accident. The result is breath-taking, with its natural beauty born of simple function.

In legends of the past, told within these homes, the Holy Grail travelled the road up the mountain from the coast to Seborga. Known to Italians as the Sacro Cantino, the treasured holy relic was believed to have first made this journey on horseback under the protection of the Knights Templar almost a millennium ago.

These crusading knights made Seborga their southernmost base in Europe for most of the Holy Wars. They sailed from this coastline in ships bound for Palestine. After two hundred years of fighting all the Europeans had returned, bringing with them relics recovered from the holy sites, including the Sacro Cantino. In the centuries that followed, the legendary chalice was lost to the imagination until it finally found its way back to Genoa.

Nearly one thousand years later, and now more widely known as the Holy Grail, it made its way up the mountain road to Seborga once again. In the place of horses and knights, this homecoming involved a bank security van guarded by Italian soldiers. The van, the type employed for collecting cash from supermarkets, was escorted by soldiers of Italy's crack Alpini-troops in armoured personnel carriers, with automatic weapons at the ready.

Anxiously awaiting its arrival in Seborga was an elite group, including a cardinal, a bishop, members of parliament for both Imperia and Genoa, government ministers of both culture and tourism, the Prime Minister of Italy, the Mayor of Bordighera, Princess Alessandra of Seborga, and her English husband, Ben. Looking on were representatives of most of the world's media.

"Quite a reception for an old bowl," Ben joked to no one in particular.

Alessandra said nothing in response to Ben's flippant remark about the Sacro Cantina, but reached down and squeezed his hand—a gesture of affection and reassurance, knowing that he was as nervous as she was, and that joking was his way of dealing with it. She could still hardly believe that this was finally happening. For as long as she could remember, stories had circulated amongst the villagers about the Templars having brought the Holy Grail here to Seborga. Princess Alessandra would be fulfilling her ancestors' dreams in seeing it return.

Most historians acknowledged that the holy warrior knights were based in Seborga, so it seemed logical that this was where they would bring their most treasured relics from the Holy Land, she rationalised. And yet, these strange tales were always told in hushed tones by the villagers. It was as if the mere mention of the Holy Grail out loud might risk the wrath of God. No other single relic of the world's largest religion is held in such awe. No icon has inspired so many rumours, wild speculation and such fantastic conspiracy theories.

Quite how an agnostic Englishman, with a less than unblemished personal reputation, had persuaded the Vatican to allow this to happen, still left many locals baffled. And yet, here it was—the Sacro Cantina, which most Italians and many others of faith believe to be the Holy Grail—being carried, very carefully, from a black van parked in Seborga's piazza Martiri Patrioti. Overlooking this scene was the near-window-less church of San Bernado, which was built around the time of the Templars.

"Had these weathered stones of this ancient church already witnessed a scene similar to this one around the time of King Richard I of England?" one American TV presenter proposed to his viewers back home.

At first sight of the Perspex crate holding the distinctive green glass chalice, a joyful cheer went up among the crowd. Hundreds of villagers and thousands of outside visitors had turned up on this bright autumn day to witness the historic event. The Grail's arrival was being recorded by at least one film crew from almost every Catholic country in the world. There were three competing

TV stations from Brazil, two from Mexico, and four from the United States.

Only the Spanish media was conspicuous by their absence, the Spanish having their own Chalice of Dona Urraca. Their glitzier jewel-encrusted vessel, perhaps more in keeping with the popular perception of the Holy Grail, is kept in the Basilica of San Isidoro in León. However, claims that the Spanish chalice was the real Holy Grail have been met with scepticism by historians and scientists. Yet, these doubts has not stopped thousands of pilgrims flocking to see it. Ben and Alex had hoped that the arrival of far-better-provenanced Sacro Cantina would bring even greater tourism to Seborga and place it firmly on the tourist map. If today was a taster of things to come, it seemed to be working.

Five years prior, Ben had been sent to Seborga by his UK university employer on the pretext of a research sabbatical. In reality, his dean had wanted him out of the way while they investigated potentially damaging allegations against Ben. By the time the investigation established his innocence, the Englishman had fallen for the Princess Alessandra and she for him, but only after a fractious courtship.

A few months after arriving in Seborga, Ben inadvertently stumbled upon a cave that a recent landslide had uncovered. On the rock walls were paintings that appeared to depict scenes from the Holy Wars, suggesting it had been used as a shelter and hiding place nearly a thousand years earlier. Inside, he discovered an ancient charter apparently issued by Pope Gregory in 1079. It was later claimed that this legal document granted Seborga its independence under the Knights Templar rule. Under its terms, the principality was also allowed to choose a prince from amongst its ranks.

The Templars ruled Seborga for over two hundred years, using it as a staging post as their knights travelled to and from the Middle East fighting the Holy Wars. From the Christian perspective, these military campaigns were all about protecting the region's holy sites and the relics they contained from Muslim forces.

A church and a monastery were established in Seborga. Nearby, a hospital was built to treat and convalesce the returning wounded, which became great in number as the course of the war went against them. Despite their considerable wealth, power and influence across Europe, the Knights Templar failed to win a decisive victory in the Holy Wars. When a strategic withdrawal from Palestine became inevitable, it was probably to this very place, close to the Pope who had called for the conflict, that the Templars brought any treasures recovered from holy sites.

With Jerusalem lost to the forces of Islam, the usefulness of the Knights was brought into question. This, coupled with their rising power and popularity amongst the people of Europe, made them a potential threat to both heads of state and even the Pope himself. These incumbent powers conspired against the Knights. False accusations led to their being excommunicated from the Church and warrants being issued for their arrest in France, from where many of the Knights originated. Seborga was abandoned to its fate and the Knights melted away across Europe, their treasures disappearing with them.

Based on this history, the people of Seborga have tried several times to re-establish their independence from Italy and be recognised as a sovereign state once again. However, a copy of Pope Gregory's original document granting independence, which would back up their claims, could never be found. Until Ben's accidental discovery of the charter, the church in Rome had consistently denied all knowledge of its existence, despite knowing that they had a copy safely secreted in their archives. It had simply not been politically expedient for the church to take the side of tiny Seborga in its claimed independence from Italy. The discovery of this long-lost evidence left the current Pope embarrassed over yet another apparent cover-up at the Vatican.

The eleventh-century cathedral in Genoa, where the chalice had rested for nearly seven hundred years, was badly in need of repairs. Its trustees had been trying for years to raise the three million euros needed to renew its leaking roof. Economic hard times in Italy made fundraising difficult. By having the project cost recategorised as tourism development, Italy's new Prime Minister, Andrea Cassini, had cleverly squeezed most of the money for the roof out of the European Union (EU).

Ben had then pointed out that removing the roof for these major works would make the Holy Grail highly vulnerable. He reminded the church of what had happened during the recent renovation at Notre-Dame in Paris, when it nearly burnt to the ground. This valid concern, along with some regret over his predecessors' cover-up, was the final leverage in convincing the Pope to sanction the Sacro Cantina's temporary relocation to Seborga. The village-state had been transformed from a rural backwater on the brink of extinction as a community into a thriving model for sustainable tourism in less than five roller-coaster years. This remarkable metamorphosis was almost totally down to the efforts of Ben and Alessandra.

Princess Alessandra of Seborga did not live in a palace, ride in a chauffeur-driven limousine or have many of the trappings of royalty. With the principality's status still unrecognised, the royal line had no wealth or revenues. Unlike some royal families, however, the princess did enjoy the wholehearted support of nearly one hundred percent of the three-hundred-plus citizens. The problem was that in a community so small, most of whom were still scratching a living from the land, no taxes could be raised to fund jewels or other finery associated with being a royal princess. Alessandra inherited all of the responsibility of a head of state with none of the trappings that usually accompanied it.

So, as soon as she was old enough, Alessandra did what most

of her teenage contemporaries were doing at that time. She left Seborga, seeking a more exciting future with better prospects overseas. In the princess's case, this meant going to live with relatives in the United States. Once there, she dropped her worthless royal title, learned to cook, and eventually earned a different kind of accolade: that of a Michelin Star chef. Claudio, her later-widowed elderly father, was left to rule Seborga alone.

By the time Alessandra returned twenty-plus years later, to care for the ageing prince, things in Seborga had deteriorated even further. There were so few young children living there that the school had closed. Former homes of deceased elderly residents remained empty and unsold, with many falling apart. Much of the agricultural land had been abandoned and was returning to nature. Brambles and weeds were strangling once productive olive trees. The village was in danger of going the way of other small mountain communities in rural Italy, and being completely abandoned in favour of city or coastal living.

The economics of artisan olive growing on slopes too steep and narrow for machines no longer made financial sense. Too much cheap olive oil was available from Turkey and Greece and other big mono-culture producers, and the villagers didn't have the marketing know-how to justify their higher costs. There was a much easier, better living for farmers to be had tending trees and shrubs in the manicured gardens of the wealthy down on the Riviera.

With the recent revival of the fortunes of Seborga, a few of these exiled residents were returning. Not yet a flood, but certainly a trickle. Perhaps more significant, younger would-be farmers were joining them. Some of these were well-educated professionals who had grown disillusioned with modern corporate life, or people who just wanted to get away from the pollution and stress of city living. In some cases, they kept their high-paying jobs but worked from a laptop in Seborga with only the occasional visit to an office or meeting. Others made the full commitment to trying to live off the land.

Attracted by low property prices, clean air, a lack of crime, and a lower cost of living, the village's empty houses were being reoccupied and restored. This inward investment of youthful vitality was beginning to revive the community. There were now sufficient parents of young children to lobby for the school to be reopened. The post office and the village store were thriving.

The chalice was safely installed in its temporary home and the Alpini troops had taken up the guard duties, which they would continue to perform for the remainder of its time in Seborga. The platoon of the elite soldiers would be barracked in the village and run round-the-clock security patrols. This was something that the prime minister had offered in order to persuade the Pope to agree to the chalice's loan.

Ben and Alessandra were relieved to have the burden of responsibility for the chalice's security taken from them. The presence of the Alpini in their traditional uniforms with the distinctive feathers in their alpine hats added to the prestige of the principality. When off-duty, they were also twenty more customers for the restaurants and bars.

In the kitchen of the village's new cookery school, preparations were almost complete for the feast that would now be served to their VIP guests. Renata, also new to the village, had cooked for movie actors, musicians, sports stars and politicians in Alessandra's New York restaurant. But this lapsed Catholic, child of a devout Mexican family, had never before fed a cardinal and a bishop.

"I suppose Devils on Horseback will not be going on the menu?" she had quipped to Alessandra when she had seen the reverential guest list.

"In celebration of the arrival of the chalice, we are going to steal an idea from my recent nemesis, Francois de Payen, and serve a twenty-first century reinterpretation of the Last Supper."

Renata looked both slightly perturbed and intrigued by the idea of recreating Christ's last meal.

"Is that even legal in Italy?" she asked, only half-joking.

"That's your challenge," offered Alessandra, knowing full well that Renata would not balk from it. She only hoped that she would invite her son, Cristiano, to contribute some of his ideas to the menu. Cristiano was already an incredibly talented sous-chef, Renata was now his mentor in hopefully achieving even greater things. Like all young people, he was impatient for success, but he also recognised the American's superior experience and skill. He knew that under her tutelage, he could rise to the very top.

The final menu for the Banquet of the Holy Grail was an inspired fusion of Middle Eastern and Ligurian cuisine which read.

Primi-mixed Meze

- Garlic baba ganoush with sesame crackers
- Beetroot falafel with whipped minted yoghurt
- Saltfish beignets with tomato, olive and ginger salsa Contorni
- Whole roasted goat 'Porchetta' style-stuffed with wild fennel, apricots and cracked wheat, served with a cauliflower and broccoli Fattoush salad

Dolce
- Warm poached stuffed figs with pistachio, honey sorbet and golden tuille
- Coffee with Baklava, halva and dates

"Bravo," exclaimed Alessandra. "The ingredients of the Bible with the methods of the moment."

With everything looking well in hand for the celebration feast,

Alessandra returned to her Osteria.

"Alcuni dicono che sia maledetto, Principessa." (Some say it's cursed, Princess.) Alessandra stopped at hearing the old lady's announcement. She sat on her doorstep, nipping the heads of dead flowers in pots on either side of it. Viola, Seborga's oldest resident, spent most of her waking day sitting on this same step. Here she held court, chatting to neighbours and interrogating strangers as to their business there. Nothing passed her by or escaped her attention. There was no snippet of information too small for her to absorb. She knew who had received letters, and often even who had sent them. Most parcels were left at her door because it was easier for the delivery drivers, and she invited them to do so. Also, because Viola was always in when others were out at work.

"Why would it be cursed, Viola?" the princess questioned the white-haired, chestnut-brown-skinned, stooped old woman, who was suffering from obvious curvature of the spine.

"They say that the Arabs in Palestine cursed it, foretelling that it would bring heavens crashing down on the infidels who took it from them. Certainly, several boats containing the returning Knights Templar were sunk in storms on their way back from the Holy Land. When they got back to Seborga, their fortunes changed dramatically for the worse. They say that the Templars were glad to finally get rid of it."

Alessandra was fond of Viola, as were all the village. She was one constant in a community that had seen much social change. She watched over the children playing in the piazza, acted as referee in their disputes, administered sticking plasters to grazed knees and issued small sweets to those with tearful eyes. No one could imagine life in Seborga without her, although they knew they would have to before too many years passed. However, Alessandra also knew that Viola had another, more personal reason, for perpetuating the myth of the grail being cursed.

Not wishing to contradict or undermine her kindly elderly neighbour's assertion, Alessandra tried to gently sidestep it. "The Templars were a long time ago, Viola. The Sacro Cantina has been safely in the Cathedral in Genoa for hundreds of years without any signs of a curse. I don't think we need to worry too much."

Viola shrugged her shoulders and turned to go inside, leaving Alessandra with a parting remark, "Ride bene chi ride ultimo."

'The biggest laughs come from those who laugh last,' was an uncharacteristically gloomy warning from someone usually so upbeat and so it stayed with Alessandra, lingering like a tiny but persistent cloud in an otherwise flawless blue sky.

2. BISCOTTI QUARESIMALI

At five hundred metres above sea level and miles from any major conurbation, the air was both clear and clean in Seborga. After years of working in London and then Newcastle, just breathing it in seemed both medicinal and therapeutic to Ben. Now that most people had gone home, the loudest noise was the croaking of frogs, of which there were hundreds in the undergrowth around the village. After five years this noise had become the familiar background to evenings in the piazza, pierced only by occasional voices, the chinking of glasses or the clatter of plates at the Osteria.

The banquet had been an outstanding success. Alessandra thought that everyone's high spirits were a mixture of elation at pulling off such a coup, and sheer relief that the chalice had been transported safely from Genoa and stored away without any hiccups. She certainly felt the sense of one weight being lifted from a shoulder, but a similar burden was still resting on the other. Despite the formidable presence of the Alpini troops, Alessandra still felt that she and Ben were now responsible for the safety of one of the world's most important Christian relics.

Long before midnight, most of the guests had departed or retired to their hotel rooms down on the coast. The proud villagers, full of roast goat and Rossese wine, were in their beds dreaming of the crowds of visitors that would soon be bringing euros to the tills of their businesses. A few staff and some new students were cleaning tables and wiping down catering equipment that needed returning to the kitchens. Some were smoking much-needed cigarettes as they worked; a concession Renata would never have allowed in New York, Alessandra thought. She was already having to make cultural adjustments.

Earlier, Ben had witnessed the prime minister standing down his bodyguards to enjoy a private stroll home with Selene in the safe streets of Seborga. They did not follow the couple, but neither did they leave the piazza. Instead, they positioned themselves at the entrance to the street down which their boss had disappeared, and kept scanning the now almost-empty village for imaginary assassins, terrorists, or worse, Italian Paparazzi.

Cristiano had brought an ice-frosted bottle of homemade limoncello so he could share a digestivo with Ben and his mother. He also carried a small plate with three orange biscuits.

"Quaresimali, how wonderful," his mother guessed correctly. "You know, these were originally made by nuns to be eaten at Lent," she explained to Ben.

"I have practiced making them, and think finally I've got it right. Blood orange and almond," Cristiano expanded.

The three sat on a wall at the edge of the piazza, looking out over the valley and enjoying the cleansing citrus flavours. It was a luminous and clear night with an uncountable display of clearly defined stars. The smoke from the dying charcoal under the spit roast mingled with the scent of orange blossom drifting up from the terraces below. The lights of Monaco twinkled brightly, outshining those of its near neighbour, Nice, a dozen kilometres further along the coast. Some strange phenomena made the silhouette of the mountains opposite appear a deep indigo blue, as they often did at this time of night.

"Look. The outline of hills against the sky looks like a reclining Templar Knight who has been laid out for burial, his hands clasping his sword to a shield covering his chest," Alessandra proposed. With her index finger she traced a line from the knight's imaginary feet to the head, as Ben and Cristiano tried to isolate the shape that she was describing.

After just a moment, "So it does. How extraordinary," agreed Cristiano.

"My father pointed it out to me when I was a child, and now I am telling you so that you can recount the story to your. . ." Realising her mistake, Alessandra let the sentence trail away but knew that the harm was already done.

Cristiano smiled. "It's OK, Mother. You do not need to worry about saying the wrong thing. Anyway, who knows-I might have children at some point. There are ways, you know."

The young chef sank the remainder of his limoncello, collected all three glasses and bid the others goodnight. After he had gone, Ben took his wife's hand.

"It must have occurred to you that the chances of an heir to the royal title looked unlikely when Cristiano accepted that he was gay?"

"Well, that wasn't my first concern, but yes, it did occur to me that my family line would probably stop with him. You and I are too old to consider starting a family, even if it were medically possible. Which, let's face it, is a long-shot."

Ben feigned being hurt and replied, "Are you suggesting that I'm past it?"

Alex smiled, and squeezed his hand but otherwise avoided the question.

"Cristiano might be able to adopt, but that solves nothing in terms of an heir. A surrogate mother would, I suppose, provide a bloodline, but constitutionally sounds like it would be a nightmare. And this ignores the fact that Cristiano is even less inclined to take over the reins of power than I was. I'm sanguine about the situation. He's healthy, happy and has a good life ahead of him in a career he loves. I have no wish to burden him with the responsibility of being Prince of Seborga. For the sake of my father, I will do what I can to make the principality great again, but after I'm gone, the citizens will have to find a new leader."

Ben stood up. "Speaking of children, my very own prodigal son arrives tomorrow. I need to be awake and away to the airport to pick him up. You need to kill the fatted calf for the welcome feast."

"It will be lovely for you to spend some time with your son. I am really looking forward to meeting him."

To temper his wife's expectations, Ben reiterated that their father-son relationship since his divorce had often been fractious. He told her that every meeting since then had ended in a row, or at best someone walking away. His wife's bitterness at what had happened only served to pour fuel on the flames of the teenager's anger. In recent years, things had got a little less volatile, but Ben wondered if this was more to do with their not speaking very often and being distanced. The prospect of finding out where they now stood during two weeks of living in close proximity filled Ben with a strange mix of hope and dread.

Alessandra looked sad at hearing of Ben's obvious pain about his father-son relationship. She rested her head on her husband's shoulder and linked her arm in his as they walked back across the piazza. Two Alpini soldiers on sentry duty clicked their heels and saluted when they saw the princess. Alessandra smiled and gave a brief wave.

"Quite nice to have them around, isn't it?" Ben smiled. "Now you have two armies at your command. Not many girls can say that."

The prime minister had to be out in time for a 9 am photocall with local children and their teachers. They would be carrying out a plastic waste survey as part of their environmental studies program. The idea was that Selene would attend with him, but in her official capacity as a journalist, and together they could enjoy a pleasant walk in the hills. She was almost certain any other press in attendance would not walk too far. They would most likely get their quotes from the PM, stage their photographs at the outset, and then return to their offices to file their material. That would leave the couple some time to themselves.

"I'm surprised to hear that there is much plastic waste in and around Seborga for the children to find," Andrea commented to Selene. "These hills around here always appear to be so pristine. I know that there is plenty of plastic thrown away along the Autoroute and down at the coast, but I'd be surprised to find a big problem up here."

"Let's ask the teachers," Selene suggested.

"It's a slightly different problem in the hills," one of the teachers explained. "It's true that there are not so many plastic drink bottles and sandwich wrappers. Up here, we find the plastic sheeting used to cover crops, off-cuts of water drainage pipes, discarded seed and pesticide bags, and other waste linked to agriculture. The other type is fly-tipping of domestic and building waste. It's a long drive to the nearest official recycling centre, and some people are too lazy, or think they are too busy, to make the trip."

"But surely the children do not pick up these types of things?" Selene said with a look of horror. "There must be so many health and safety issues."

"No, it's a lesson in what is out there and why it's so wrong. We collect small items that can be picked up with one of these," the teacher said, pointing to the metre-long rod with a sprung claw at one end. "They count, estimate the size of, and record the presence of the other waste, which we report to the local authority."

The party did not have to go very far along the road before excited children were competing to be the first to point out a red plastic screw top from a cola bottle on the road itself. Further along, in the ditch beside the road, was a fertiliser bag filled with plastic plant pots. With a clipboard with a pencil attached to it on a string, one little boy recorded each entry and its location using a GPS device.

When they thought about it for a moment, Andrea and Selene realised how many aspects of learning this exercise covered. It was not merely an environmental lesson. There was numeracy, estimating volume and scale, map reading, record keeping and working as part of a team. The teachers had devised a scale of deterioration of the plastic from one through to five, easiest to measure on bottles with thin walls. The lowest number was attributed to newly discarded bottles with no wear. The other end of the scale were bottles worn down by cars running over them or from being washed down the rocky stream beds, which were beginning to break down into plastic microbeads even before they reached the ocean.

The fascinating lesson came when the children were asked where they thought the plastic bottles' missing bits had gone. The teachers had brought some harmless coloured dye, into which they mixed some granules of sugar to represent the plastic microbeads. They filled several of the bottles they had collected with water from the stream, and the teachers added the other ingredients. On a given signal, four children poured their pink liquid back into the stream and watched as it was swept away down the hillside toward the river they could see far below. When it was pointed out how that river ran into the not-too-distant sea, the children's hands were shooting up as they wanted to be the first to answer questions.

These simple but powerful lessons were not only influencing the children's thinking, but they were also having a profound effect on Andrea and Selene. What had previously seemed such complex and distant challenges suddenly appeared clear and immediate threats to the environmental legacy being created for these children.

3. SARDENARA

    Were all of the western world's airports designed by one firm of architects? Ben wondered, as the glass doors slid silently open to Nice's Côte d'Azur. As an English Francophile, he had taken only a few international flights in his life, but every airport he had ever been in looked exactly the same. Using almost identical materials, construction, layouts and palettes of colours, they were simultaneously familiar and yet disorientating.

    Familiar meant he could find his way around airports easily, but once inside these buildings he always felt detached from the city, country or continent they were situated in. He had often thought that if he inadvertently got on the wrong flight thinking it was to Bordeaux but ended up in Bangkok or Bogota, he probably wouldn't notice that anything was amiss until he got outside of the airport.

    Airports seemed to him to be exciting places because they were filled with expectation. For those departing there was the expectation of new horizons—holidays to be enjoyed, business deals to be done, or even new places to be lived in. For others there was anticipation of the arrival; of much-missed family, lovers, colleagues and old friends. For almost everyone there, a visit to an airport was not an ordinary day.

    Ben scowled when he saw the arrivals board. His son's budget flight from Gatwick to Nice was delayed by thirty minutes. He had arrived at what he thought was the last minute and parked in the expensive short stay car park. Vincenzo had recommended that he bring Alessandra's car with Claudio's private number and diplomatic number plate, allowing Ben to park anywhere.

It went against his English sensibilities to use an advantage he did not believe he deserved. Ben had told Alessandra's chief guard – only half-jokingly - that it would be tantamount to queue-jumping, a crime second only to murder in an Englishman's eyes. Now, with at least an hour to kill and the parking metre ticking, he regretted his decision. Ben bought a copy of the Nice-Matin newspaper and a café macchiato to pass the time.

He had lost track of time when he heard some commotion further along the airport concourse. Passengers hauling cases to and from flights were scattering to allow four French paratroopers to pass through them, running at full speed. A couple of women screamed and grabbed their children in panic at seeing the armed troops primed for action. Several family groups started heading for the exits at a half-trot. With all the recent terror threats in France, everyone was extremely jumpy. One hundred metres ahead of the human projectile of green combat fatigues, dark sunglasses and claret berets, Ben could now see a uniformed customs officer. He was waving with one arm, and with the other holding open a door through to the airside area of international arrivals.

The four soldiers with their automatic weapons burst through the glass door, nearly knocking the customs man off his feet. No alarms were sounding in the airport, and with the door firmly locked behind them people began to go about their business again, but with perhaps a bit more haste and heightened awareness, Ben thought. Like him, most guessed that the scare was probably nothing more than someone leaving their hand baggage unattended while they used the toilet.

When Ben looked back at the arrivals board, his son's flight was flashing as 'Arrived.' A few minutes later, a flurry of passengers began emerging onto the concourse. He wondered how it was possible for him to know with reasonable certainty that this was the London flight. After all, their faces were not all pale, they were not all carrying Marks & Spencer carrier bags, nor were they drunk and singing football songs: the usual stereotypes of the English abroad.

But then again, this was the Nice Côte d'Azur Airport, where 'tourist' is a dirty word to the thousands of wealthy British ex-pats who pass through it regularly. These travellers all looked well-off but in an understated way. There were few artificial fabrics to be seen. They wore linen, cashmere and leather, but without any overt branding. They all looked self-assured but without any swagger. Their appearance made a statement, but in a whisper rather than a shout. Whatever it was that gave them away, the passengers being greeted or rushing out the doors to waiting cars were for the most part Brits, Ben concluded. As the numbers dwindled to a trickle, there was still no sign of Tom.

Ben caught sight of himself reflected in the plate glass and realised that he blended right in with the passengers he had been observing. A few short years ago it would have been hard to pick him out from the hundreds of other commuters trudging to work up Grey Street in Newcastle. Pale-faced and with his scarf pulled up over his neck to stave off the biting wind whipping up from the River Tyne, he had also blended in there. His handmade shoes had long since seen a cobbler and the seat of his Saville Row suit was now shiny with wear. A navy cashmere coat was still an effective windbreak, but it was shabby at the cuffs. At a distance, Ben might once have passed for chic, but on closer inspection he was now very definitely shabby.

Transformed by a new lifestyle, weather and wife, Ben was today just another Riviera ex-pat. His hair was longer—much longer in fact. And whiter. Or was it the deep tan which made his hair more of a contrast? He was unsure. Deck shoes, shorts, and button-down Oxford shirt were the uniform of the Côte d'Azur and all you needed to get into some of the best restaurants in the world. Not that Ben ate in such places because his wife ran what he, and many others, considered the best restaurant in Liguria. It was there where he would be headed for lunch as soon as he could collect Tom.

Another thirty minutes passed before the opaque glass doors from arrivals slid open again. The four paratroopers emerged, causing everyone around them to move well back out of their path. One soldier was on point and another was bringing up the rear, their eyes scanning the concourse for anyone who might be foolish enough to challenge them. The other two soldiers each had an arm under the elbow of a man whose bound feet were dragging behind him. His wrists were fastened together in front of him with the same plastic ties and his head was bowed. He looked barely conscious. From his sturdy build and the shock of unkempt blonde hair, Ben at once recognised him as his son.

Instinctively Ben slipped from his stool and rushed toward the approaching paratroopers, but even as he was doing so, realised this was an ill-judged move. The soldier on-point shouted, "Arretez!" in a manner that sounded as if he was certain his command would be obeyed. The lead trooper simultaneously levelled his automatic weapon at Ben and clicked off the safety catch.

Ben did as he was instructed and stood stock still, as did every person within about one hundred metres. The two men carrying Tom dropped him unceremoniously on the floor, where he hit his head on the polished marble and groaned.

While Ben was interrogated, the other three turned to form a protective circle, weapons levelled and eyes scanning back and forth.

"Identifiez-vous immediatement mais ne bougez aucun muscle."

Although not a fluent French speaker, he understood this instruction 'to freeze' clearly enough.

"Je Suis son pere." His brain fogged by what was happening, Ben had to think hard for the next sentence. "Je suis ici pour le recoperer."

There was what seemed like an interminably long silence while the trooper assessed the threat. After glancing around to check on his subordinates, the officer mentally downgraded the threat and spoke more softly.

"You are also English?"

"I am, and that is my son arriving from London."

"Put both your hands on your head and do it now." Ben did as the soldier told him.

Some imperceivable communication passed between the leader and the soldier furthest away, who now swept around the group towards him. He swung his weapon over his back to free his hands and started patting Ben's thin summer clothing. He could feel his fingers probing his skin like a masseur, leaving no crevice unsearched. When he was satisfied there was no threat, he told Ben to lower his hands.

"Marcher. Walk," the soldier corrected himself, indicating with the barrel of his gun in the direction of the exit doors. The two soldiers who had been carrying Tom picked him up again and continued dragging him along, with the fourth soldier operating as rear guard.

Once outside in a designated security area, it took Ben fifty five minutes of persuasion and a last resort phone call to his daughter's boyfriend, the Prime Minister of Italy, to finally get himself and Tom released. They were escorted back to Ben's car and watched out of the airport, but only after Ben had paid thirty euros in parking charges. They had instructions to head straight for the French border and into Italy, from where Tom would need to exit and return to London via some route other than Nice Airport. He was effectively banned from the Côte d'Azur.

There was silence in the car for the first few kilometres. Once they had passed the road toll and were on the autoroute that sweeps around Nice towards the French border with Italy, Ben finally felt calm enough to speak.

"Bloody hell, Tom! What planet have you been living on for the past five years? You haven't heard that France is on a virtual war footing after numerous terrorist incidents? Or that French paratroopers are world-famous for their lack of a sense of humour? They eat nails for breakfast instead of croissants. Getting pissed on a flight, threatening a French immigration officer and refusing to open your hand baggage in this tense climate was only ever going to end one way."

Ben glanced across at Tom to judge his ignominy level, only to realise that Tom was sound asleep. A little trickle of dry blood ran from the corner of his lip. Bright red weals had appeared around his wrists where the soldiers' plastic ties had bound them together. His left cheek was swollen, presumably where he'd received a blow from a rifle butt to shut him up, Ben assumed. His clothes looked neither washed nor ironed, and his trainers had no laces. The age of his stubble was indeterminable but certainly older than a week. He looked like a homeless person, his father thought. How could he take him home to meet his new wife and pass his neighbours with him looking like this? he pondered.

In the thirty minutes it took to reach the Italian border, Ben had come up with a plan. He took the first exit in Italy down to Ventimiglia while Tom snored like a pig. Parking the car at the large Carrefour supermarket, he left his son sleeping while he went inside. Ben paused in the foyer to message Alessandra, who was expecting them for lunch. He told her that the flight had been delayed–partly true, he justified to himself–and that he would call when he knew their ETA, but that they were unlikely to make it for lunch.

Ben's mental shopping list consisted of two long-sleeved shirts, sandals, a pack of white t-shirts, a pack of boxers, jeans, joggers, a towel, and a sports bag to put them all in. He guessed Tom's size to be one greater than his own. They were about the same height, but Tom was bulkier, especially since he appeared to have lost some of his muscular tone since Ben had seen him last. At school, he had been a pretty good rugby player. Tom had continued to play until a couple of years ago when he was kicked out of the team for repeatedly not showing up for matches.

When he returned to the car, Tom was still asleep, his body apparently having gone into partial shutdown to recover from the alcohol and the beating he had received. Ben drove to the seafront and parked next to one of the beach showers. He pulled, shoved, and bundled the reluctant, drowsy young man onto the beach and turned on the shower of cold water.

"Fuck. Fuck. Fuck...," was all he heard for about two minutes while the cool drenched Tom's hair and clothes. Yet, he did not attempt to move away from the spray of water. Instead, he revolved his head, letting it into his ears and eyes – even into his mouth.

Ben shook his head in apparent despair. "It's gratifying to see that a hundred thousand pounds' worth of private education has at least endowed you with a varied and colourful vocabulary."

The shower did the trick. After a few minutes, Tom sounded more like himself and started to make eye contact with his father. Ben decided it would be more effective to repeat his earlier reprimand from the car some other time, when he was more receptive and might take in the enormity of his stupidity. Ben held out the towel. Tom went to grab it, but it was pulled back from his grasp.

"Clothes off and then the towel," was Ben's offer. Without any thought or sign of embarrassment, Tom peeled off his wet t-shirt and dropped his cargo pants, under which he was ironically commando. Ironic, because Ben could now see the clear imprint from a soldiers' boot on his left buttock. Either he was stood on, or non-verbally encouraged to move forwards. Throwing the towel at him, Ben picked up the wet clothes and wrang the bulk of the water out of them.

Food and coffee were next on Ben's agenda, and they didn't have to go far to find them. On the other side of the seafront was an array of restaurants and cafes, including one with the unmistakable smell of pizza, called Margunaira. As a hangover cure, this would be almost as good as an English breakfast, Ben decided. After wrapping the wet clothes in the towel and placing them in the car, Ben guided his son across the street, which was busy with Italians whizzing by at speed as if they had a reputation to keep up. Tom limped slightly, suddenly aware of the emerging bruise on his buttock.

During the rapid demolition of a large pizza with prosciutto and salami, little was said. Ben sipped sparkling water, not wishing to order alcohol under the circumstances. He had one of best slices of sardenara he'd tasted anywhere outside of his wife's kitchen. The base was light and almost crumbly—the tomato sauce, rich and slightly spicy. Fragrant and piquant capers, along with Taggiasca olives, were scattered unusually liberally on the top.

"What's that you're eating? It looks good," the now revived young man commented.

Ben explained that it was a local speciality and asked if he would like to try some.

"But of course. I'm still starving."

Two slices of sardenara and two americano coffees later, Tom started returning to what Ben remembered as his usual self. It was at this point that Ben was reminded that his normal self was not always very nice. So far, he had treated the waiter with disdain and blatantly ogled the young waitresses. His first words approaching a conversation were neither a thank you, nor an apology, but a complaint.

"These plastic chairs are a bit cheap and nasty. I thought you'd be eating in nicer places than this now since you're married to a princess."

Ben held his temper until he was in the privacy of the car. The remainder of the thirty minute journey to Seborga consisted of shouted rallies of accusation versus recrimination, and allegations met with retribution. It was not pleasant listening for either father or son, and certainly not a way to rekindle their relationship after a five year break.

When Ben had been asked–nay instructed-to leave his family home by his then-wife's lawyer, Tom was only in his early teens. Much of what was said harked back to what Tom saw as his abandonment by his father. This male vacuum in his life was inadequately filled by his mother's new partner, a man to whom Tom took an instant dislike which only grew stronger with time.

A few years older than Tom, his sister, Selene, had only had to endure less than a year in the new family unit. Against all predictions, she won a writing scholarship to become a residential boarder during the sixth form, from where she went straight to university. After graduation, Selene moved directly to London, rarely returning to the family home.

In stark contrast, Tom's schoolwork went downhill-only his skill at rugby saving him from expulsion, and assisted in gaining him a place at a university where sporting prowess counted more than qualifications. He spent several bitter and miserable years there, during which time he rarely spoke to or saw his father. Failing to gain a degree at his first attempt, he scraped through in his fourth year. The resulting low pass mark in sports science was unable to help him into a career, and he bounced from one casual job to the next. His strongest family bond was with his sister who, although continuously exasperated by his behaviour, always forgave him quickly and offered a sympathetic ear when he was low.

By the time the car turned into the main piazza of Seborga, several long-buried demons had only been partly exorcised and there remained a tense silence. Both men had reached a state of contrition about things they had either done, not done, said, or left unsaid. As unpalatable as this confrontation had been, both now had a clearer understanding of the other's position. It was a platform upon which they could perhaps start again, Ben hoped. The air was clearing, if not yet entirely cleared.

Tom would be staying at the apartment above a shop which his sister had recently inherited from a man who everyone in the village referred to as the 'Crazy Dutchman.' Her brother never questioned this strange nickname because his insanity was evidenced by the fact that he had given an entire building to his sister, someone he hardly knew.

Selene and Rikki—the erstwhile Crazy Dutchman—had met during Ben's daughter's first visit to Seborga. Despite apparently having nothing in common and being almost a generation apart, they had become unlikely friends, albeit nothing more than that. Or at least, there was no prospect of anything other than friendship as far as Selene was concerned. She rented the flat above his shop when she stayed in Seborga two years prior and borrowed his strange yellow VW Kübelwagen Jeep if she needed to drive anywhere.

The odd couple could often be seen having a coffee, a drink or a meal together when Selene was in the village. She found the charismatic, eccentrically dressed, dope-smoking, fifty year old Dutchman was easy company. He seemed to have no personal agenda and so made for entertaining, unthreatening male companionship. The journalist in her was fascinated by his dramatic stories of drilling for oil in wild, faraway places, dealing with local bandits and paying off corrupt politicians. It was possible that some of these stories had been his ultimate downfall. Ben assumed that Rikki had spent so many years in the company of hard-drinking, tough-talking engineers, that the Dutchman simply craved female company and Selene was easy to talk to. Whatever it was, they both seemed to get something from their odd relationship.

About a year later, Rikki went off on one of what he called his 'RnR' trips, which everyone understood to be his periodic need to get drunk and/or high in 'colourful' female company. San Remo was his usual local RnR destination, but he was also known to fly much further afield. Having worked for oil and gas companies all over the world, Rikki knew many people in a lot of exotic places. The problem was that many oil and gas people did not like him because he had turned whistle-blower on some of the industry's shadier practices later in life.

He had never returned from the last trip overseas, and no one in Seborga knew what had happened to him. His store remained locked, its mailbox filling up with post, and his strange old car sat for the time accumulating dust. Almost a year later, a letter arrived in Seborga addressed to Selene, care of her father. It was from a lawyer in the Hague informing her that Rikki was deceased. The letter informed her that he had left his property in Seborga, including the Kübelwagen and his extensive vinyl record collection, to Selene. There was no further explanation.

**Looking down on
the bay of Bordighera from Alta:
a scene also painted by Monet.**

Drawing by Linda McCluskey

4. PANSOTTI CON SALSA NOCCI

Ben sat at his favourite table under the faded canvas canopy of the Osteria. From here, he could see out over the valley towards Negi, and get advance warning of any weather fronts approaching over the Alps. He could also watch all the comings and goings of people in the village. There was only one road up to, and down from, Seborga, and all streets radiated off the Piazza Martiri Patrioti. The Osteria was literally and socially the hub of village life.

When Ben answered his phone, the prime minister's first words were, "The bill has been passed."

"Wow. To put that in context, that is the first new law specifically relating to Seborga since the Knights Templar ruled this land more than nine-hundred years ago," Ben observed.

He was told that legislation to give Seborga the power to create unique local taxes, planning laws and inward investment rules had been passed without serious opposition.

"There was a bit of bleating from the left-wing parties about perpetuating outdated autocratic regimes, but they did not put up much of a show," Andrea added. "The Green parties supported us because of the environmental aspects of the legislation."

"Thank you, Andrea. We can use this opportunity to both fast-track Seborga's economic recovery, and hopefully find a suitable model to revive other hilltop communities facing similar challenges."

The PM responded, "You understand that I did not do this just for Seborga but for the greater good of Italy? It will be a ground-breaking experiment in sustainable living."

Andrea Cassini had become Italy's youngest-ever prime minister after his predecessor's sudden arrest on corruption charges. It was unlikely that the handsome Sicilian would otherwise have been elected to lead the conservative centre-right party.

Cassini was not an obvious candidate for Italy's top job, due to his age and because he was what many of them saw as a 'loathsome southerner' in a country still harbouring an irrational north-south divide. What's more, Cassini was the son of a union man, he was an environmentalist and, most recently, a champion of women's rights. Ironically, his predecessor had chosen him for precisely those reasons, believing that he would mop up enough votes from these groups to tip the balance of power. It had worked. However, as his boss's deputy, Andrea got his new job by default. He was now seen as just too popular amongst the voters for the conservatives to get rid of-at least by most, if not all, of his colleagues.

As soon as they heard the news, Alessandra called a meeting of the ministers of Seborga to enact their pre-prepared tax legislation. The documents had been drafted in Rome by Andrea's civil servants. The new laws created highly attractive zero-tax windows for inward investment into targeted areas of Seborga's economy. There were some stringent criteria to be met to weed out money-laundering, green-washing, and other nefarious schemes which had emerged in recent times. But for those who could tick all the right boxes, these were ground-breaking incentives.

One such business in London had been alerted to the opportunity by Cecily Noble, the English entrepreneur and recent friend of Ben and Alessandra. The multi-million-dollar, international fair-trade cosmetics business which she had built up single-handedly had recently been sold, although Cecily retained a small niche product line based on blood oranges to keep her busy during her premature semi-retirement. This rare fruit, with its antioxidant properties, had more than ten years earlier brought her into contact with Roman, a Sicilian orange grower who would later become her lover. An experienced sailor, Cecily chose to live aboard a large, renovated, classic yacht so that the couple could conduct their then-secret affair in out-of-way destinations.

Their clandestine affair was a compromise which allowed Roman to care for his wife, who was suffering from early-onset dementia. The Sicilian was married with two teenage children who were at that time still in education in America. The couple had previously separated and were in the process of a divorce when Roman had met Cecily.

However, on hearing of his wife's out-of-the-blue, and ultimately terminal diagnosis, Roman had taken the decision that he could no longer leave her, and his daughters, alone under these new circumstances. As difficult as it had been, he had encouraged Cecily to forget about him and get on with her life. Instead, she had settled for meeting as and when they could, and then basing herself on the boat made that distanced relationship easier.

Cecily's home port for her yacht was Menton, the nearest French harbour to Monaco, where her commercial office was based. The port provided easy access to Nice Airport, from where she could fly anywhere in the world. The pretty harbour town with its regular market offered quite a different lifestyle to that in Monaco. Although just inside the French side of the border, it was more Italian in appearance and atmosphere. It was to Cecily's boat in Menton that first Alessandra's father, and then later her and Ben, supplied their artisan olive oil to her onboard chef. This relationship led to the two couples becoming friends and Ben learning about the high commercial value of blood oranges.

Cecily had been one of the founding members of a small

private club in London. A dozen years ago, it had been set up to fill the gap between the oversubscribed Groucho Club and the other stuffy, old-school gentlemen's institutions. It was hipper, more egalitarian and served better food, but was still strict on privacy for its many celebrity members. The Club had quickly attracted a new kind of customer from digital media and other emerging technology sectors. The Club grew to open a dozen such venues in major cities around the world. They had even started to branch out into out of town, country club-like destinations with food and rooms. Cecily used the Club's city venues as a drop-in office and meeting place when she had business abroad.

The Club's directors had been watching an emerging hospitality trend in Italy and France for something that had become known as Albergo Diffuso. This type of deconstructed hotel had emerged in a few ancient hilltop villages, like Seborga, which were also facing depopulation. The model made use of small, abandoned properties scattered throughout villages to breathe new life into the communities.

Rather than all the hotel rooms all being in one building, a central reception provided a hub where guests checked in, but the accommodation radiated throughout the village in individual properties. These often quite different units were all renovated to a consistent, exacting standard and equipped with twenty-first century features such as high-speed broadband, air-conditioning, and so on. To blend into their communities, they looked like traditional village houses but inside had luxury hotel standard features and services.

Alessandra thought that the Club's marketing director had summed up their approach well when he described it as, "A kind of contrary back-to-basics approach, where things are designed to appear rudimentary but are in fact just understated opulence."

The major factor driving the phenomena was a growing desire for a more authentic holiday experience. The properties were all fully immersed in the community in which they were situated. Guests lived alongside the locals and enjoyed experiencing their culture up close. For the community, the Albergo Diffuso model brought construction and service jobs, rejuvenated neighbourhoods, and filled seats in local restaurants and cafes. The affluent visitors also tended to buy plenty of local produce to take home with them.

The Club's CEO and a couple of directors visited Seborga, held meetings with Ben and Alessandra, and viewed some of the potential properties. The directors and investors were very excited about the new opportunity. They saw the Albergo Diffuso model as an opportunity to diversify their offering, attract new members, and expand their asset base without the high costs of city centre sites.

Since first hearing of the opportunity, the slow pace of Italian bureaucracy in drafting the tax legislation had allowed the Club's directors the rare luxury of time with which to plan. They had used the year to fully assess the scheme, draw up proposals and have the investment in place. They were ready to proceed as soon as the legislation that would facilitate it was passed. A local surveyor and a notaire had been appointed to act as their agents in the property transactions, and an Italian subsidiary company had been set up to hold the freeholds.

The tax 'carrots' for the investors included no local property rates and zero corporation tax on profits for ten years, allowing them to keep their overheads down and allowing quicker recovery of their investment. Ben pointed out to the doubters in the village that they were only giving away tax revenue they would never have received had these properties remained empty and the Albergo Diffuso not been there. He had explained that the village got many of its vacant and dilapidated properties renovated, jobs created, locally grown produce sold, and spin-off tourism revenue generated. It really was a win-win.

When they received the news that the bill had passed, the Club instructed their agents to make their first purchase offer. To everyone's surprise, this offer was to Selene for the property; the one that had been bequeathed to her by Rikki, the Crazy Dutchman. They wanted this purchase agreed first as it was the only traditional property in the village with a shop front that could be used as the reception for the Albergo Diffuso.

They also wanted this property because they had discovered that the shop was still packed to the ceiling with Rikki's stock of local antiques and bric-a-brac. There were numerous brass bed heads, copper pans, granite sinks with brass taps, crockery, old coffee pots and almost everything they would need to achieve the authentic, rustic Italian look they wanted for the new guest rooms. Rikki had once sold all these items at hugely inflated prices to foreign holiday homeowners on the Riviera for their retro-chic kitchens. The Dutchman had revelled in the idea that the stone sinks and brass taps which Italians saw as old-fashioned junk, the wealthy northern Europeans thought to be the height of stylish vogue.

When Alessandra heard about the unexpected offer, she put her head in her hands and exclaimed, "What a disaster. All that planning and we are tripped-up at the first step by that Crazy Dutchman. Even from the grave, I bet he's laughing at this."

The phrase, 'just slightly above market-value offer' at once rang alarm bells with Alessandra, who recognised that it could look like nepotism on two counts. Firstly, Selene's father was the instigator of the inward investment initiative. Secondly, it was her own lover, the prime minister, who had pushed through the legislation of which she was to be the first beneficiary. It did not look good from any angle, she concluded.

When Selene had learned about her surprise inheritance, she was delighted about the idea of having a holiday home in the village she had come to love. However, she did not have any money to carry out any of the renovation work required, or to convert the ground floor shop into living accommodation. However, if she sold the property now and pocketed the cash, it would look like profiteering.

Summarising what he saw as their dilemma, Ben said, "The Club needed this property to make their business model work, but if Selene sells it and anyone finds out the parties involved, it could scupper our whole ship before we've got underway."

Alessandra's frustration at one hurdle appearing after another was beginning to boil over. "Scupper. Scupper. What the hell does scupper mean? You bloody English and your insistence on using language from your colonial power days. Well, if you haven't yet heard, Britannia no longer rules the waves and Spitfires do not control the skies over the White Cliffs of Dover. Welcome to the twenty-first century."

Ben knew that in normal circumstances, Alessandra loved his quirky Englishness and revelled in his funny old-fashioned sayings. But this was clearly not one such time.

"Let's speak to that guy, Richard, in London; the commercial director of the Club who, like me, loves your pansotti con salsa nocci so much. I'll explain our dilemma and see if he has any ideas."

Ben made the call and was promised a call back within twenty-four hours. It only took an hour and a half before Richard phoned back with a proposal, which Ben relayed first to Alessandra and then to his daughter. He openly admitted that they knew that Selene's property was pretty much a deal-breaker, so they had set aside a generous budget to acquire it. They had also put a rough estimate on the market value of the furniture and antiques inside the shop.

"We see this as a true value that we can justify to our investors. It is not a gift or a bribe. However, I see how it could be misconstrued."

During their visit to Seborga, the Club's director had been shown a smaller property on the edge of the village that the owners had already renovated. It was a two bedroomed place with about the same floor area as the shop with its flat above which Selene had inherited. Whilst they liked this property, they had discounted it from their list for several reasons-mainly its distance from the village and their desire to use it to provide reception services. Their proposal was that the Club acquired this ready-to-move-in home, but then simply swapped it with Selene's property without any cash changing hands.

"That way everyone gets what they want, and only we know how," Richard had reassured Ben.

Ben later rationalised to Alessandra that Rikki had no family in the village and so no one knew the contents of his will, or indeed, at the moment, even that he was dead. The whole village knew that Selene had stayed in the place many times in the past and was also often seen driving his quirky old car. For now, Tom staying there and driving the Kübelwagen would not in any way look out of the ordinary. When the Club became the official owners, the news of Rikki's death could be revealed, and everyone would assume that the Club had acquired his shop and flat from his heirs. No one would connect it to Selene's acquisition of a house outside the village.

Once the arrangement was put to her, Selene looked online to view the property they proposed to offer her in exchange and fell in love with it. It had an airy first-floor bedroom with a Juliette balcony which provided wonderful uninterrupted views across the valley. Outside were a stone-paved terrace and a small garden in which there was an ancient, gnarled olive tree, plus two others of lemons and cherries. It had all been newly renovated and painted in neutral colours. The asking price was only slightly more than the Club had offered for her run-down property in the village and the contents. It could hardly have been more perfect for her circumstances. Without speaking to Andrea or visiting the property, she agreed to the exchange.

5. FRISCEU DI BACCALA

From her Clapham flat, Selene could be at London's Gatwick Airport quicker than going into her office. From here, there were several flights every day to most of the major airports in Italy with a journey time of an average of two hours. She could leave home at 6 am and be having coffee in Milan by 10 am. From her newspaper's office it was an even shorter journey to London City Airport, albeit with a more restricted number of departures and destinations.

Selene was spending regular weekends in Italy. She was able to take budget flights on Friday nights to wherever the prime minister was working in Italy and be back at work on Monday morning. He would arrange press passes for her to gain access to whatever function he was attending. The events were seldom in the same place twice. Any public guests would be different each time, and so only the PM's closest staff and colleagues would know what was going on.

The mainly Italian journalists who attended several such events would not think it too odd that they saw a familiar face with a press badge. Reporters seldom interacted much, for fear of giving away some vital snippet of information to a competitor. Andrea and Selene had conducted their blissful international love affair for almost a year in this covert way. It was Rome one weekend, Milan the next, and even the occasional few days in Lake Como. Prime ministers worked long hours but get many invitations to some lovely places, she had learned.

The couple had first met at a festival in Seborga when Andrea had only just been appointed as second-in-command to the notorious head of the then opposition, Tricolore Party. The leader was an entrepreneur with a murky past, who soon after was elected Prime Minister of Italy. In a few short weeks, Cassini moved from being a low-level local Sicilian politician to the land's second-highest office. Before they had time to make that nameplate for his office door, Andrea Cassini would himself be promoted to prime minister. The chequered past of the man who had briefly been his boss finally caught up with him and he had been arrested.

Mastroianni had spent a lifetime scheming, manipulating and cheating his way to the top; first in business, and finally politics. He had appointed the young, liberal Andrea Cassini because he was the antithesis of everything that he himself represented. The Sicilian's youthful sincerity put a shine on Mastroianni's otherwise much-tarnished image. For Cassini, it was a pragmatic, if not an altogether comfortable, partnership, which would in time move him into a position where he could get things done. At the time, he had no idea just how quickly that moment would come.

The initial attraction between Andrea and Selene was immediate, and it had grown into them being completely besotted with each other. When he and Selene were attending public events it was very difficult for them to resist touching each other, something they more than made up for when on their own later. Their future together had been discussed but any prospect of marriage quickly put aside. There were already too many potential conflicts of interest. Andrea had previously played a key role in supporting her father's initiatives in Seborga, and continued to do so. Her role as a journalist on a UK national newspaper could be compromised by too obvious a connection to a foreign country's PM. They would just have to wait until either he left office, or she gave up her job. Neither of these events looked in the cards for the immediate future.

The next event in the couples' hectic and exotic calendar was the launch of a four hundred foot super yacht in Genoa, as the guests of a specialist Italian boat builder. Italy ranked amongst the most prolific superyacht builders in the world, and many of those built in other northern European countries were brought here to be fitted out. The small European nation still led the world in luxury goods exports and its designer brands, from cars to clothes, were some of the most desirable anywhere.

Andrea had told Selene that, "The world apparently can't get enough designer bling, and we are very good at providing it."

Since her first work-related visit a year ago, Selene had become very fond of Genoa. This trip would also allow her to visit her father and brother in Seborga. It was less than a two-hour drive along the Italian Riviera to the mountain village where her father now lived with his new wife, Alessandra. They could all enjoy an Italian Sunday lunch together, and she could get a flight back from Nice on Sunday night, or even early Monday morning.

Selene had envisaged the huge yacht sliding down a slipway into the waiting sea after having had a bottle of champagne smashed over its bow. In the event, the glistening white and metallic black boat was already sitting waist-deep in the water, and the prosecco was merely poured over its nameplate to avoid knocking a chunk out of its shiny new plastic skin.

Although the launch itself was something of a damp squib in Selene's eyes, the party was a chic affair. The client, whose name no one had so far been allowed to mention, was there - albeit in a roped-off area away from the press and most of the guests. Even from thirty metres away Selene could see who it was. Two waiters appeared simultaneously, as though they had been poised in the wings waiting for a customer. One was proffering prosecco in frosted glasses from a tray, and the other canapes.

"What are they?" Selene asked of the waiter, but it was Andrea who answered.

"Frisceu di baccala, fried cod fritters. A delicious local appetiser made with dried cod, potatoes and herbs."

"Wow. This is an A-list gathering," Selene exclaimed.

"You mean the rapper?" Andrea asked. "They had to explain to me who he was and the names of a couple of his hits. Music that you certainly won't be hearing played in my car," he joked.

"Do you have to go and meet him?"

"Apparently, I do. And tell him that I love his work. I might tell him that my journalist friend is his biggest fan and has bought all of his downloads. What I am really going to do is get him to sign up to my Green Seas Charter."

"This is the pledge not to discharge untreated waste at sea?" Selene remembered Andrea discussing this idea a few months earlier.

"Well, yes. That, and to only use biodegradable materials on board. Superyachts often use harmful chemicals and then discharge their waste tanks into the sea. It's very damaging to the oceans."

"My bet is that he doesn't give a damn and won't do it. Or at least, he will agree to it here in public but then forget all about it afterwards."

"You are such a cynic. That is the journalist in you. You just watch me at work."

Andrea strode purposely in the direction of their famous and outrageously dressed host, causing consternation amongst two respective sets of minders. The rapper's men bristled and bulked up their frames as a signal to the approaching strangers. Andrea's bodyguards spoke into their lapel microphones and unbuttoned their jackets just enough for people to glimpse the weapon holsters. These signs were sufficient to identify them as the prime minister's party, who they had been expecting. No one else would be allowed to be armed in public.

Andrea sidestepped the Ukrainian rapper's extended hand and went in for the more physical bear-hug he knew that Eastern European men preferred. He placed one hand over Zeno's right shoulder and the other around his waist in what looked the precursor to a wrestling hold. It was easy to see how this greeting had come about as a way of testing the strength of a potential ally or opponent. This completely un-politician-like greeting somewhat disarmed their usually ultra-sure-of-himself host. Andrea kept up the initiative with his opening greeting of, "Big love from me and all your fans in Italy. A style ambassador for Versace would only choose one place to have their yacht fitted out. She looks fabulous."

As he spoke, Andrea reached back for Selene's hand and pulled her gently to his side.

"Speaking of looking fabulous. This well-known English writer is also a huge fan, but told me that she was too shy to approach you. Selene, meet Zeno."

"Truly beautiful, man. Italian politicians, their babes and even their policeman are more stylish than anywhere in the world. I bet your bodyguards have Armani gun belts. I love this place, man," the rapper replied, with more than a tinge of an accent giving away his ethnic origin.

Any potential frost had melted in this possible cultural no-man's land. They both knew the reason that the prime minister had agreed to attend the opening was because the boatbuilder had told him about its unique recyclable construction methods. Zeno was also smart enough to know the environment was a growing cause of concern and would tick many boxes with his fans. Both men would benefit from the photographs now being taken and shared around the world on social media.

"That was very slick," Selene conceded. "You really are a Sicilian fisherman. You certainly hooked that one."

"Of course. I also caught you, didn't I?" Andrea tried to

whisper above the noise of rap music resonating from the Bose sound system. "But unlike him, I won't be throwing you back."

"Throwing her back to where?" asked a voice which was suddenly far too close.

"Ah, Amara. You are never far away from a conversation that you shouldn't be listening to," chided Andrea in a way that was supposed to sound jokey, but which also hinted at his displeasure.

The raven-haired, underdressed, over-heeled Junior Minister for Culture seemed to Selene to be omnipresent when Andrea was on official business.

"Exactly what is the connection between superyachts and culture, Amara?" the PM asked.

"Ah, that I can tell you. These floating status symbols are designed by the highly cultured and discretely well-off for the distinctly uncultured, vulgarly super-rich. Ironic, don't you think?"

The woman, who was perhaps a couple of years older, and currently two inches taller than Selene—mostly due to the heels— was striking looking. If she were describing her in one of her columns, the journalist might say something like, 'Beautiful in a uniquely Italian way. Like a Ferrari; both highly desirable and potentially menacing.'

Selene was uncomfortable about the degree of familiarity between Andrea and his Tricolore party colleague but was determined not to let that show. Although, she suspected that Amara had an inkling that something was going on between her and Andrea. She was always hanging around them and, according to Andrea, was a world-class gossipmonger and political manipulator.

When pressed about Amara, Andrea later admitted that five years earlier, there had been a one-night-stand after a party to end a highly successful party conference. When the regretful Andrea had sobered up and then failed to call her about another date, she had sent him abusive messages. Next time they had met, she had confronted him and made a big scene in public. He had told Selene that he was contrite about his role in the affair and that it had been a judgment failure. To his credit, he apportioned no blame to her. He said that he had acted badly and that she had deserved greater respect.

Now that their respective careers had taken off and they found themselves public figures, they were always looking over their shoulders. Relatively minor misdemeanours in the past had a habit of coming back to haunt politicians. They could be either leverage for the needy, or weapons for the angry. Amara unsettled Andrea. Despite ostensibly being on the same side, he couldn't help feeling she was waiting for payback and wondered just when it might come.

"You looked dressed for dinner somewhere far better than this, Selene," Amara probed, looking the Englishwoman up and down and then gesturing around at the crowd made up of the rapper's hangers-on, local bureaucrats, and journalists.

"You're quite right. From here I am going to meet an old friend in Genoa. We have a lot of catching up to do."

Resisting the urge to wink at Andrea, Selene kept her eyes on Amara, avoiding his gaze as he was also trying hard not to give anything away. "In fact, if I don't leave now, I will be late. So, you will have to excuse me, Prime Minister. Amara, it's interesting to have spoken to you."

With no more than a polite wave, Selene backed away from the two politicians and disembarked from the boat via the neon-illuminated walkway. After another fifteen minutes at the party shaking hands and being photographed with the other guests, Andrea also made his excuses and left. When he got back to the car which was parked out of sight of the yacht, Selene was already inside behind the blacked-out windows. It was early enough for them to drive to their destination in the ancient city and have a relaxing dinner.

6. ARANCINI AL RAGU

After saying goodnight to his son, Ben's parting advice had been for him to put some cream on his wrist wounds and sleep off his hangover, adding that he would see him the following day. Assuming Tom still possessed a rugby player's appetite, his worried father arrived at Selene's apartment the next morning carrying a parcel of Alessandra's focaccia plus a couple of brioches. When he let himself in through the unlocked door, there were no signs of life except for lights, apparently left on from the night before, and clothes were strewn around the floor. There was also a distinct smell of marijuana and some suspicious-looking butts in a foil food tray.

After filling the Bialetti coffee pot, he turned on the gas ring and went to wake his son. Asleep under a mop of unkempt blonde hair, Ben was briefly reminded of happier days when Tom was a young schoolboy. When awoken, however, Ben was reminded that the little boy had turned into a belligerent young man.

"What the hell? What bloody time is it?

"Ten o'clock European Central Time or nine am in London, from where you arrived twenty hours ago."

Having been roughly frisked and nearly arrested at Nice Airport, Ben had been forced to cancel both the lunch and dinner Alessandra had prepared especially for him. It had cost him over two hundred euros to equip his son with a basic wardrobe of clothes. Soon he would have to explain to his wife and his neighbours why Tom looked like he had just played in a rugby scrum against the All Blacks. Then, when this holiday ended, he would not be able to drop his son off at nearby Nice but would instead have to drive several hours to an Italian airport, where he would doubtless also have to pay for a new return ticket. Ben was in no mood for diplomacy.

"Now that you are twenty-five and supposedly an adult, I am finally going to start treating you like one. If you don't like what I have to say and are unwilling to behave responsibly, you need to leave. I will drive you to the train station, pay for your tickets home and, reluctantly, say goodbye. You decide."

There was a long silence. Tom leaned forward and took a sip from the coffee his father had brought to his bedside.

"I can't go back," Tom mumbled, barely audibly.

"What do you mean, you can't? I've just told you that I will take you and I will pay for your tickets."

Sitting on the edge of the bed, Tom looked his father in the eyes, knowing that this would hurt him.

"I can't go back," Tom repeated louder this time. "People are looking for me."

"People are looking for you. What kind of people?"

"Bad people. People I owe money to. At least two different bailiffs and a Turkish drug dealer."

The young man's head dropped again, and his sad eyes stared into the cup of coffee. Ben realised he was close to tears. He could not remember his son ever looking so totally defeated. Instinctively, Ben dropped onto his knees and hugged his son. Tom's muscles resisted at first but then relaxed as he started to sob quietly. They stayed in this position for a minute or so. It seemed longer to Ben, as his knees had begun to ache.

"It will be OK, Tom. We will work something out. I'll speak to your mother and..."

"I wouldn't if I were you," the young man warned, now sitting bolt upright.

"Why on earth not? You're still our joint responsibility. At least morally, if not legally."

"That's what one of the bailiffs told her when they turned up at her house threatening to take away her jewellery if she didn't pay them two and a half grand on the spot."

Ben screwed up his face at the thought of his ex-wife confronted by a couple of neanderthal bailiffs threatening to enter her house and take away her prized belongings. A part of him also wished he could have been a fly-on-the-wall to witness that scene.

"And she paid?" checked Ben, assuming she would have.

Tom explained that his mother had rung him straight away when it happened, but that he saw her number come up and had not answered her call.

"She screamed a message into my voicemail about my never setting foot in their house again until I had repaid the money in full, as well as apologised to her and her new husband." His red eyes were growing angry again and Tom added, "Two things that are just not going to happen."

"Bloody hell, Tom. That's just not taking responsibility for your own actions, once again. You can't keep running away from the consequences of what you do. Where will you run from here? This is the last stop at the end of that line, Tom."

There was a pause before Ben asked, "How did you end up owing all this money, anyway?"

The young man's anger mellowed to contrition when he had to face up to the unavoidable fact that he had borrowed from a couple of payday loan companies and gambled most of it away online. With the interest compounding daily, he'd looked for another way to get out. He had accepted some dope to resell to friends, but then gambled the proceeds so couldn't pay back the dealer.

When it all started coming home to roost, he had fled to his sister's flat in Clapham. But then somehow, the dealer had heard he was living in South London. Someone must have spotted him in a pub, he rationalised, and now they were looking for him. Not wanting them to find out where Selene lived and drag her into it, Tom had rung his father, finally taking him up on his offer of a free holiday in Seborga.

"Faced with the prospect of telling you and your new wife, the princess, my sorry tale, I got off my face on duty-free booze between checking in at Gatwick and arriving in Nice."

Ben's mind was already racing through the various scenarios, possible best and worst-case outcomes, and searching for potential solutions.

"So, bailiff number one was taken care of by your mother?" Tom nodded.

"Bailiff number two is still looking for you and wants how much?"

"With costs and interest, I think it's risen to eighteen hundred pounds and some change. Say another £2k"

"And I dread to ask, but the dope dealer?"

Tom looked indignant and pleaded, "He only gave me two hundred and fifty quid's-worth but says he wants four times that back because of the wait and collections costs. He's a thieving Turkish bastard."

"That's why he is in his chosen profession," Ben observed. "So, the sum of your current indebtedness is three thousand pounds, plus the two that you now owe your mother. Is that correct?"

Tom hung his head again and went quiet while he weighed up whether to reveal the full scope of his stupidity. After a few minutes more interrogation, it turned out there was also unpaid rent at his flat. He had simply walked away, ignoring bills for council tax, utilities, and two credit card balances. There were also overdue repayments on a designer watch he'd bought on credit and later pawned for cash. All-in-all, the extra debt was another seventeen hundred pounds.

"So, by my calculation, you need to earn something over ten thousand pounds just to clear your current debts."

The young man looked angry and frustrated again. "No, just short of five K."

Ben sighed. "Tom, firstly, to end up with seven after tax, you need to earn ten. Tax is how adults pay to keep the world around us working. Secondly, you seem to have discounted repaying your mother, or more likely your stepfather, the two thousand. My first condition for agreeing to help you is that you do just that."

"But he's...," Tom started to argue, but his father stopped him mid-sentence.

"Tom, you can only negotiate when you have bargaining power, and you currently have none. This is a take-it or leave-it offer. I will help you on my terms or take you to the station. You decide. I'm now going to tell Alessandra your tale of woe and ask her if she is willing to help me with this. If she agrees, I will return, and you can tell me if you wish to stay here with our support or go back to London and face the consequences of your actions on your own."

At this, Ben left the forlorn young man with his emotions interchanging between embarrassment and resentment as he sought someone else to blame for his predicament. But even Tom found his rationale for each potential contender flawed, and had to absolve them all from blame. In the meantime, Ben called Selene on her mobile, and it rang with a reassuring overseas dial tone. This sign indicated that she was in Italy this weekend as she had told him she would be. Explaining what had happened to her brother, the anxious father asked her to make a couple of phone calls to London on his behalf.

Alessandra took the news about Tom with the sense of resignation that only a betrayed employer, wronged wife, or disillusioned parent could. It occurred to Ben that you needed a strong emotional connection with someone to feel a deep sense of disappointment and feeling of hopelessness at their behaviour. The misdemeanours of strangers are viewed in isolation and not as part of a greater malaise. Without the background of previous transcreations, people seem more capable of redemption. Also, when you have weathered the challenges that Ben and she had during the last five years, Tom's seven thousand pound indiscretions seemed like small change. Alessandra agreed to help unreservedly. Ben remained more circumspect.

After making some phone calls of his own, Ben returned to the flat to speak to his errant son. In the first sign that things might improve, he had picked up and roughly folded the new clothes. Tom was wearing the new denim jeans and the long-sleeved Oxford shirt. He looked presentable and possibly even handsome, Ben thought.

"I can see why you bought this now," Tom said, holding up the buttoned-up sleeves so that the red welts on his wrists just became visible. He still had that winning cheeky smile that seemed to make men forgive him, and women melt, which would no doubt come in useful when he finally met Alessandra. Tom had not attended their wedding or even replied to the invitation. These were actions which had hurt and had upset her at the time.

Ben explained that Alessandra was busy working in the Osteria at lunchtime, but that they would meet tonight. Selene was driving over from Genoa later, and they would have a family dinner together.

"I have brought a packed lunch and you and I are now going for a walk." Ben dropped his own walking boots at Tom's feet. Both men wore the same size, so Ben had put on some old trainers that he used when working in the fields. Tom began to argue against unnecessary exercise but Ben just ignored him and turned towards the door, waving the prospect of lunch over his shoulder.

"If you want to taste the best arancini al ragu in Liguria, you had better catch up."

With Tom's appetite whetted from the amazing focaccia and pastries at breakfast, he pulled on his boots without bothering to lace them and traipsed after his father. The latter was already going down the stairs into the shop below.

As they passed through the ground floor shop, Tom asked, "What's with all the junk?"

"These antiques were the stock-in-trade of the deceased Crazy Dutchman." Ben gestured with his arms to suggest the whole building, "He left all this to Selene in his will. I'll explain as we walk."

"Bloody Hell. If my sister tripped in the street, she would land on a twenty-pound note."

Ben countered with, "Your sister will also have inherited the Dutchman's hashish stash, which you have apparently found and smoked. So, you now also owe her for that as well. But you will know the going rate for dope," he added with more than a hint of sarcasm.

Tom had no reply. As they crossed the piazza heading for the road north out of the village, the young man's blonde head panned around taking in all the sights he had missed when he had arrived the previous day, still half-drunk. He realised how high the village was, as the land dropped away steeply on all sides, except for the ridge they were walking along heading north. He could see the red-tiled roofs of houses scattered on the other side of the valley, nearly all of them at a lower elevation.

Ahead of and above them, there were few signs of habitation. Above the line of the road was little except a wild forest of mixed pine and some deciduous trees. Below, were the silver-green leaves on twisted branches that even Tom recognised as olive trees. Nothing further was said by either man until they reached the Passo del Bandito sign when Tom guffawed aloud.

"I speak no Italian except Birra Moretti, but that sign must surely mean, Bandit Street?"

"That's precisely what it says. This path, and many other trails leading into the hills, are thousands of years old. They were used to move between villages but also for trade over the mountains. They are so remote that they were almost impossible to police. Robbers were able to attack traders carrying goods or money and disappear into the hills. During the last two wars, thousands of partisan soldiers hid up here and fought a guerrilla war for years against the Nazis."

The younger man was surprised at how his father was striding ahead while his own breath was getting short. It seemed as if Ben was deliberately pushing the pace to make conversation more difficult. He wanted them both to have time to adjust to their respective changed perspectives and think about a way forward. During regular pauses to look around him, Tom began to acknowledge the natural grandeur all around them.

Ben felt encouraged that this outing looked like being a good idea. He had always found that these walks helped him to put things in their right places. When you are sitting looking down from what seems like the roof of the world, big problems seem smaller somehow, he had learned. It was now Ben's turn to halt progress. He removed two chilled bottles of water from the backpack. Only when he saw the bottles did Tom realise just how desperately thirsty he was. Partly it was dehydration from yesterday's booze, but mostly it was the exertion of the hike.

They both drank deeply but said little, conserving their breath as there was no sign of an obvious endpoint for this upward sloping path. They soon reached a fold in the hillside. Here, a narrow stream flowed down and under the path, emerging from a stone arch on the other side. Ben ducked under a tree next to the main trail and held up the branch for his son to follow him down. Now, under the canopy of trees, they could see a trickle of water descending a gradient more than double that of the trail they had been walking on. Using the stream bed as a path, Ben started to climb.

"Be careful-the wet stones are slippery," he warned.

The larger exposed stones of the riverbed created a natural, if irregular, staircase, without which the slope would have been almost impossible to climb. There was little more than a drizzle of water flowing off the mountain at this time of the year. Even Ben, who had done this many times before, had to drop onto all fours for some of the more challenging parts. It took fifteen minutes to reach a flat grassy clearing which had sunlight streaming through sparse leaves. Tom collapsed on his back on the grass, breathing heavily. Ben remained sitting on a rock, for he too was a little breathless. One word at a time, Tom asked, "How. Much. Further?"

"Another thirty minutes but with much less incline now. That was the hardest part."

Without the watch he had pawned, or his mobile phone that had been cut off for unpaid bills, Tom had no idea of the hour of the day, except that his stomach told him it was lunchtime. As his father had promised, the remaining walk was more leisurely, but still took a further forty-five minutes because of Tom's slower pace. As they reached the end, the trees became thinner and expansive vistas began to open up around them. Azure blue skies with the occasional wispy cloud formed a stark contrast with the green all around them. An occasional passing passenger jet left its smoke-grey trail across the blue.

At last, they reached their destination and a clearing opened on one side to a rocky ridge. A boulder about a metre in circumference and two metres long looked as if it had been rolled from the mountain into the centre of the grassy plateau. Here, someone had set about carving symbols into it, including a large cross, with two numbers on one side and a letter on the other.

"Boundary markers of the Knights Templar," Ben offered as

an unsolicited explanation. "The numbers indicate the distance to Seborga and the letter the direction, S for south. Carved nearly a thousand years ago."

It was not the most impressive ancient ruin Tom had ever seen, but the view from the ridge took his breath away even more than the climb had. He had been at this kind of altitude before whilst skiing, but not in clear sight of the sea. The coastal ribbon of human development scored a clear horizontal grey line between the green and the blue in the middle distance. Beyond that, the azure sea blurred into the sky without a visible join.

From reading some of his sister's coverage of events in Seborga, Tom was broadly aware of its history and the recent tumultuous events. He still found it hard to believe her luck at being right there when the document proving the principality's independence was discovered-a piece of good fortune that had kickstarted her career in journalism. Not content with that, in Seborga she had since met and was now dating the Prime Minister of Italy. When Tom recently heard about her inheriting a house from a virtual stranger, he resigned himself to believe that any good fortune in their family was clearly destined to be hers.

However, much as he envied her, begrudged her prosperity and hated her smugness about it all, his love for his sister had been brought home to him last year when she was threatened. Tom had witnessed the security video, where the former PM, Mastroianni, assaulted her and was apoplectic with rage. If he had been there, and not Cristiano, he had told anyone that would listen, the 'fat pervert' would not have escaped with his manhood intact, as was the case.

Ben shuffled himself up to sit on the Templar stone and, with tapping his hand on it, indicated for Tom to join him. Out of the knapsack he extracted two small bottles of beer which he passed to his son. Four packages appeared from the bag, neatly wrapped in greaseproof paper. Ben deftly popped off the bottle tops on the rock and let them fall onto the grass.

"Pick those up before we go, Tom. We will leave this place as we found it."

Ben passed him two packages with the advice to open them and spread the contents on their rock table. Amazingly, the arancini were still slightly warm, making them soft and moist inside. The rich red ragu almost dribbled out like jam from a raspberry doughnut when they bit into them. The clean mountain air amplified the meaty smell. There also was a homemade frittata, freshly baked bread, a wedge of hard cheese, prosciutto and peaches.

"So, these are the famous arancini?"

"They are. And your verdict?"

"Well, obviously, I am not yet an expert, but these are the best I have ever tasted."

"Good. Tell Alessandra that, but leave out the bit about not being an expert, and all will be well in her world."

They ate the remainder of their lunch in silence, both considerably calmed by the serenity of their surroundings. Before they set off, Ben bent down, picked up the previously discarded bottle tops and placed them in the knapsack without comment. The alternative route back was circuitous but not as steep, allowing more opportunity for conversation. After more than six years with minimal contact, there were many gaps in Ben's knowledge of what his son had been up to. Most of what he learned on their journey only fuelled his concern. With each kilometre, Ben's frustration, and the weight of Tom's guilt, grew until neither were happy with their burdens.

Selene was expected to arrive in Seborga at about five thirty. She was to meet Tom at the apartment before bringing him for dinner at the Osteria. He had been instructed to wear the long-sleeved shirt his father had bought to hide the wounds on his wrists. It struck Ben as an extraordinary coincidence that now his son and his wife each carried evidence of violence on their respective wrists.

Alessandra's scars had been inflicted in a drug-fuelled rage by one of her kitchen staff who she had caught having sex with her now ex-husband. The girl had lashed out at Alessandra with a boning knife that she had grabbed, leaving deep scars on the undersides of both wrists. The scars left her looking like she had attempted to take her own life, making them doubly embarrassing. She had finally come to terms with this disfigurement when in the company of friends, but was still uneasy about it in front of strangers. Ben did not want her attention drawn to it by having to explain his son's own version.

Alessandra dearly wanted to make a good impression on Ben's son. She was overcompensating for his assumed lack of experience with traditional Italian cuisine by selecting the most anglicised menu she could think of. It consisted of bruschetta, spaghetti pomodoro, Bistecca Fiorentina and tiramisu, served with Ben's Rossese wine. She had run it past Selene in a text message, and she had replied, "Spaghetti, steak and tiramisu. Tom will fall in love with you, as his father did." But at once she qualified this response with, "Well, maybe not quite in the same way," accompanied by a smiling and winking face emoji.

Selene was not very sympathetic to her brother's plight. She was horrified to learn that his drug dealer had people looking for Tom in Clapham while he had been crashing on the couch at her flat. Over the years, Tom had acquired a habit of turning up on her doorstep when he fell out with their mother, stepfather, flatmates, or had just run out of money. Selene had previously been forgiving of her brother's teenage angst but when he got into in his twenties, her patience, like their father's, wore thin. His falls from grace had become increasingly serious, and now it seemed that they were beginning to threaten her personal life.

Andrea had only stayed at her flat on two occasions, but one of them was quite recently. On those nights he had been able to sneak away from official meetings in London, but there had not been enough notice for her to arrange time off work and a discrete rendezvous location. So, the Prime Minister of Italy had worn a baseball cap to disguise his distinctive blonde, wavy hair and taken an Uber to her flat, so they could grab a few precious hours together.

What if this Turkish thug had turned up during one of these liaisons demanding his money, she had agonised? Andrea certainly would not have paid him, even if he'd had been carrying the cash on him to do so. She envisaged the international headlines following what would have been the inevitable fracas between the Italian PM and a London drug dealer taking place at the flat of a British journalist. Tom's shameful behaviour had to stop, she decided.

After an uncomfortable conversation with his sister, Tom turned up for dinner at the Osteria in a foul mood but wearing his best smile and a white t-shirt, despite his father's instructions. Selene thought that her father looked like he had aged since they'd last met just a month or two ago. Tom held out his hand to shake Alessandra's, and she immediately said, "Oh my God, what happened to your wrists?"

Ben had decided that, along with the debts and running away from them, the incident at the airport was one too many disasters to burden Alessandra with all in one go. Tom's explanation of what happened was at variance with his own recollection, but he was in no mood for another confrontation before dinner. He would tell her later. Cristiano, who was helping in the kitchen so his mother could have the night off, came out to say hello. The junior chef was in his clean, pressed whites wearing his trademark bandana to hold his black wavy hair.

Cristiano greeted Tom with a huge smile and open arms, offering a bonding hug and, "Great to finally meet you. Welcome to Seborga." In stark contrast, Tom barely managed a smile, which to Ben looked more like a smirk, while proffering an unenthusiastic handshake and nothing more than, "Hi. Any chance of a beer?"

"Well, this is going well," Selene said to her father under her breath.

Alessandra decided that food was needed to improve the atmosphere, and everyone was happy for the distraction of her handing around bruschetta. Ben used some of his frustration wrenching the cork out of a bottle. Selene started telling Alessandra about her weekend in Genoa, about meeting Andrea, and the dinner they'd had after the yacht launch. The mood lightened somewhat, and Ben poured wine into everyone's glass.

"These are the last two bottles of my first ever vintage, from two seasons ago."

Tom took his glass held it up to the light, sniffed it briefly and then downed it in one gulp. "Pretty good stuff, Dad. Anymore?"

Ben took a second to gather his thoughts. He decided that he'd really had enough of Tom in the last twenty-four hours.

"Yes, Tom. There is another bottle. I believe it's thirty euros per bottle here at the Osteria. Oh, but I forgot, you don't have any money, do you? Which fast-forwards us nicely to the conversation that I was going to save until after dinner. My wife, your sister and I have discussed your self-inflicted perilous situation and are willing to help you, but only if you agree to some simple conditions.

"We will pay off your current debts if you agree to stay here in Seborga and work to pay us back, and then make enough to repay your stepfather. We think it will take about six months, but you will have gained some much-needed work experience for your CV and be out of debt. You will be able to go home, where hopefully things will have calmed down. We will give you somewhere to live and feed you while you are here."

Tom stared into his empty glass as though wishing he had sipped it. "What kind of work?"

"I don't think you are in any position to be picky about your employment, but it might be working in the orange groves, cutting wood, or washing pots for Cristiano in the kitchen. Whatever needs doing that someone is willing to pay you for."

Tom stood up, pushing his chair backwards until it tilted and fell. "Washing pots for Cristiano? I don't think so. Does your first offer still stand?"

"Which first offer?" Selene asked, looking puzzled.

"A lift to the train station and a ticket back to London."

Without hesitating, Ben confirmed that it did. Tom grabbed two handfuls of bruschetta from the plate, said, "I'll take that offer," and stormed off in the direction of Selene's flat, dropping pieces of tomato and basil leaves as he went.

After a moment, Selene observed, "Well, that was a total disaster."

7. OYSTERS AT BENTLEY'S

Back in London, Selene exited from the rear of Kings Cross station, the final part of Selene's daily commute was a pleasant ten-minute stroll alongside Regent's Canal. It housed a strange breed of narrowboat dwellers who were now familiar figures, with the detritus of their minimalist lives often laid out for all to see. In Central London these upcycled steel, floating homes had become the most affordable real estate in the city.

As she walked along holding her takeaway coffee, Selene often wondered what it would be like to live aboard. Certainly, in terms of square meters, it did not appear to be much smaller that her Clapham flat and would save her almost two hours a day on her commute to work. As she walked and pondered life afloat, her phone vibrated with an incoming message. "Are you screwing a Prime Minister?" was the first WhatsApp message of what would turn into a steady stream from her work colleagues over the course of Selene's day.

The first message had been from her editor in with a link to Instagram post clearly showing Selene in a restaurant, with who the author suggested looked 'remarkably like Andrea Cassini, the dashing young Prime Minister of Italy.' The image of the person sitting opposite her was far from clear. The baseball cap pulled low over his brow cast a shadow over most of his face. However, the man clearly had Cassini's build, with locks of wavy blonde hair protruding from under the hat. There was no denying a likeness.

Andrea had chosen 20TRE (twenty-three), a restaurant in the

backstreets of Genoa. It was close to the historic Via Giuseppe Garibaldi, a UNESCO World Heritage site. The decor was intimate with moody lighting and had plenty of pillars to hide behind. He had also heard that the food was amazing. Their deconstructed take of the classic Genoan dish of cappon magro was famous amongst the city's discriminating foodie elite, as was their millefoglie with chocolate mascarpone cream.

The restaurant was run by one of a new generation of entrepreneurial young restaurateurs serving modern, reinvented versions of traditional Ligurian cuisine. However, it was hard to get a table, especially if you could not reveal that you were the prime minister. Andrea had booked it through the Minister of Tourism who had said it was for a magazine restaurant critic who insisted on the utmost discretion.

Selene was tagged in the post, indicating that the author knew exactly who she was. She had already weighed up the possible consequences if this went any further. After all, Andrea was an unmarried man, who was young and handsome with a track record of being seen with beautiful women on his arm. Nobody would think there was anything remarkable or controversial about him being out to dinner with a young woman. No one except the diners who found themselves on a nearby table, who must have thought they recognised Andrea. For them, it must have seemed like their moment in the spotlight.

Selene decided to make light of it and typed a reply to her editor, "You know that there is nothing I would not do to get a scoop for our newspaper, and if Mr Cassini so much as looked in my direction, rest assured I would jump into bed with him." Selene could easily justify this statement if pressed because it was pretty much what had happened. She edited a slightly different version of this same story for other friends and colleagues who had seen the post. She hoped not to hear much more about it.

Still dealing with the fallout from her brother's financial

fiasco, Selene received a similar sarcastic message from one of her older male colleagues who worked on the news desk. Seeing the reporter's name gave her an idea. She called him, joked about the Instagram photo, but then moved to ask a favour of their newspaper's new crime correspondent. Briefly explaining the background, she asked if he could find and contact the Turkish dealer looking for her brother.

From the detailed description Tom had given, the seasoned reporter was sure that there was a fairly good chance he could find him. Selene said she would transfer a thousand pounds to him but asked that if he had any leverage he could apply, to try and negotiate a deal closer to the actual debt. With something of a crush on Selene and so relishing her personal challenge, the journalist agreed. He said it was better not to make a traceable bank transfer. Instead, he would use his own funds and get it back in cash from her later.

"Can you do it sooner, rather than later?" Selene pressed.

"I can get on it today, but it will cost you a lunch of oysters and fizz at Bentley's," came the reply.

"Agreed," she confirmed, happy to spend an hour dodging her colleague's advances to get rid of the even-less-wanted attentions of this Turkish criminal.

By the following day she received a message saying he had identified the dealer. Later that night, another message read, "Met him. Done deal. Almost half price. Lunch soon."

Concert for the locals by Yannick.

Drawing by Linda McCluskey

8. CACCIATORE

The rattle of a metal-wheeled trolley on the flagstones outside the window told Ben that the time was gone 8 am, when the shop opened. Every item sold in Seborga's few shops had to be pulled by handcart from the piazza, which was the closet any vehicle could get to the narrow alleys of the village. Each truckload might need several journeys back and forth using the trolleys, providing a wake-up call to those who needed it.

Most older villagers were already up and about. Sitting with a coffee, or even a glass of Vermentino, watching the drivers from the cities arrive, manoeuvre around the narrow bends, fight over limited parking spaces and argue over trolleys, used to be a welcome spectator sport in an otherwise uneventful day. However, with the arrival of the Grail, its Alpini guards and the return of tourists, the old men now had plenty of other distractions.

Ben hardly slept the night after what he had hoped would have been a wonderful family reunion. His emotions swung from anger at his son's behaviour-embarrassing both him and Selene in front of Alessandra and Cristiano-to terrible guilt for any contribution that he might have made to his son's apparent feelings of isolation. Ben rationalised that leaving the family home when Tom was at a difficult stage of adolescence had not been his choice, but rather his then-wife's insistence. He also had no control over her moving in a new partner so soon after he'd gone.

Ben subsequently wondered if his wife's relationship with this other man was already going on behind his back and whether his own much-exaggerated misdemeanour was just the perfect excuse to get him out of the house. Ben had no factual evidence for this theory and would probably never know for sure.

Ben tried to keep in touch after he moved out, but Tom was so upset and angry that their phone conversations usually ended with the boy hanging up without saying goodbye. His subsequent move three-hundred miles away to Newcastle must have seemed like the final desertion, he now realised. So, the long night had passed with him going over and over ways that things might have worked out for the better, without coming to any conclusion. He must have finally fallen asleep because Alessandra woke him with a cup of his favourite Earl Grey tea at gone eight o'clock.

"How are you feeling?"

Ben thought for a moment. "Sad, angry, disappointed, let-down, despairing and frustrated," he listed.

His wife replied, "Tom too, I suspect. Plus, maybe, abandoned, lacking confidence, and worst of all, desperately lonely."

Ben scowled. "If you're lonely, you don't push people away. If you're offered support, you don't throw it back in the faces of the people who clearly love you enough to make it."

Alessandra set on the bed and leaned back, close to her husband. "Ben. Ben. You can't just apply your English academic logic to human emotions, especially where family are concerned. It's much more complicated than that. Cristiano and I went through something remarkably similar to this when I took him away from New York, leaving his father 'to rot in prison,' as he saw it. Later, I brought you into his already upside-down life. Fortunately, you were kind, generous and forgiving, and eventually won him over."

Ben began to argue his point, but Alessandra interrupted him, "You're a pragmatic problem-solver, Ben, and there's no one better at that. But in this case, you are focusing on the effects of the problem and not the cause. That is like building flood defences against climate change. Failing to deal with the root cause only moves the problems somewhere else. It's a treatment, not a cure."

It was hard to argue with his wife's analysis or her conclusion, but Ben was simply bereft of ideas of where to start.

"If he insists on still leaving this morning, let me take Tom to the station. I'll see if I can talk to him. At the very least, I will try and get him to call you and set things straight. You can't part not speaking to each other."

What Ben didn't know was that after he had gone to bed early last night, still fuming from the ruined dinner, Alessandra had taken a plate of the leftover food around for Tom. They had chatted, cautiously, for nearly an hour, and Alessandra came away feeling she had gained a degree of trust. However, Tom insisted that he wasn't staying to be a kitchen slave to someone his own age.

"Did you know that he has real issues with gay people?" Alessandra asked.

Ben looked surprised. "No. I had no idea. What makes you say that?"

"The way he treated Cristiano last night. He looked like he thought that he was shaking hands with a leper."

"That would be that bloody snobby school they sent him to after I was gone. It was part boarding school, and there are always polarised factions of the rugby guys versus those few boys still figuring out their sexuality. Teenagers can be cruel and brutal. Later, if they go on to play club rugby, where they're always immersed in that very macho environment, those prejudices are perpetuated."

Alessandra sighed. "This is the twenty-first century. Tom needs to get over it."

"That and a lot of other things," Ben added, looking forlorn.

The couple agreed that Tom had two generous options in front of him. Also, that it was time that he stood on his own feet and accepted responsibility for his actions and decisions. Alessandra would drive him to the station, but Ben would come and say goodbye before they left.

Unlike Ben, Alessandra could see what she thought was the root cause of Tom's anger. She believed that he had been made to feel homeless and rejected by all his family. He felt that his father had abandoned him to his fate. His sister had left home soon after his stepfather moved in, and he was then sent to boarding school and had not been made particularly welcome if he went back for holidays. For a teenager, already coming to terms with so many other changes in his life, this was just too much uncertainty.

Alessandra picked Tom up from Selene's flat in her late father's old Fiat. Selene had left very early in the morning to get her hire car back to Genoa Airport and catch her flight to London. When Alessandra drove by her own house a few minutes later, Ben was sat outside on the doorstep looking glum and stroking Don Gateau, the friendly three-legged cat. The cat was arching his back and rubbing up against Ben's leg. When Alessandra's car came around the corner, he stood and tried to put on a brave smile. His wife got out of the car, but Tom stayed firmly in his seat with his seatbelt buckled. The windows were down as it was already hot inside. Ben gave Tom an envelope containing some cash and then offered his hand. Tom shook it with only slightly more sincerity than he had Cristiano's the previous night.

A quietly spoken and grudging, "Thanks," was all he would offer in return.

"Take care."

After a peck on the cheek from his wife, the pair set off for Ventimiglia. Ben looked at Claudio's battered gold watch, which she had given him after her father died. It was only 8:30 am and there would be no train until 10:30 am. He assumed Alessandra must have some other errands to run in town. Sitting back down on the doorstep, the cat, who had been lying in a sunny spot, retuned for some more attention from Ben.

"It seems that you're the only one who needs my affection today."

Ben decided to spend the day in the vineyard where the work usually made his troubles evaporate. When he arrived, Vincenzo and Marius were already hard at work in the early morning sunshine. They had spent over a year gradually repairing the terraces on Ben's vineyard in between their other jobs. The stones which had been scattered over several decades by foraging cinghale (wild boar) were first gathered into heaps. Then the painstaking work of rebuilding the dry-stone walls began.

Starting with the biggest stones – many too big for one man to lift – a solid base was created along a runner line of string which was stretched between two points to ensure a straight line across the terrace. Inclined wooden lathes placed every few metres gave the wall a uniform, slightly backwards tilt. This design would ensure the weight of the wall offered resistance to the ground pushing against it. These were techniques practised over thousands of years. For a similar amount of time the hooves and snouts of wild boar, most weighing much more than a man, had been ploughing the walls down. It was a never-ending battle, until the advent of electric fences. But even these were not foolproof.

After an hour or so, Vincenzo's mobile phone rang with his easily recognisable and much-too-loud Nessum Dorma ring tone.

"Pronto. Si," followed by a long pause with some head nodding and shaking and then, "Princepessa. Si. Si. Si. Abiento."

After pocketing his phone, the big Italian bent back down to his work. Apparently, no explanation was going to be offered, and so Ben did not ask for one. Forty-five minutes later Alessandra's car appeared on the track below the vineyard. Two figures got out and Ben could see that she had brought Tom back with her. Taken aback, he ran through a mixture of emotions including delight, trepidation, and finally relief. His wife stayed at the car but handed Tom a neatly wrapped package which Ben at once recognised as lunch. Ben now looked to Vincenzo for an explanation of the phone call.

Alessandra's right-hand-man shrugged his shoulders as if to ask, 'What was so surprising?' "She asked if we could use some help. I said that we could. She asked me if I would teach him, I said that I would. She said not to tell you who'd called, so I didn't."

Ben smiled at Vincenzo as if acknowledging his dilemma. He set off to meet his son halfway, in a gesture of compromise that was instinctive rather than planned. In the minute it took to walk a hundred metres down the sides of the terraces, Ben decided just to start over as if last night had not happened.

"We are glad that you decided to stay and help us. This is a mammoth task. So long as you're here to take my place, I'll take a lift back with Alessandra. I have other things to do. I'll leave you to get on with it."

Vincenzo waited for Tom to reach them. Marius introduced himself and started showing him which stones to collect and where to stack them. There was half a pile already in place from which Vincenzo was placing stones in the wall. Marius also started building further along the terrace, but they quickly ran out of the material. When Tom came back to the pile carrying just one medium-sized stone, both men stood with their hands on their hips.

Realising that his collection speed was limiting their progress, Tom stopped daydreaming about the morning's events and stepped up the pace. His efforts were still not providing enough stone for two men laying it, so Marius went back to building his own pile. After just ten minutes, Marius had accumulated a pile more than twice the size of the one Tom had created for Vincenzo.

It was past eleven thirty in the morning and the sun was

approaching its highest point. Tom's back hurt, he was getting blisters on his thumbs, and his t-shirt was soaked in sweat. Not long after, they could hear the sound of church bells from across the valley. Without checking the time, Vincenzo and Marius knew by the bells' peel that this was noon and so lunchtime. With both piles of stone almost depleted again, they stopped work. Vincenzo turned on a tap which he had rigged up at the end of a pipe fed from the spring up above them. Both men washed their hands and splashed water on their faces.

"Come and have your lunch, Tom," Marius invited.

Being competitive by nature and realising that he appeared to be losing this race, Tom declined. "I've not long had breakfast, so I'll work through." His thinking was that if he could build up some stocks of stone, he could get ahead of their work rate. He took off his shirt, revealing his pale skin, now with reddened arms.

"I'd put that shirt back on, take a rest and have a good drink of water," Marius advised, but Tom ignored him.

After their lunch, Vincenzo and Marius made themselves comfortable, pulled spare shirts over their heads and napped in the midday sunshine. Tom worked on, collecting and piling up the stones in heaps along the terraces. Despite the discomfort, he was finding solace in the work which caused his worries about problems in the UK to dissipate into the heat of the afternoon. After almost exactly an hour had passed Vincenzo stirred from slumber, as some internal clock knew it was time to get back to work. In what seemed like no time at all, the piles of stone had disappeared into the terrace walls and Tom was struggling to keep up again.

The last hour seemed like three to the young Englishman, and when Vincenzo finally stood up, straightened his back and said, "Abbastanza," Tom was nearly ready to collapse. He looked at his now burst blisters on his hands and could feel the tightness of the skin of his back. His back ached and the muscles in his arms throbbed, but strangely, he felt better than he had a long while yet in a way he could not really explain. There had been virtually no conversation during the day, yet so much had been communicated between them.

Tom learned that Marius worked with an economy of movement that it made it look like he was not doing much, despite the all the evidence proving otherwise. The dark-skinned Romanian deferred to Vincenzo in all matters, despite appearing to know as least as much about everything they were doing as his elder did. Vincenzo conveyed that he thought Tom was lazy, weak and feckless just by his body language. Marius seemed more friendly and less judgemental. Tom liked his quiet confidence, he decided. He seemed like a young man much more comfortable in his own skin than he was.

Together they travelled back along the valley in Vincenzo's Ape. As they bounced along the road in the back of the old pickup, Tom took in the scenery of the mountains above and the breathtaking views down to the coast. The sea looked very inviting, and he would have given almost anything to run down a beach and plunge into it right now. He finally opened the lunch package Alessandra had given him earlier. Inside was another of the wonderful arancini, this one filled with soft cheese and ham. There were also some small salami sausages, cheese, and a big slice of salty focaccia.

Tom saw Marius looking at the package and so reluctantly offered up the package to him. He shook his head, causing his long, curly hair to shake from the bandana he'd been wearing. He deftly caught the blue cotton handkerchief in one hand before it blew out of the Ape on the breeze. Declining the offer of food, he reached into his pocket and handed Tom his pocketknife to cut the salami.

"Cacciatore," Marius said, nodding at the wild boar salami. "It's our way to get back at the cinghale (wild boar) who knock down our walls and eat our crops. We make them into sausages."

Tom managed a half-smile, cut some chunks from sausage and offered the knife back. Marius said, "Keep it. You will need a knife every day, and you'd have to go all the way to Bordighera to buy one. I have another at home for myself. I can bring it tomorrow."

The Englishman began to decline this act of generosity but was stopped by a simple raised hand gesture. "I insist," was the end of the matter.

Vincenzo pulled up outside Selene's and waited for Tom to climb out which he did with some difficulty, his muscles and burnt skin now tightening up. Although Alessandra had told him that he could eat twice daily at the Osteria, Tom could only think of his bed.

9. PANINO CON VERDURE ARROSTA

On this occasion, it was Selene who spotted herself in a photograph with Andrea in the Instagram post before her colleagues did. Someone had snapped them at the rapper's boat launch in Genoa, just at the moment she was introduced to Zeno. It was the only time that she and Andrea had touched, at a public event, as he had reached back for her hand and pulled her forward to meet their host. But in the photograph it looked like they were hand-in-hand, smiling like star-struck lovers.

They might have been able to explain this photograph away had it been in isolation, and not deliberately linked to the image posted the day before showing Selene having dinner with a man who also looked like Andrea. They were clearly wearing the same clothes, except for Andrea's ineffective baseball cap disguise, indicating that these images were probably taken only hours apart.

Selene knew that these photographs were going to achieve a massive audience in Italy. In Andrea's brief time in office, he had gone from being an unknown local politician to the most popular PM in living memory. A movement for change was in the air and his policies were striking a chord with voters on both sides of the political divide. His support for environmental issues and women's rights had won him fans who would previously never have supported a centre-right government. But it was his battle with the European Union over sustainable fishing that was his cause celebre.

Even those who were indifferent about the fishermen's plight liked the idea of him standing up to the EU. This made for some previously unthinkable alliances with the Green parties. As a responsible father, being seen to be doing the right thing by his ex-wife and child, even the traditionalist Catholics forgave him for his now ten-year-old divorce.

Giving the media almost as much access as possible, always stopping to provide a photo-opportunity and giving a quote, they had so far treated him kindly. He was also happy to flirt with any female celebrities he met at events which provided endless material for the gossip columns. It also had, so far, distracted any attention from his actual relationship with Selene. Outside and inside his party, his opponents were furious about his golden boy image and a seemingly endless honeymoon with the media.

Was all this about to hit the buffers, Selene wondered? It had been the most wonderful year of her life, and she did not want it to end. The taking and publishing of these photographs could have been just a coincidence, but Selene had an uneasy feeling that someone had a malevolent hand in it somewhere. She just could not think of who or why, although she acknowledged that there would be no shortage of candidates with Andrea being in politics. Anticipating an escalation of interest, Selene rang him to suggest a cover story and then she rang her editor to obtain the backup for it.

Andrea pointed out that the cover story's problem was that, if the whole truth came out, they would look worse than if they just admitted it now. The journalist could see his point. A cover story, if blown, would look like they really had something terrible to hide. However, if they went public, Selene's newspaper's coverage of anything related to Italy would appear to be undermined. She would probably be asked to resign. Andrea's continued support for her father's Seborga projects would suddenly be seen in a new light, and likely retrospectively scrutinised. It seemed that they were damned if they didn't and damned if they did.

In the end, they agreed to go with the cover story that Andrea had given her newspaper's Sunday magazine supplement-a UK exclusive focussing on 'the man behind Europe's best-loved politician.' This gave a very plausible cover for Selene being seen with Andrea outside of his political appointments, but the big problem was that this excuse would come to an end when the feature was finally published.

Although she could probably spin it out for a while in order to obtain her editor's backing for her story, she would ultimately have to deliver a substantial article. At least a few more months of privacy was worth it, they calculated. By then, all the Seborga initiatives would be in place and Andrea could back away from any public connection to the principality. Her colleagues had assumed that her regular trips to Italy had been to see her father, and now she had gained the added justification of the property she had inherited there.

She had barely got the agreement in place for the exclusive magazine feature when the first Italian journalist rang Selene at the office. Sat at her desk, she had taken one bite from a verdure arrosta (roasted vegetable) focaccia sandwich from a new Italian takeaway near her office. Their delicious produce reminded Selene of San Antonio's panettiera, her father's favourite lunch stop when he was in Bordighera.

"Selene Morton? My name is Carina Esposito from La Stampa newspaper. I want to talk to you about the photographs that appear to show that you and our prime minister are in a relationship."

Selene did her best to muster a convincing laugh and then countered the accusation with, "I wish. Isn't he just gorgeous? As flattered as I am that anyone thinks he would be interested in me, I am just like you, a journalist doing my job."

Selene told herself that although this was a highly misleading statement, it contained no facts that could not be justified. She was indeed flattered by his attention, and she was doing her job when she met him. Before she could explain the cover story she had rehearsed in her head, the Italian dropped her bombshell.

"Your father is Professore Ben Morton and his wife Princess Alessandra of Seborga, are they not? Is it also the case that between them they have been the recipients of millions of euros in grants from Senor Cassini's government?"

Selene hung up.

10. BAGNA CÀUDA

The Fiori Autostrada (highway of flowers) snakes along the coast between the French border with Italy and the city of Genoa. It is one of the most spectacular driving routes in the world. As the Maritime Alps were pushed up from the floor of the Mediterranean Sea millions of years ago, they formed dramatic folds of rock along the coast. In some places, these rock protrusions continued pushing upwards until they formed the highest peak of Mount Argentera at over three thousand meters.

The dips between these ridges rising out of the sea became sandy bays around which fishing villages sprang up. Many of these have today grown to be bustling seaside towns with working harbours and pleasure marinas. To traverse this, the undulating terrain more prosaically known as Autostrada 10 alternates between tunnels, bridges and viaducts, twisting and turning along its route to follow the coast.

One moment travellers are in a kilometre-long tunnel through a mountain, the next they suddenly exit into bright sunshine one hundred meters in the air. Implausibly high concrete columns support a roadway that often appears in the sky above towns and villages. It is as spectacular as it is sometimes alarming, but the views are also breath-taking and the driving exhilarating.

After forty-five minutes on the Fiori Autostrada, it was mid-morning when Alessandra and Ben arrived at the tiny hilltop hamlet of Colletta di Castelbianco, located halfway between Seborga and Genoa. Although the village was situated at a similar elevation to Seborga, it was several kilometres further inland and so did not enjoy the same views of the Mediterranean. It was also even smaller than the tiny principality that the couple now called home, with fewer than thirty houses.

What was strikingly different, now they were up close to it, was just how uniform the buildings' condition appeared to be. That is to say, the houses were all unique in size, shape, and elevation outlook, but their exteriors looked to have been recently restored, apparently using their original materials. There were no partly rendered and painted walls, only beautifully hand-laid stone ones. No plastic windows, modern extensions or replacement roofs using modern materials - only old clay pantiles, copper gutters and oak window frames could be seen on all the houses. There was not a satellite dish anywhere to be seen.

The use of copper as a waterproof, and rustproof, material in roof architecture goes back to the Romans. In highly industrialised northern European communities, it was later replaced by cast iron and finally by plastic. In remote rural Italy, where people often had to build and maintain their own houses, materials were chosen because they could be formed by hand. Copper can easily be bent into almost any shape and sealed with solder without much expertise or the need for anything but basic tools. For reasons lost in time, in Seborga the ends of copper gutters are sometimes formed into elaborate dragon head shapes by local artisans. When it rains, they look as though these mythical beasts are spewing out water.

One of few common features were the green wooden louvre shutters on all the windows. Each leaf of the side-hung shutters contains another top-opening panel. The purpose of these is not obvious until someone has lived in these houses during summer. By noon, these shutters are closed to keep out the baking rays of the sun. The smaller inset panels are often opened slightly, their carefully angled louvres still offering shade but also catching any breeze and directing it upward into the room. Although today, new shutters are usually made of green-painted aluminium, this cleverly evolved design feature has been retained.

Like all the others in this region, this community would have grown and evolved over hundreds of years. It had probably never looked quite this pristine at any time in its history. It was as if it had all been built within the same couple of years by one builder, using identical specifications. In fact, that is almost what had happened there a few years ago, it would later be explained. Already in economic and social decline, the entire village had been abandoned after an earthquake sometime in the fifties. It had been left to deteriorate even further in the intervening half-century. Twenty years ago, a visionary architect had raised funding to restore the entire village, sticking strictly to traditional materials and practices.

When finished, the unique project became a destination for architectural students: almost a place of pilgrimage for those favouring sympathetic restoration over new build. To meet one of those very graduates was the reason Alessandra and Ben were here today. Alberto Cannavaro was now based in San Remo and was the London Club's chosen architect behind the Albergo Diffuso planned for Seborga. He had invited them here to show them what he planned to do with the buildings his clients were acquiring there.

Like everyone else, the couple had to park outside the village as it was now entirely pedestrian, apart from some small electric carts used to transport baggage, for maintenance, or for any medical evacuation. All the tarmac and concrete paths had been replaced with stone slabs and cobles. The young architect pointed out the black marble door heads, steps and windowsills used on all the buildings. Also, the traditional-looking windows all had triple glazing and integrated internal shutters to maintain the internal temperate-winter or summer.

"It is wonderful craftsmanship," Ben acknowledged.

The young architect then took them out to the perfectly restored and maintained olive groves surrounding the hamlet for what he called his mentor's piece de resistance. He stopped and asked, "So, what do you think of this feature?" A gurgling noise could be heard, and there was a slight chemical smell, but otherwise there was no clue what he was referring to.

"Of which feature?" they both asked, almost in unison.

He urged them both to stand on the tips of their toes and look over that terrace wall. Immediately on the other side was a swimming pool that had been entirely invisible until now. It was long and narrow because they had limited it to the three-metre width of the original terrace. It had just enough width for a couple of people to swim lengths for exercise. Everything was either hidden at sub-ground level or made to blend in with the surroundings. The shower looked like a garden hose with a sprinkler on the end casually slung over the branch of an olive tree. In fact, it was permanently fixed and connected to a water supply heated by the sun on the roof of a nearby building.

"It is all mightily impressive," Ben acknowledged. "Of course, in Seborga we will not be renovating every single building, so the effect will not be so uniformly immaculate as this."

"Maybe not a bad thing," observed Alessandra. "Although undoubtedly very authentic, this does look a little too clinically organised for Italy."

"I tend to agree," the architect acknowledged. "The Club wanted their guests to stay in an authentic environment and not in a museum. But you get the idea of a sympathetic, light-touch restoration?"

They all agreed that there were plenty of buildings in Seborga that would benefit from this treatment. After his tour, Alessandra and Ben thanked him for his time and they parted company. Now approaching lunchtime, Alessandra suggested a slight diversion to San Lorenzo al Mare, where there was lovely restaurant that she knew called Emy, next to a tiny beach. Like her own Osteria, it was run by a female chef. Ben, of course, took no persuading.

They ordered the spada (swordfish) because they were told it was fresh and local, plus some Bagna Càuda and vegetables to start. Two glasses of local Vermentino would go down well with this, they decided.

"Bagna Càuda?" Ben queried, reading it from the menu. "That's another new dish for me."

"The Piedemontese claim it as their own, but there has been a Ligurian version for as long as anyone can remember. It is simply anchovies blended with olive oil and garlic."

"Surely Piedmont is a landlocked region, and so isn't this much more likely the invention of coastal people?" Ben suggested, in academic support of the Ligurian claim.

Although reluctant to concede the advantage to their near-neighbours, Alessandra acknowledged, "We tend to eat our fish fresh after the catch, but anchovies preserved in salt, from which this dish is made, have always been traded with Piedmont for their wheat and pasta, so their claim that it is their invention is not entirely without merit."

When the small bowl of brown dip arrived, Alessandra tested the temperature of the contents with her finger.

"If it's cold then it's probably been made previously in a big batch and kept in the fridge. Warm means they just made it fresh." It was served with slivers of raw peppers for dipping, plus some crusty bread. Ben declared it, "Another triumph for the Ligurian less-is-more philosophy."

While they munched their salty vegetables looking out over the picturesque Italian seaside scene, conversation drifted back to Seborga.

"Tom appears to have settled down and be adjusting to his temporary home, don't you think?" Alessandra suggested.

Ben looked thoughtful for a moment and then replied, "He's so exhausted when he finishes work that he can't get into any trouble or upset anyone at the moment. He gets home, eats and sleeps. What keeps him going is his determination to prove Vincenzo wrong and match or even surpass Marius's work rate. It was the same with sport when he was at school. If a coach replaced him in a team, he would train and train until he could beat that person and win his place back. Having then done that, he would lose interest and stop turning up for matches. As he saw it, he'd made his point. So, I'm not celebrating yet," Ben added.

"People are motivated by many different things, Ben. You should know that."

He smiled, "You proved that when you got him to stay after everything he'd said about leaving. It was an inspired idea, offering to take him to the beach in Ventimiglia for breakfast. He'd go anywhere for food. Then choosing the beach where all the young waitresses go to swim and sunbathe before starting their shift was just genius."

"It's true. I can't deny it," Alessandra said, laughing. "After an hour of watching them arrive on their scooters, undress, swim, shower and then apply sun lotion, Italy was looking far more attractive than rainy old London, even if staying meant that he had to eat his words. There's a carrot for every donkey, as my dear father, Claudio used to say."

As well as the weather forecast for London, Alessandra had said that she was concerned about how he would avoid the people looking for him and where he was going to live, questions to which he'd had no answers. She had flattered him about his athletic physique, saying that it would not only impress the girls, but could eventually get him a better-paid job here working outdoors. After all, to date these girls he would need transport, plus money for petrol, drinks and pizza, she had pointed out. That was when she had phoned Vincenzo to check he would take him under his wing.

"So, it was essentially the same offer that I made him, just in better packaging?" Ben observed, wryly. "And it's me who's supposed to know about marketing," he joked.

Their spada steaks arrived with big chunks of fresh lemon, slightly caramelised on the surface from being placed on the grill. They smelled of the sea and olive oil.

Squeezing lemon over her fish, Alessandra concluded, "It was you who taught me to work out my customers' needs and wants, so I applied that same logic. And what does a twenty-five year old single man want?"

"Exactly what you offered him," Ben conceded.

After his first mouthful and murmur of pleasure, he remembered, "I had a message from Tom's mother this morning, saying that she had finally tracked down the other bailiff who was looking for Tom and paid them off as well. I will send her the money for that today. She only agreed to do this after I personally guaranteed that she would get back the previous two thousand pounds within six months."

"So, with Selene taking care of his drug debt, he is now solvent and no longer on the run?" said Alessandra, sounding relieved.

"As far as we know," added Ben, sounding sceptical. "But let's not tell him just yet. I don't want him thinking the coast is clear to run back home. I'm determined to make up for the time I have lost with Tom. I want to see if I can change his ways before he gets into real trouble."

"Remember needs and wants," his wife taunted.

"And the appropriate carrot for the donkey in question," he joked.

For the remainder of their lunch, the couple returned to the subject that had brought them there. Impressed with what they had seen at Colletta di Castelbianco, Ben wondered if they could not adjust the rules of their inward investment zero tax scheme for Seborga. He proposed that they could include some regulations to promote sympathetic restoration and the use of more environmentally friendly materials. He knew that in UK

National Parks, they had similar rules about using such materials and even paint colours. He said that he would ask Andrea, who he felt sure would welcome such an initiative.

Alessandra pointed out that without forcing residents to restore or rebuild in exactly the same way, the new Albergo Diffuso buildings would 'set the bar high' and give them something to aspire to.

Alessandra said, "I believe it will drive up standards, albeit slowly, this being Italy. When is Selene moving into her new house?"

"As soon as the paperwork is complete. Well, it's Tom who will be moving, because Selene is too busy to come at the moment. Maybe less than two weeks. The Club wants someone to get in there and start work the next day. I thought I might ask Richard if there was work for Tom."

"Better still, why don't you suggest Vincenzo to Richard as a contractor for building work? No builders are living in Seborga, and he has stonework and basic construction skills. He can always use some extra money. During Richard's visit, he told me that the Club pays well and offers early completion bonuses. If they accept, let Vincenzo offer Tom that carrot, keeping his new mentor as the one holding the reins. Distancing the job offer from any perceived interference by us will also sit better with Tom."

"You are good at this parenting thing, aren't you?" Ben said, only half-joking.

"Where men are concerned, maybe," Alessandra allowed, "but I'm not so sure I could handle girls quite so well."

Ben gave her a knowing smile and then washed the last morsel of swordfish down with the remainder of his Vermentino.

"A nap on the beach before we drive back?"

11. CARDI ARROSTA

With no previous business experience and just a second-class degree in History of Art, Cecily was both a reluctant and an unlikely entrepreneur. Her first husband had left her for a younger woman he had met on the Internet and moved to live in America. Left with a mortgage she could not afford, she had been forced to try and make some real money or move out of the garden flat in Chiswick that she loved.

Looking south over Kew Gardens and guarded on three sides by the snaking River Thames, the London Borough of Chiswick is an enclave of smug affluence. Some of its 18th century inns actually deserve the label 'gastropub'-unlike the hundreds of formulaic pastiche versions that have bred like rabbits in neighbouring boroughs but would never dream of putting 'bunny' on the blackboard menu.

Working from home, is another term that might have been invented in Chiswick by an earlier generation. Populated by media-tech foodies with flexible hours and high disposable incomes, residents meet in its West End cafés with East End post-industrial décor to discuss their next must-have kitchen implement. If Clapham is where those starting their clamber up the greasy pole begin, Chiswick is where those who make it come to raise families. If all goes well, the next and final stop is Chipping Norton in the Cotswolds.

An Olympic-standard networker with a can-do attitude, Cecily had soon mobilised a small army of her time-rich neighbours. They helped sell her homemade, chemical-free soaps and shampoos to their friends and family. Before she knew it, she was working twelve hours a day making and wrapping orders. Other products soon followed, and later her kitchen table was replaced by an outsourced factory while she concentrated on marketing.

Cecily's years of experience of growing her fair-trade cosmetics business had given the elegant Englishwoman an in-depth understanding of exactly what went into modern beauty products. She had spent her waking hours avoiding the types of toxic ingredients that her environmentally aware clients would find unacceptable. Banning the inclusion of ethanolamine, parabens, formaldehyde, and other harmful chemicals also gave her products a genuine point of difference from her mainstream competitors.

After leaving London to live on her yacht in the Mediterranean, Cecily applied the same rigorous environmental controls to everything used onboard. She knew that, like all boats, the waste from the drains ended up in a storage tank, along with any chemicals and plastics used in the products themselves. Skippers could legally open valves to discharge this waste into the sea, but responsible ones only did this in the deep open ocean, at least five kilometres offshore. So long as all the tank contents were purely organic material, this is an acceptable practice. However, most modern discharges contained harmful chemicals, microbeads, sanitary products and cotton buds – all of which are clearly harmful to the environment and the wildlife. This meant that even a boat made from wood and powered by sail, like hers, could still leave a disastrous environmental trail in its wake.

During the last year, Ben and Alessandra had learned about the poor environmental practices of other ships from Roman during several short sailing trips with the couple on Cecily's boat. Cecily, already a seasoned sailor, was well aware of the importance of respecting the nature of the ocean. Cecily's unconventional relationship with Roman had been the catalyst for her to purchase the classic ketch and to take up permanent residence there. It gave her the ability to stay close to Monaco with the perfect mobile office and provided a rendezvous location for her secret meet-ups with Roman while he was still committed to his cataleptic wife. Roman now a full-time resident, brought his eco-friendly practices learned from lemon farming to the vessel as well. Their combined knowledge proved to be a treasure trove to Ben and Alessandra in their own search for balance with agriculture and the environment. With the passing of Roman's wife, he and Cecily could look towards the future and were making plans to build a house somewhere between Seborga and Menton in close proximity to where the boat was moored. This would give Ben and Alessandra even greater opportunity to pick Roman's brain for more helpful environmentally sound practices.

Roman had also been asked to join the new Seborga environmental working group because his expertise as an orange farmer in Sicily was deemed extremely valuable by Ben. His friend had declined, citing that 'committees were not really his preferred way of working.' However, he did offer to provide advice whenever it was needed, channelling that through Cecily. He further conceded that, if his attendance were thought to be vital at a meeting, he would come along, with the proviso that Alessandra was cooking lunch afterwards.

The prime minister had floated the idea of using the new limited legislative independence of the tiny principality to experiment with untested environmental policies and practices. His thinking was that he could experiment with small-scale, low-cost, and therefore reduced risk, Green projects without making changes to national law. Any which proved successful could be rolled out across Italy. Cecily seemed like precisely the kind of person they needed as part of an advisory group.

Having recently sold the bulk of her cosmetics business,

keeping only a small niche range using blood oranges, she had some time to spare. Because some of the rare oranges she needed were now coming from Seborga, Cecily also had the motivation to look after the environment in which they grew. Even without a vested interest, the multimillionaire entrepreneur would have been happy to help her best friend, Alessandra, and new friend, the Prime Minister Andrea Cassini.

This morning was to be the inaugural meeting on the Environmental Committee of the Principality of Seborga. It would take place in the Osteria, after which everyone would enjoy lunch there. Everyone except Andrea, who could only join them via video from Rome, much to his own disappointment about missing Alessandra's pasta. They had invited Alain Cassel, a young marine scientist from the Monaco Oceanographic Institute, and the chairwoman of a Riviera environmental group. A representative of the Slow Food Organisation in Piedmont and a couple of their students who were now on placement in the village would also be joining the group.

Ben was acting as chairman and already had quite an agenda of things to discuss, and that was before any additional matters were raised by the other members. Today's objective was to come away with a list of potential policies to be researched and costed, ready for the next meeting in thirty days. Before the meeting, the members were asked to provide a list of what they believed to be their main environmental concerns, in order of priority, and any suggestions for tackling them. Ben then aggregated these into the agenda. Andrea was to open the meeting with a few words about his aspirations.

"Almost uniquely, you have the opportunity to reshape the community in which you live. By adjusting taxation, we can reward, punish and eventually cajole people into acting in certain ways. It can attract, but also exclude, certain types of economic activity. What you have to decide is the type of place you want to live in and how its economics will work."

The politician paused to let this sink in.

"Let me be clear that I accept that some of these experiments might not work. After all, that's what experimentation is. But, to borrow a phrase, let us fail fast and often until we find something workable. I don't know how long I will have in the office of the prime minister–historical precedent suggests not that long. I want to try and make a real difference in the time I have."

"Let me get this straight: you're asking a chef, a winegrower, and a food-loving cosmetics expert to reinvent a nation and change the habits of its citizens?" replied Cecily, only half joking about the enormity of the task.

"Exactly. We need to create a recipe for a nation. One that makes the most of local resources, can be created quickly, is sustainable and will attract diners to partake in it. In effect, we will be cooking up a country."

Cecily thought it was a clever analogy, given the audience, underlining once again what a natural leader Andrea was. He would have excelled in business, she mused, had that been his calling.

"If I am to roll out any of the initiatives during my term in office, what we try here needs to show measurable results in months, not years. Please do not propose anything that will take four years to build, a billion euros to fund and a decade to show results. Small-scale, short timeframe, and therefore limited cost projects are what we want, but within those parameters we can afford to be bold."

"I think you'd be better with an alchemist, a wizard or a genie in a bottle," Cecily joked.

"Or a fairy-tale princess and her knight in shining armour," Andrea countered, smiling broadly.

Ben decided this was a good time to wrap things up. He thanked the prime minister, conscious that, as his daughter's secret partner and potential future husband, Andrea probably also had other worries about people's perception of their respective roles in this, should they became widely known. Nevertheless, the members pressed on with the meeting and ninety minutes later had what Ben thought was an excellent shortlist of potentially feasible, economically-sound environmental initiatives.

Cecily had proposed a trial using some of the personal hygiene and domestic liquids on her boat. They were supplied in large containers which could be decanted into smaller reusable glass or stainless-steel bottles available from the village store. This would have the dual effects of significantly reducing single-use plastic bottles and preventing harmful chemicals from being discharged into the land through the soak-away drains and septic tanks still widely used in the village.

"These toxics and plastics will eventually end up in the olives, oranges and grapes that we otherwise think of as organic, and the bottles end up in landfill, or worse, in the ocean."

Andrea said this was precisely the type of initiative they wanted and immediately suggested a zero rate of purchase tax rate on products with no plastic packaging sold in Seborga. Cecily advised them that the loose product already cost less, and with a further twenty-two percent tax removed, customers should not need much more persuasion to try it.

Alessandra said that she would speak to the people behind the new Albergo Diffuso to ask if they would commit to using the refillable organic toiletries. She was confident that it would appeal to their customers' sensibilities.

Anticipating some Italian conservatism and resistance to change, Alessandra proposed an initiative to get the school's children involved - a slight modification to the curriculum to cover specific local environmental issues which would build on the annual survey of discarded plastic in the vicinity of the village. She argued that the children would educate their parents and shame those not complying into good practices.

"When parents and grandparents hear the children's heartfelt concerns about the planet that they will inherit from them, it will move even the most die-hard traditionalists to action," she predicted.

There was much discussion around private car use, and the potential of electric vehicles in particular. Everyone knew that there was currently limited employment in Seborga and only one food store, making regular journeys to the coast essential. However, even those working in Monaco only had a thirty minute commute, which was within the range of most electric cars. Most residents' journeys were only as far as the town of Bordighera, just twelve kilometres and all of that downhill on the outbound leg.

Ben advanced the idea that with the village open to the sun during all daylight hours, solar panels might provide much of the power needed to fuel these journeys. Alain, the scientist, said that these cars were now extremely popular in Monaco, but warned that the cost of acquiring them might be prohibitive to the average Seborgan.

"Then there is the solar infrastructure needed to recharge them," he added.

Andrea said that the government was already in talks with Italian car manufacturers about their industry's future. Without promising anything, the prime minister said that he would speak to Fiat about this problem and also to someone from a green energy supplier before reporting back.

Ben moved on to the problem of all the new construction going on in the principality. He had no previous experience of this building industry but could not help noticing all the plastic materials being used, concrete being poured, and tarmac being laid. The marine scientist added that the latter could increase the potential for flooding by covering previously porous surfaces with impermeable drives and carparks.

Not having even thought of that aspect, Ben added, "When we get storm rain rushing off the mountains around us, the informal network of gulleys that must carry it out of the village and down to the river below already become overwhelmed. The consequences of any further strain on the existing ad-hoc infrastructure are completely unknown."

The incidence and severity of rainstorms had increased, even from the first years that Ben had been in Seborga. The first intense storm, not long after his arrival, had caused the landslide which led to Ben's discovery of the charter given by Pope Gregory to the Templars. In a cave revealed by the landslide, he and Selene had found the long-lost document which proved the principality's independence from Italy. That event had started a chain reaction, leading to Seborga's partial-autonomy, and ultimately to this meeting today.

No one from the Slow Food organisation had so far made any contribution to the meeting, and Andrea was keen that they should be involved somehow. The truth was that the young academics were somewhat in awe of the charismatic Italian leader, the first ever with a clearly stated environmental agenda. They were more used to fighting to have a voice for their cause but now that they had one, they had gone strangely quiet.

The PM said, "Ben is restoring vineyards in Seborga and encouraging other villagers to do so, by joining a wine cooperative. He tells me that one barrier is that the land is often poor or has either been neglected or overworked by people raising other crops. What is needed is a natural fertiliser. This terrain cannot sustain grazing animals that would produce manure. So, I would like you, Slow Food guys, to come up with suggestions to revitalise the land, without compromising the organic status of the end products. Can I leave that modest task in your capable hands and look forward to a report with outlined proposals by the next meeting?"

The Slow Food spokesperson agreed that they would

investigate fertilisers.

On hearing about the revival of wine growing, the representatives from Slow Food were also prompted to describe a recent phenomenon they were aware of known as 'crowd-farming.'

"It might be something that the new wine growers could investigate to help fund their initiatives," they suggested. They explained that the model leveraged social media to facilitate the advance purchase of products by individuals from growers who used sustainable methods. Using the analogy of investment brokers who trade commodity 'futures' to provide investment, they pointed out that it reduced all parties' risk.

He explained that funding typically came from city dwellers bereft of access to the countryside who felt too distanced from the source of what they ate and who had environmental and food integrity concerns. This new breed of consumers could connect with individual farmers almost anywhere in the world, whose food ethics they supported, and order part of a future crop–a box of oranges, litres of olive oil, wine cases, and so on. When it was harvested, the produce would be delivered directly to their homes by a carrier. It offered a direct connection to an artisan grower where people could invest in their success and share their produce, they explained. Customers shared a small part of their risk in return for a percentage of their crop.

"Consumers feel as though they are part of something worthwhile, and it makes a great dinner party story when they finally eat or drink the produce they have invested in. It's a global initiative that is growing exponentially," the student spokesman added.

"Armchair farmers who don't even have to get their hands dirty," joked Andrea. "I love it."

Ben was making notes, already highly excited by this crowd-farming idea and determined to find out more. Only his lack of prowess with Internet technology was casting a shadow over his ambitions. He wondered if Tom might be able to help him in exploiting this idea.

Lunch was roasted cardoons in bechamel sauce with a parmesan breadcrumb crust which had been baking slowly for over an hour.

"A member of the artichoke family, the cardoon can be found wild and cultivated in Liguria and so is found in traditional recipes of the region, but little used these days," Alessandra explained to her now-hungry diners.

12. LINGUINE AL RAGU DI COZZE

The Osteria's shuttered kitchen window looked out over the valley towards the sea. A three-generation-old stone sink with a copper and brass tap had been placed in front of the window. The glass panes were perpetually obscured with stains of splashed pasta water and so during the day were usually open. It was there Alessandra worked on her food preparation, looking out over the landscape which produced the ingredients.

Cecily had arrived early for their meeting, so had taken over scrubbing mussel shells under running water while her friend ground a paste in the mortar and pestle.

"Not a bad view from your office window," Cecily observed. "What are we cooking?"

"La cucina di strettissimo magro (lean recipes). This dish was created many years ago by a Ligurian priest to make on 'sacrifice' days when the congregation were forbidden to eat meat. The pasta sauce I'm cooking is the result that one might expect from an Italian coastal community. It includes mussels, anchovies, pine nuts, garlic and a lot of olive oil, with a little parsley to finish. It is perhaps a sign of changing times that this is a rare dish these days. Only a few small places are keeping old Ligurian recipes like this alive, and here at the Osteria we are one of them."

"Roman will be so cross when I tell him about this dish, Alessandra. It is exactly the type of thing he loves."

"Good," she replied, joking. "Maybe that will persuade him to attend future meetings."

Ben had found some equally unusual rosé wine made with the Rossese grape in Piedmont which he was keen for everyone to try.

Rosé wine was something he was eager to experiment with. Italian rosé is often quite different from the light pink wines of the south of France. It is usually darker, stronger and drier. Until recently, little had been sold in Italy and even less exported, although that was changing as they acquired a better reputation. Ben thought that if he could create a Ligurian rosé with more of the Cote de Provence characteristics, he might find new markets for it. Regardless, he was enjoying the research.

A week earlier, when Ben and Alessandra had eaten spada (swordfish) for lunch in San Lorenso Mare, she had noted that they had used a liberal sprinkling of small capers in the sauce, which seemed to work well, adding some sharpness to the otherwise simple fillet. That morning, her fisherman friend had offered her freshly caught albacore tuna so she decided to try her own version, including a splash of Ben's rosé wine for extra aroma. Ben declared it to be sublime and no one present disagreed.

Alain congratulated Alessandra on choosing one of the more sustainable fish for her dish, pointing out that swordfish had been overfished in the Mediterranean in recent years. However, he also acknowledged that the Italians were not the worst culprits in this depletion of Mediterranean fish stocks. He explained that their smaller boats generally used traditional nets, keeping and selling almost everything caught. Virtually nothing was thrown overboard and wasted. These methods were far less damaging than the larger, industrial-scale trawlers favoured by other nations.

The young scientist from Monaco said, "You have a real opportunity to create something unique here. You have an unspoilt area that has changed little in hundreds of years. Traditional farming practices have been gentle on the land. That is why I was delighted when I was asked to join this group. Andrea Cassini has a genuine will to try new and better ways of doing things. His willingness to take risks to get quick results does not sit too comfortably with my scientific training, but I also understand the need for him to see measurable progress."

Alain now turned to Cecily, saying that she must be aware of the use of harvested seaweed and algae in cosmetics. Mid-way through a mouthful of tuna, the Englishwomen was caught off-guard and could only nod her agreement. Alain explained that, although what had become known as ocean farming had been taking place for hundreds of years, it had always been an informal industry. Coastal farmers desperate for nitrates to reinvigorate their land had always used seaweed washed up on the shore to bring life back to the soil.

"It seems to me, that although a landlocked nation, Seborga needs to look to the nearby ocean for means of sustainably strengthening the make-up of the soil."

Ben could immediately see this suggestion's logic, but any obvious method of putting this into practice eluded him and almost everyone else around the table. However, Cecily seemed to enjoy a light-bulb moment and quickly washed her food down with a gulp of wine.

"There are many thousands of boats moored along the Côte d'Azur, all of which need de-fouling every few years. My own boat was done last year and what looked like a ton of algae was scraped off the hull. This was just washed back into the sea."

Ben interjected, "So your yacht is cruising around the ocean unwittingly harvesting algae as it goes?"

"Mine and every other yacht. If you don't clean your hull below the waterline regularly, the drag that it causes gradually reduces your speed under sail and increases fuel consumption under power. Surely that algae could be a source of fertiliser? It's free, and boat owners want rid of it."

The marine scientist had already spotted the flaw in this theory. He explained that it had been the general practice for many years to paint boat hulls with antifouling paint below the waterline. This coating often contained potent chemicals to discourage the algae from attaching to the hull in the first instance. This antifouling paint had previously been identified as a marine hazard. Power-washing off the algae would inevitably take with it some of these chemicals, thereby rendering the algae tainted.

He acknowledged the merit of the idea in principle, but suggested that they discount it, for now at least adding, "Once again, man's attempts to resist the forces of nature has solved a human problem, only to create an environmental one."

Over dolce, the conversation turned from future initiatives to what had already been achieved. Alain complimented Ben and Alessandra on their achievements so far.

"In just a few years you have almost transformed this village from a failing community to a thriving one, with lots of projects as-yet unrealised. Farming oranges is now a sustainable business, with a spin-off benefit of raised brand awareness for the remaining olive growers. Winegrowing has been reinstated, and the resulting products are showing promise. The Slow Food outreach cookery school and restaurant are up and running. By the time the hotel and spa are finished, this community will be unrecognisable from what it was."

"Not to mention now being the home, albeit temporarily, to the Holy Grail," added Ben, putting aside his usual British understatement and natural modesty for a brief spell.

As much as Alessandra relished a moment of self-congratulation, she was keen to focus on the remaining challenges. No one was more aware than she how the fickle hand of fate could suddenly throw plans out of the window. While Andrea was in power and very much fighting their corner, she was determined to capitalise on this situation. She raised a glass and offered a toast, "Like our English St. George, we Templars can slay these environmental dragons with courage and cunning."

Those around the table raised their glasses while a chorus of

"San Giogio," was mixed with, "Saint George," responding to Alessandra's toast.

Gianni delivering his zucchini flowers to local restaurants on his trusty scooter.

Drawing by Linda McCluskey

13. SCIUMETTE

A wooden box overflowing with canary-yellow flowers balanced on the footrest. With nowhere to rest them, Gianni's long legs hung over each side of his Vespa, his trainers skimming the stones of the piazza on his way to the Osteria.

"Fiori di zucha?" Ben asked as he disembarked, balancing the box on one arm, his helmet dangling by its strap from the other. The obligatory headgear was permanently dangling from his arm and never seen on his head-as if the mere act of having it about his person fulfilled the letter of the law.

"Si, Professore. Your Italian is getting better," he complimented, adding, "but slowly."

"So, I need to, veloce?" the Englishman suggested.

"Più veloce," Gianni corrected.

The pair had been going through this ritual most mornings for nearly five years and Ben's Italian was still woefully inadequate for a permanent resident. One of the problems was that although he spoke English, Gianni only supplied vegetables. Their short conversations were therefore limited to what grew in these hills, the seasons, the weather, and the elderly Vespa that served as his delivery vehicle. The meat supplier and fishmonger spoke little English, so his guesses at the names for the contents of their deliveries usually went uncorrected. Despite this, Ben had acquired invaluable restaurant Italian, and could now at least translate almost any menu with reasonable accuracy.

Only ten days after their initial discussions with Richard, a director of the London Club considering creating the Albergo

Diffuso, an agreement was in place. Vincenzo could now begin work on converting the shop, which Selene had owned briefly, into the reception. This was an unfeasibly fast process by Italian standards but the project was already fully funded, and the decision-making team had been small. The Club was used to rapid decision-making, were good at delegating, and were willing to rely on email to record any initial agreements. However, they were yet to encounter official Italian bureaucracy where success is measured by the volume of paperwork generated and progress is more often counted in months, not days.

Ben had allowed all three men to cease their restoration of the vineyard terrace walls. They had made much progress but it was not urgent work, and Ben was running low on resources to pay them, having unexpectedly had to finance his son's debts. The Club was paying the men a far better rate than he could afford, and the more Tom earned, the sooner he could repay everyone who had loaned him cash. The young Englishman was now fit again, had calloused hands, and had acquired some basic construction and masonry skills.

The conversion of the Crazy Dutchman's former antique store into a reception for the deconstructed hotel concept was not a complicated job. They would first have to remove all the contents into a shipping container delivered to a nearby carpark as temporary storage. It was then merely a case of supporting the floor above before demolishing all the internal walls and removing the stone residue. It was physical, dusty, but not incredibly skilled work which Tom was now equipped for. The work required little more than a sledgehammer, a shovel, a wheelbarrow and some muscle.

Vincenzo knew that these works required a building inspector's consent but were also aware of the consequences of asking for permission in terms of the timescale. The Club had offered a twenty percent success bonus, based on each phase meeting its projected deadline. It was a sizeable incentive.

Vincenzo had explained to Ben, who had in turn told London, how he suggested they proceed.

Vincenzo had learned from the San Remo architect that the Club wanted all work done to the highest standards and using best industry practices. This meant they would build everything to at least meet, and more often than not exceed, the minimum building regulations. If they stuck rigidly to the rules and took photographs of all critical work in progress, they knew that they could not fail to obtain retrospective approval, even if that meant it would ruffle a few feathers among officials later.

This way of working meant that the construction and the application could proceed in parallel. However, it was a strategy bound to create friction with the bureaucrats whose jobs it was to administer the process. Alessandra and Richard had agreed that they would manage the human factor using tried and tested methods. Ben would previously have had all kinds of ethical concerns about the plan, but after all he had witnessed in recent years he had learned to keep those concerns to himself and be 'more Italian' in his approach. He justified his stance in knowing that no corners would be cut in construction, and no one bribed, at least not with cash.

The Club was making informal invites to those officials involved to attend an official ribbon cutting of the first phase in just six months' time by non-other than the prime minister, who was also their ultimate boss. Between now and then, Alessandra would host a monthly update meeting at the Osteria which would take place prior to a fine lunch. The inspectors could still produce all the paperwork that they wanted for their superiors, albeit retrospectively. They would just be doing so after a good working lunch every month. Ben had to admit this plan had managed to combine both carrot and stick neatly.

Although he had yet to admit it to anyone, Tom was enjoying the construction work. He found it emptied his mind of any worries he might have, and that being physically fit again felt empowering. His fair skin had adjusted to the sun, and he could now work in shorts without a shirt and not get sunburned. He was getting along well with his workmate, Marius, and even beginning to respect Vincenzo, if only for his physical strength and purposeful character. Alessandra had been exceedingly kind to him, bringing him free beers on an evening and making him packed lunches. She had even been dropping him at the beach on a Saturday morning so he could take a swim and chat with the locals while she went shopping for ingredients in Ventimiglia's famous food market.

Ventimiglia sits just on the Italian side of the border with France. The inevitable cross-border trade meant that the produce on offer blurred the respective cultures. Goods are available in Ventimiglia market that one would be unlikely to find elsewhere in Italy. Also, the disparity in wealth and taxation rates between the French Riviera and the Italian meant that things were often cheaper there. More than half of the customers at the food market were French people looking for bargains. It was a bustling, vibrant cornucopia of flowers, food and wine. Alessandra loved it.

Tom's evening meal arrangement's informality meant that he often ended up chatting to his father during dinner at the Osteria, or over an aperitivo afterwards, without either of them explicitly arranging to meet there. By learning to avoid talking about his mother, his debts and his future career prospects, they had even managed to get through several evenings without disagreeing over something. Both men were finding the process restorative, and Alessandra was feeling pleased with herself for her role in the peace process.

It was after one such enjoyable dinner which went on too late for his father, who had already gone home, that an attractive young woman entered the Osteria and ordered a drink. Tom enjoyed the last scrapings of what Alessandra had told him was Sciumette, or 'floating islands' dessert, another old Ligurian recipe.

"The islands are made from meringue floating in a sea of custard, flavoured with pistachios," she explained.

When Alessandra took the young woman's order, she spoke in English, which promoted Tom to say, "Hi." Although it turned out that she was Italian, the girl spoke excellent English and chatted for a while. She said that she was a journalist drafting a story on bringing the Holy Grail to Seborga.

Tom's response to hearing the subject of her work was to ask, "Do people really believe all those stories about the Holy Grail? It sounds like a fairy story to me. Yet another myth perpetuated by the Church to keep people putting money in the donation box, in my opinion."

The pretty reporter had the most enormous dark eyes that Tom could ever recall seeing, and she kept them engaged with his own continuously during their conversation. So enamoured was he that he did not notice that, after his dismissive opening, she asked very few questions about the Grail. However, she did want to know a great deal about all the restoration and building projects that were going on. She wanted to know who was involved and how that came about. Tom told her what he knew, which was extraordinarily little. Then, to appear more knowledgeable and seem more important, he embellished the facts with things he'd assumed or made up. The more he talked, the longer she stayed.

When Tom had run out of things to say about Seborga, he turned his attentions to what he saw as far more important matters and asked the girl to come back to his place for a digestivo. The flirtatious reporter suddenly transformed herself into a 'good Catholic Italian girl,' feigning modesty. She did leave him her business card and asked him to message her if he remembered anything more about the Seborga projects. Before she had left the Osteria, Tom was already trying to think of an excuse to call her.

"She was pretty," Alessandra offered when she came to clear the table. "A new friend?"

"I would like to think she could be. She's a reporter here to write about the Grail," Tom explained.

Alessandra pulled a face at hearing she was a reporter, as they were not her favourite group of people. That said, through Ben, she had learned that they could be manipulated, always provided that you were aware of the rules of engagement. In such matters they both now deferred to Selene, who had become adept at acting as both poacher and gamekeeper, as Ben would say.

Alessandra looked puzzled. "The Grail has been here for weeks now. The story has died down everywhere else. She is a bit behind the curve for a reporter."

Tom shrugged. "Who knows? Well, grazie and buona notte," he said, practising the little Italian he had learned on Alessandra.

As he left the Osteria, he spotted Marius and Cristiano entering the piazza from the other side. They were laughing and joking. He was then astonished to see that they were holding hands, although they dropped their grip as soon as they spotted Tom. The embarrassed Englishman looked away and walked on, not acknowledging that he had seen them.

Shocked, it had never occurred to him that Marius might also be gay. The Romanian fitted none of the stereotypes Tom had formed over the years. He was annoyed at his own naivety of having grown to like and trust his workmate, enjoying his company during and after work. He had no idea what he would now say to Marius when they next met.

14. SARDE A BECCAFICO

Unusually, Alessandra had a morning to herself. There was no preparation to do for the Osteria, as Cristiano was stepping in for her today. Ben had gone to meet Vincenzo at the vineyard where he wanted to show him some slight signs of blight on the vines furthest from the water supply. He was proposing they put in more irrigation to feed water from Lorenzo's Spring–as it had become known locally. Alessandra used the time to care for own neglected plants on her doorstep and veranda, as well as tidy the house in case Roman and Cecily came back later that afternoon.

Cecily had invited Ben and Alessandra out to lunch. Their hosts would pick them up, and they were told it was even less informal than the Osteria and so to dress casually. Roman drove up to Seborga in his old Mercedes Ponton, partly because it had been stuck in the garage for weeks and needed a run to charge the battery, but also because it had four doors and generous luggage space. They arrived to collect their friends from the Osteria at noon. From the time chosen, Ben had guessed that they weren't travelling far.

"Why the mystery tour? It can't be a new restaurant because I would have heard on the chef's grapevine by now," Alessandra quizzed.

Ben was correct about the distance; they had not travelled a kilometre out of the village when Roman steered the immaculate old car onto a dirt road and parked. Alessandra had also been correct, in that this was not a restaurant. It was a parcel of ground, flat for the first twenty metres or so, then dropping steeply away into the valley below.

Roman opened the boot of the Mercedes to reveal a picnic table and four folding chairs. He invited Ben to carry what he could manage, and he followed with the remainder. Cecily lifted out a cool bag and handed it to Alessandra before taking the large bamboo basket that remained. Ben had noticed with curiosity that a garden spade was also in the boot.

"A picnic in a bramble patch. How lovely. We can pick our own dolce," Alessandra said with a sardonic smile.

The two women had become the absolute best of friends, which was strange considering how little they'd had in common in their lives until recently. However, what they had shared was a focus on their respective careers that had made making and keeping friends difficult. What had finally broken the career cycle for both was finding new love at a time in their lives when they were starting to question what was important to them. It was probably no coincidence that this opening up to a new partner also resulted in their finding new friendships.

Both Cecily and Alessandra had worked extremely hard but had also enjoyed success early in their twenties before either woman had much self-confidence or experience. Some level of fame and money had brought with it people whose motives were not always what they seemed. Both had fallen foul of this. These bruising encounters had caused them to retreat from the limelight and busy themselves with work, which, ironically, brought even further success.

Today was to mark a significant milestone in Cecily's journey. After ten itinerant years, she had finally put down roots with her man in a new country, as a neighbour to her new friends. With the table laid and glasses at the ready, Roman removed the champagne bottle from the cooler and expertly poured four glasses.

In his wonderful English with a Sicilian accent, Roman proposed, "A toast to our first home, my soon-to-be wife and our good friends." To which Cecily quickly added, "And our new princess."

It was all too much for Alessandra to take in. She burst into tears and hugged her friend, seeking acknowledgement from her own lips, "You're getting married?"

"We are," Cecily confirmed. "And building a house right here where we are standing. Roman, get the spade. We have work to do."

Ben had shaken Roman's hand, but the Italian had decided an embrace was more appropriate. The Englishman's stiff upper lip was quivering a little and he too was a bit teary, but he hoped no one had noticed.

"I'll get the spade," Ben offered, welcoming the diversion. "You top up the champagne."

Roman dug the spade into the ground and placed Cecily's hand on the handle under his own. They lifted a pile of earth and then passed the spade to Ben and Alessandra to do the same. With a permanent marker, Roman wrote his own, and Cecily's, names, along with the date on the champagne cork. Cecily took a small tin from her bag and placed the cork in the container along with a little soil from each spade full.

"Our little time capsule which we will bury under the house. Right; let's eat. We have a wedding to plan."

"And a house to plan," Ben added.

"It's all planned," Roman announced. "Cecily and the architect that you introduced us to have been working on it for weeks. After lunch, I will show you the drawings, and my soon-to-be wife has a virtualisation on her iPad."

Roman rolled out the paper plan and then turned it so that it aligned with the house's actual position in the landscape. There were two main structures to be built in an arc following the contour of the land. One would sit above and behind the other, mirroring the terraces into which they would sit. On the lowest level, a wide but narrow pool followed the same curve. In the front elevation drawing the stonework was drawn to match that of terraces on either side, as well as above and below it.

"From just metres below the whole structure will be almost invisible. Looking up from Bordighera no one would know it was here," Roman said with some satisfaction.

Ben and Alessandra stood imagining themselves looking out from the terrace above the pool. The view was down the valley, slightly east of the village and out over what was known as locally Fisherman's Beach. It derived this name from being immediately beside the small harbour of Bordighera. This made the aspect of the house south-east, meaning they would enjoy a sunrise over the coast and have sun most of the day until the early evening when it would dip behind Seborga.

"That evening sun bakes the house in the summer, and the residual heat makes for uncomfortable nights," Alessandra pointed out, trying to be helpful.

Cecily looked slightly smug and said, "That will not be so much of an issue because this will be a Passivhaus, where the temperature inside is carefully controlled with extremely high standards of insulation and clever climate control technology. The triple glazing has a coating to reflect the heat and will also be shielded by programable vertical louvre shutters."

"Sounds expensive," Ben commented, but then realised that this was unlikely to be an issue for Cecily.

"The structure is being built in a Czechoslovakia factory, so not as expensive as you might imagine," Roman countered, not wishing to seem extravagant. He explained that it would be made of engineered timber, with specially laminated sections to create the curves. He also acknowledged that the expensive parts were the windows, doors, heating, and cooling systems, which cost more than the structure itself. "The windows alone cost most than the average house in Sicily."

"What did I work eighty hours a week for and rack up tens of thousands of airmiles if we can't spend our money on some comfort and enjoyment in our retirement?" Cecily admonished her partner. "Anyway, enough of houses. It's lunchtime. Take those plans off the table."

Cecily's onboard chef had prepared the picnic which she was now unpacking from the basket. There were Sicilian arrancinette mignon–small rice balls filled with prosciutto and mozzarella. Roman's favourite dish from Palermo followed this; sarde a beccafico–rolled sardine fillets stuffed with breadcrumbs, raisins, pine nuts and anchovy.

After two southern Italian classic dishes, the pudding was, like their hosts, an English/Italian affair: summer pudding made with Valpolicella wine – strawberries, raspberries and blackberries cooked in vanilla flavoured wine and placed in a stale bread-lined bowl until the juices turned the casing red. Alessandra picked four juicy brambles from the nearest bush and some nearby wild mint, placing this garnish on each portion.

"It's just perfect," Cecily announced. "I could not be happier." Just then, her phone rang.

"Don't you dare answer," said Roman, looking suddenly cross.

"It's Selene. I'd better answer."

Cecily's smile instantly evaporated. "She's been trying to get hold of you two," Cecily said, looking glumly at Ben.

Ben explained that they had both purposely left their phones at home so they could enjoy an uninterrupted lunch. Cecily handed the phone to Ben, who listened, nodded, shook his head, and finally closed his eyes as though he had a headache.

"I'll take a look and call you back," was all he said before turning to his wife and announcing, "It's out there on the Internet. Andrea Cassini is in a relationship with the daughter of the recipient of millions of euros of government money. In another report, Selene is also further implicated as the recipient of a free house from a developer with interests in Seborga. She believes that both their careers are about to fall off a cliff."

15. BASTONICI DI POLENTA

The city of Rome sat baking in the Tiber basin, smouldering in a heat wave. The old, pale cream stones of the ancient buildings retained the warmth of the sun, releasing it again at night so there was no respite from the cloying heat. With few of the covered walkways of Turin or Milan, most Romans went about their business in the city in the full rays of the sun. Still, Italians dressed like it was spring. The care they invested in their appearance suggested they were heading for a first date, or the most important interview of their careers. Even the traffic officers all looked like poster models for a police recruitment campaign.

Amara sat in her air-conditioned office in the city centre, savouring the consequences of her actions and anticipating future outcomes with glee. She calculated that she had earned an indulgent treat and so had picked up some Bastonici di Polenta (polenta sticks) dipped in Fontina cheese from the deli near her office. Munching on these delicious snacks, she watched the media acting like sharks in a feeding frenzy, snapping at any snippet of information relating to the PM, Selene or Seborga. The wily Minister for Culture had several such tasty morsels ready to toss into the pool whenever the media interest looked like it was waning. For now, Amara was happy to let them chew on this feast of intrigue.

The journalist she had tipped-off about the relationship enjoyed her scoop, her newspaper publishing, and creating a Twitterstorm amongst Andrea Cassini's supporters and detractors. Amara had briefed her allies to re-tweet and share the stories. She had supplied the journalist with the first photograph of them together at the yacht launch. The second snap of the couple taken later the same evening was just a lucky break. It had persuaded Amara it was time to go public with her suspicions.

The second photograph had been taken by a friend of one of their Tricolore Party junior colleagues at a birthday celebration. The young researcher had attended several events during the last year with the PM, at which the English journalist was also present. Selene's pale skin, blonde hair and English clothing style made her quite noticeable. She spotted the Englishwoman in a friend's Instagram post, and after closer examination of the photograph, she also thought that she recognised her boss. Initially, she had not considered the frequent attendance of this foreign journalist particularly significant. She knew the PM to be single, and that Selene was in Genoa that day for the boat launch. Why should they not be having dinner, she had thought?

The next morning, when chatting to Amara at the coffee shop, she mentioned the photo her friend had taken in the restaurant. She knew that Andrea and Amara had worked together for a long time and, from the way she looked at him, suspected that Amara held a candle for the prime minister. Her superior asked to see the image, but then contrived disinterest and told her colleague that she did not believe it to be their boss.

"However, it does look a bit like him," she added as an afterthought. "Please forward the photo to me and I will tease Andrea about it later. Just between us though," she had added, holding one finger to her lips. Later, to distance herself from its public release, Amara would claim that she had shared it with other colleagues in her office. "And from there, God knows where it got sent," she would later say.

Even the media at the centre and right of the political spectrum struggled to see how to put a positive spin on the breaking news. It only took a few minutes of cursory research on

Google to tie Selene to her father and him to the substantial Seborga cash grants. From there, the money trail led back to Andrea. At best, it was a grave error of judgement for a PM to expose himself to such obvious accusations of appearing to be handing out personal favours. If Andrea eventually acknowledged the relationship with the English woman, he was surely handing his opposition a stick to beat him with. Their reactions would be predictable, and Andrea's fate would be sealed.

For many in the opposition, as well as some in his Tricolore party, Andrea was just too young, too radical, and far too handsome for his own good. For the media, he had also been annoyingly squeaky clean up until now, with no apparent skeletons in his closet and so little of substance to write about. Cassini's only apparently newsworthy aspect seemed to be his left-leaning policies, them being somewhat at odds with the leader of a traditionally right-wing party.

Andrea Cassini simply did not generate the kind of juicy gossip that provided journalists with salacious copy to write and sell newspapers. Most political reporters would rather have seen the return on a Mastroianni-type character, who created a new scandal almost weekly. For all the reasons that his detractors disliked him, the public loved Andrea Cassini. No prime minister in living memory had garnered such high approval ratings and been so well respected.

He had spoken to Selene only very briefly on the telephone since the news broke. She had been in tears for most of the short call and he was due into an urgent meeting with his press secretary. He was being bombarded with phone calls and messages, essentially asking the same question: was it true?

They both knew that it would not take much investigation to place Selene in the same place as the PM on at least a dozen occasions over the past year. A little further digging would probably find a member of staff at a hotel or restaurant that the couple had visited who would tell all to the press for a moment of fame. Denying the relationship now would only make Andrea's position untenable when the truth finally came out. And it would. Of that, they were both quite sure.

The press secretary's meeting did not take long, mainly because the civil servant did not have a viable proposal to offer his boss. The best he could suggest was to say that his personal life was his own business, that he was a single man and had nothing to hide as far as Seborga was concerned. Even as he said it, the press secretary knew that he would be crucified in the evening news and tomorrow's daily papers if they went with this. After a few minutes, the PM instructed that a news conference be called at 6 pm that evening, at which he would speak live to the Italian public.

"That's just three hours from now," his press advisor pointed out. "That is not enough time to draft a statement, get it agreed by the party or for you to learn it."

"I don't need a statement, and I certainly don't want to speak to anyone from the party. Just call the briefing. I will adlib. The truth is clear. It's only lies that are difficult to remember."

The press secretary looked ashen at hearing these instructions, now certain that this would be his, and his boss's, last day in their jobs, with no lucrative PR job in the private sector to follow for him. Henceforth, he would be known as the press secretary who oversaw the downfall and public disgrace of two prime ministers in a single year. Quite a record, even in Italy.

Amara could not hide her joy at hearing the news about the press conference. She was convinced Andrea was going to offer his resignation. She had even started drafting her own press statement distancing herself from the prime minister, his policies, and his actions. The scheming minister had already pulled strings to have the junior researcher who gave her the photograph of Selene with Andrea promoted to her own Department of Culture - a promotion which came with a sizable salary uplift. This should ensure her loyalty and silence, Amara calculated. In her new role, the young girl's first job was to fact-check the press release she had prepared and get it ready to email out to the list of favoured journalists.

However, the press briefing had somewhat wrong-footed Amara, as she was expecting official denials to drag on for days, or even weeks. She had heard about the imminent press conference from her journalist friend, rather than unusual internal government channels. Slightly panicked that events were running ahead of her; Amara instructed her newly appointed assistant to email her the edited press release and make another Instagram post at 5:50 pm. She wanted to attend the briefing in person and witness the PM's annihilation up close. Moments before the news briefing was due to start, a second post appeared on Twitter saying Selene's brother had been awarded lucrative construction contracts in Seborga, without going through any tendering process. Amara and the other journalists had seen it, but the PM and press secretary were too busy preparing to field the questions they knew would soon be raining down on them from the gathered media. They had been told that the PM would make a statement. After this, a microphone would be passed around so that questions were dealt with one at a time. No time limit had been placed on the briefing and so they could all wait their turns without missing out.

As the hour approached, every available press badge had been allocated according to the traditional media pecking order of their respective audiences' size. The room was packed with faces familiar to the prime minister, and all were smiling, waving and nodding to him as he entered. They were all hoping that he would favour them by singling them out to ask their question. Andrea knew that any one of them would bury him with the power of their pen given the slightest chance.

With his head slightly bowed, he took a deep breath and began somberly, "I have made a big mistake," Raising his head so that he faced directly into the lenses of the cameras, he went on, "I failed to trust you, the Italian voters, to judge me solely by my actions and not listen to gossip and hearsay on the Internet. However, you should know that I had committed myself to support Seborga before I fell in love with the English journalist Selene Morton, and I will tell you why. Seborga represents what's left of the Italy we all love, but which most of us have lost. I saw this tiny rural principality as the antitheses of Milan's pollution, the traffic jams of Turin, the fast food of Rome, the pickpockets of Florence and unemptied bins in Naples. It's the Italy we all remember from our childhood and that tourists come to experience. The air is clean, the streets are safe, people look after their neighbours and the food is both seasonal and local. There are still hundreds of places like Seborga all over Italy, but we are losing them fast. They're being killed off by globalisation, where price and profit are valued more than quality and sustainability."

Andrea paused to take a drink of water. He could see from the expressions on the faces of the journalists that whilst they were eager to get to what they saw as the dirt that had been thrown at him, they were not expecting this line of defence. They were also aware that the PM was not addressing his speech at them, but rather directly at the viewers online and on television.

"Seborga is a microcosm of all that used to be right, but which is now going very wrong with Italy, and the rest of the world. Here was a community that was still clinging to much of what was good. They have resisted change and so far, have succeeded. I saw an opportunity to not only preserve what remained, but to see if we could build a new type of more sustainable community. One that is fit for the twenty-first century. Those initiatives I have put in place in Seborga which prove successful can be rolled out in other small communities, as part of a rejuvenated Italian way of life."

Pausing again for a drink of water, Andrea took stock of his audience's mood, and thought that once again they looked more intrigued by his story than they were frustrated at his avoidance of the reason that they thought they were here.

"In an effort to turn the tide towards a carbon-neutral society we have given Seborga a unique tax system, to incentive the private sector to invest, experiment and innovate. Using innovative technologies and techniques, we intend to reinvigorate farming and create organic produce. Italy has eight thousand kilometres of coastline but dwindling fish stocks. Seaweed could be used to produce fertiliser, fuel and food. We can turn our fishermen into seaweed farmers and allow our fish stocks to recover. Two different private companies will be running trials of solar-powered car re-charging in Seborga for a fleet of pooled vehicles. Tax-free shopping for produce with plastic-free packaging is being trialled, which will save the authorities the increasing costs of collecting and disposing of waste."

The relatively inexperienced politician realised that he was beginning to find a voice that was resonating with a younger audience, such as most of the journalists in the room, but knew he also needed to eventually address the question of a potential conflict of interest.

"Most of the money being already invested in Seborga came from the EU, more from the private sector, and very little from the Italian taxpayer. We have spreadsheets to hand out containing all the figures. Any public funds have been channelled through the Slow Food Movement, a registered charity, independent of myself and the government. Not a single euro of that money was paid to, or through, the Morton family or Princess Alessandra. What is more, when I obtained the latest figures, I was astonished to learn that the man who devised the plans, raised the money and is putting them into action has not, so far, been paid a Euro in salary. Ben Morton, Selene's father, has so far worked for nothing to help his community."

There was a murmuring, apparently of disbelief at this revelation, but as the press were being promised the detailed accounts, they held off baying for blood.

"If you'll excuse the pun, the jewel in the crown of Seborga will be the Albergo Diffuso luxury accommodation, which will see many ancient Rustica houses restored without a euro of public funding. The only obstacle to this project getting underway was the lack of a commercial building large enough to house the hotel rooms' reception and services. Selene was approached and agreed to exchange her one hundred and fifty square metre property in the village for a much smaller, but already restored, cottage outside the village. That exchange is recorded in public records any of you can check with a like-for-like valuation. No money changed hands and Selene made no financial gain. She was merely facilitating one of the key projects."

More murmuring and headshaking suggested that the press would indeed be checking this fact, but they also sensed that this front page story was evaporating before their eyes.

"However, returning to my big mistake, what I now recognise I should have done is to have told you about Selene as soon as we got together. Instead, and also because of a potential conflict of interest with her job as a journalist, like yourselves, I decided not to go public with our relationship. However, because of the exposure of our private lives on the Internet today, she has now lost the job she loved. But for me, that is good news because it removes that obstacle to our being together permanently. Although there is so much that I want to do for Italy, I have decided today that if the price I must pay to have the woman I love, is my job, then I will give that up."

The until-now quiet audience now began shouting, "You are resigning for this woman, Prime Minister?"

Andrea shook head in a deliberately exaggerated way, "I am saying that if the Italian voters do not accept that I have acted honestly, and I am forced to choose between this job and the woman I love, I will step down for her. Furthermore, as I have been accused and tried on social media, the public can also use that method to tell me what their verdict is. Unless there is an overwhelming expression of public confidence on social media by noon tomorrow, I will stand aside as prime minister."

"What about the big contract awarded to Selene Morton's brother's construction company?" shouted one TV journalist. The prime minister's press secretary stepped forward to show him the Twitter post containing this latest accusation.

Smiling at what he saw as the sheer ridiculousness of this apparent revelation, Andrea responded, "That story had no basis in fact. Selene's brother is a young man employed by a private company as a builder's labourer, at fifteen euros an hour. He does not have a construction company. Last time I saw him he had a hammer, a shovel and a wheelbarrow, plus lots of sweat on his brow. Go to Seborga and check for yourselves. That is a made-up story."

Amara was trying to make herself small and inconspicuous at the back of the room. For the first time, she was aware that Andrea and others would be starting to wonder who was behind this deliberate campaign of misinformation. If it were ever to be linked back to her, it would be the end of her career in politics and any hope of becoming Italy's first female prime minister.

As she was moving discretely towards the door, one of the members of the press spotted the Minister for Culture standing behind them in the crowd. A microphone was thrust at her, "Minister, the email that I have just this minute received suggests that you are not backing the PM's support for Seborga. It says that you opposed moving the Sacro Cantina there and suggested that EU funds could have been better spent on other projects. Can we take it that you believe the PM should now resign over his alleged deception?"

A look of horror followed the realisation that her own press release had now been sent to the media by her new assistant.

16. GENOESE RAVIOLI

Walking down Clapham High Street, Selene was struck by the difference in the pace of life between the UK and Italy. Everyone here looked gripped by a sense of urgency to get where they were going. There was no strolling, meandering, or window shopping. Few people stopped to chat, or even exchanged a hello. More coffees were being sold in takeaway cups than were being leisurely sipped in cafes.

When she reached Clapham Common station, Selene asked herself, where had the newsstand gone? How long had it been missing, without her noticing? Every Italian station still had a kiosk selling newspapers, magazines and lottery tickets, but Londoners had gone almost entirely digital. Then she realised that she hardly ever bought a paper copy of the newspaper she wrote for. The newsstand in Clapham was now a pizza slice takeaway, which was perhaps an irony, Selene mused.

Selene had been summoned by text to her London office by her editor. She attended with a heavy heart, knowing full well what was coming. Selene even imagined the phrases her somewhat acerbic boss would use to end her short-lived career as a journalist on a national newspaper. It turned out that she had not entirely foreseen what the editor had in mind for her.

Looking genuinely pleased as she entered the glass-walled office, she was greeted with a broad smile, "Congratulations. You seem to have hit the jackpot and scored the real dolce vita."

Thrown by her surprise warm welcome, Selene forced a smile and thanked her but with less sincerity than she had intended.

Outside she could see all her workmates-or were they already former colleagues - pausing to watch the show. She imagined what slaves facing the gladiators in the Colosseum much have felt like, waiting for the thumbs-up, or down.

"You'll have to work your notice, but you already knew that. But that's not too high a price to pay to start sharing a limo, and much else no doubt, with the most handsome politician since JFK. Lucky you."

Selene struggled to understand her boss's position on the revelation that she had been conducting a covert affair with the Italian Prime Minister. She was focussing on the loss of the job she had struggled for years to get. Unbeknownst to her, the seasoned journalist-turned-senior-manager saw it as a business opportunity.

"Selene, darling. You're not a bad writer, but let's face it, the world if full of wannabe Kate Adies and Katharine Grahams. I can replace you tomorrow with an even more eager, younger model and for probably 10k less salary per year. Serendipity has placed you in the right place twice – no, actually, now three times – in just five years, and we have both benefited hugely from that. However, this part of your life is over."

Waving Selene to a chair which she flopped into looking very confused, the editor opened the glass door and called for drinks to be brought in.

"The news business that I have known all my life, and that you thought you were joining, is now over. We're the last dinosaurs left on planet 'News'. Our chairman has openly admitted that this company will never buy another newspaper printing press. In other words, when the current one stops printing in however many years from now, that will be the end of ink on paper news. The business of news has changed. You are fortunate to be getting out now, ahead of the final demise. Too few people today value the truth enough to pay for it. They have settled for sensationalism that they can have for free. Or, more accurately, for what they believe to be free. In fact, they are paying by sacrificing their privacy."

Selene instinctively wanted to argue the moral case for quality news media to keep government, business and criminals under scrutiny. Still, deep down she knew her boss was right and that she was wasting her time.

"You and I need to have our last hurrah and think to our futures. Myself, to retirement at my cottage on the Northumberland coast, and you to your hunky politician in Rome. But before we do that, we have one last scoop to negotiate, and the serialisation of your book to agree upon."

"Book. What book?" asked an astonished Selene. A tray containing prosecco and two glasses arrived and the editor held her finger to lips until the bearer had placed it on her desk and closed the door.

"The book, or maybe books, you will start writing about the crazy goings-on in Seborga. I can visualise the Netflix series now—it will be like a mash-up of EastEnders, The Crown and Inspector Montalbano. Even I'd watch it and I hate TV," added the editor, laughing at her own joke.

The vision of a new life and writing career that was being painted for her did not sound altogether unappealing, and Selene wondered why she had not thought of it herself.

"I've written a number on this piece of paper that I think I can get you from this newspaper for the final exclusive story, plus the rights to serialise the book. If it is acceptable to you, I will go upstairs and see the CEO now. I should be able to get you a verbal agreement right there and then. Then you can get back to your desk and start writing your last ever story for this newspaper. If I can get the nod from 'God' upstairs, I'll get the lawyers to draw up the paperwork. You can sign it later, and we open another bottle of this fizz and all go home happy."

Selene opened the folded paper, nodded without hesitation

and then finished her drink in absolute shock while the editor left the room. She sat in a something of a trance until a knock on the glass partition stirred her from her thoughts. A colleague was waving her out of the office and pointing to her computer screen, around which several other reporters were already gathered. Showing was the live TV feed from Rome, where her lover, Andrea, was holding his briefing.

She joined them as all her colleagues watched TV. Soon tears began to roll down Selene's cheeks as the man who she loved publicly offered to give up everything for her. Even some of her hard-nosed reporter colleagues were looking teary as they digested the significance of the commitment they were witnessing. It would later transpire that similar scenes were being played out in front of TV screens in kitchens, cafes, bars and workplaces all over Italy. Andrea's speech struck a nerve with everyone who'd ever been in love.

Even Italian men were moved by Andrea's evident passion for the English reporter. Some news agency had found a year-old photo of Selene in their archives, which was widely used to accompany the stories now circulating. It had been taken on the night that Andrea had first met Selene in Seborga, when she had been wearing the clinging, backless dress that she borrowed from a designer in Monaco. This image alone convinced most Italian males that their prime minister had made the right decision.

The significance of Andrea's impromptu speech was also being analysed with great interest for reasons other than the revelations about his personal life. This was the first time they had heard concrete plans to address some of the environmental concerns he had previously only alluded to. Many younger voters had become disillusioned by politicians paying little more than lip-service to growing worries about climate change, pollution, and the effects of globalisation. Without planning to, his words had galvanised all kinds of groups from across the political spectrum into a concerted and very vocal force.

These were also the same young, tech-savvy groups who almost exclusively used social media to air their grievances and champion their causes. Andrea now became one such cause-and they took to Twitter, Instagram and other online media to support him. By morning it would be clear that Andrea would not only be keeping his job, but that he had also probably garnered even more support for his policies and his party from the opposition. He would have the mandate to act boldly and even more decisively.

In Seborga, with all the orange blossom now in bloom, and the hired-in bees busy fertilising them, Vincenzo had been keeping an eye on the weather forecast. While political storm clouds had been gathering in Rome, very real and potentially more dangerous ones were gathering over the French Alps. For the second time in recent months, the jet stream had slipped down towards northern Scotland, deflecting an Atlantic weather front in over the Bay of Biscay, ultimately heading for Italy. Unfortunately, this was the remains of a tropical storm that had already caused devastation on the east coast of America and still had plenty of pent-up rain looking for an outlet.

Ben and Alessandra watched Andrea on TV at the Osteria, along with Vincenzo who was waiting for his order of Genoese ravioli. The generously filled veal and pork mince parcels were one of his favourites. Of the three, only Vincenzo seemed impervious to the emotions of the moment. Alessandra had a growing concern that she could guess the source of some of some of the wilder accusations in the media but could not speak of this to anyone. Typically, Vincenzo avoided discussing the events on TV by completely changing the subject.

"I have been watching those builders from Ventimiglia who are working on the other projects in the village. On Fridays, they finish work early as you would expect, at around 3 pm. But instead of heading back down the road to the coast, they drive their truck inland towards Negi. About twenty minutes later, they drive back and then head for the coast. They are up to something," Vincenzo declared with absolute certainty. "First thing in the morning, Ben, I think you and I should go and take a look."

There was only one exit from the road to Negi within ten minutes of driving time, and it did not take Vincenzo long to find where the builder's truck had been going. Bright white chunks of plaster, shards of metal and plastic fragments indicated where they had stopped along the Passo del Bandito. The route had been carved into the hillside, leaving a steep side of the left and an unguarded drop to the right. Ben and Vincenzo left the Ape and looked over the edge of the road into the forest below.

"Bastardi," Ben exclaimed, leaving Vincenzo looking slightly shocked at his uncharacteristic bad language.

"As I suspected," Vincenzo said with resignation. An area of previously pristine forest about thirty metres wide and a truck's width was covered in an avalanche of paint cans, empty silicon tubes, packaging, offcuts of plastic pipe, insulation sheets and plasterboard. There was even an old PVC window frame complete with glass.

"They should be taking all this waste to the reclamation site at San Remo. But that is an hour round trip for them, and they have to pay by weight to leave it there."

Ben was lost for further words at this act of wanton irresponsibility but was also determined to shame those responsible. He took plenty of photographs on his mobile phone.

"On Monday, we will go and confront them with this evidence."

"Not so hasty, Ben. If they deny it, we have no real proof it was them. They will stop doing this, but we won't get this cleaned up. Wait until next Friday and I will come and catch them in the act."

Men playing scopa
at bar-restaurant Da U Triu in Sasso,
with aperitivo in the foreground.

Drawing by Linda McCluskey

17. PICAGGE VERDI

Tom managed to get through the days after his encounter with Cristiano and Marius in the piazza by avoiding working alongside him and not mentioning the event when they did meet. He was sure that it must have been evident to both Marius and Vincenzo that something was wrong. Although it had occupied his thoughts, Tom remained unsure about his feelings on the situation. He had thought he'd found a great friend in Marius but now had no idea what to say to him. He had even considered speaking to Alessandra about it. His stepmother had become something of a confidant: a maternal figure that he could talk to who he felt did not judge him. However, as she was also Cristiano's mother, Tom decided it was too complicated.

Alessandra was facing her own dilemma. She was almost sure that the information that had caused Selene to lose her job, and Andrea to almost give up his, had come from Tom's recent conversation with the attractive young journalist in her own restaurant. She knew that no harm would have been intended but still felt sure that he should come clean about his indiscretion to his father and sister. However, she also felt certain that he would be disinclined, having started to gain a little credibility in their eyes. She did not want to fall out with him by being the one to suggest a full confession that he was unlike to agree to.

Ben was already enjoying an aperitivo in the Osteria when Tom arrived for his dinner. By the time he took a seat at his father's table, Alessandra had set another cold beer down before him. As the days had turned into weeks, there had been a gradual thawing of relations between them. Most observers would describe the current relationship as normal for father and adult son. They still held widely differing views on many things but had learned to stay clear of these topics. Ben had also decided only to offer specific advice when specifically asked for it, which was virtually never. Conversations that revolved around food, beer, sport, cars and work gave them enough to talk about, and the latter normally dominated.

Tom was pleased with both the new practical skills he was learning from Vincenzo and the physical fitness that the work had brought him. He'd turned a couple of kilos of fat into muscle and, with his growing golden tan, was attracting some attention from the girls at the beach. He complained to his father about Vincenzo pushing him hard, but Ben could tell his grudging respect for the Italian was growing stronger with each day.

Ben had laughed, perhaps a bit too enthusiastically, at Tom's story of Vincenzo standing on the edge of a terrace, below which he had just rebuilt the retaining wall. Vincenzo knew Tom had not listened to his instructions about filling all the small gaps with stone wedges to make it solid. In his haste to keep up with Marius's work-rate, he had cut corners. With Vincenzo's weight on it, a one-metre section of the wall he had just spent two hours building collapsed into a heap of rocks with the merest pressure from his boot. He pointed to the bucket of smaller stone wedges and said, "Meno velocita, piu forza," (less speed, more strength). Tom had been furious, but also embarrassed at what he knew was his folly.

Alessandra appeared with two dishes of the night's main dish, which was picagge verdi (green noodles with sausage). It was the type of substantial pasta dish that Tom loved. The young man's mood brightened with his dinner's arrival and he enjoyed having some conversation to distract his thoughts from what he should say to Marius.

After placing the steaming bowls on the table, Alessandra

warned them that she had baked a walnut cake with honey and ricotta for dessert and that they should, "Leave some appetite for dolce."

Ben had been watching clouds appearing over the mountains in the distance. This water-soaked mist poured like liquid over the ridge and down the slopes, beginning to cloak the valleys like a grey curtain. A breeze got up and started to ruffle the Seborgan flags on the houses around them. The first big spot of rain fell into the dog water bowl left outside the Osteria for customers' pets. It was a drop so large, and struck with such force, as to almost empty the bowl of its original contents. Slowly but surely other drops fell around it, bouncing off the stone slabs of the piazza. In less than a minute the sky had gone black and rain fell in sheets, soaking everything it touched in seconds.

Although they sat under the canopy, Ben and Tom were getting splashed by rain bouncing off planters and tables that were not undercover. They had to move their dishes to another table further inside where they could be dry. Every paved surface was now under a couple of centimetres of water. The gutters on the houses around were overflowing, adding to the deluge. The Alpini troops who had been operating patrols were running back to their temporary barracks on the other side of the piazza, apparently not wishing to spoil their immaculate uniforms or polished weapons.

"These storms do not usually last long," Ben said. "In ten or fifteen minutes, it will probably all be over."

Tom looked outside and sceptically at his father. "You think so?"

Twenty minutes later, the intensity of the rain had not diminished. If anything, it had got worse. Waves of wind drove the rain even harder down the valley. This was a storm of biblical proportions, Ben realised. He witnessed plants and their terracotta pots washed out of a side street by a torrent of fast-flowing water. These were the plants which most residents used to decorate their doorsteps, too heavy to be moved by any storm they had seen before. Then a waste bin came tumbling down, followed by an advertising banner that had been torn off the side of the road. Hearing the noise of the wind and rain, Alessandra came outside to see for herself.

"I've never seen water washing things down the streets like this before. I wonder if the Cookery School is Ok. Parts of the building still only had a temporary roof." She looked at her watch, "Renata could still be working in there, maybe Cristiano too."

Seeing that Alessandra was concerned, Tom volunteered to go and check on them. Tom's t-shirt was soaked through to his skin and sticking to his body within two steps outside. His blonde locks were washed into his eyes and he had to sweep his fringe back to see where he was going. As he made his way down the narrow streets towards the lower part of the village, the water flowing down was getting deeper and faster. It was like no storm he had ever experienced.

Turning into Piazza Monastero, he was shocked to see that the Cookery School, a few steps down from street level, now sat in what looked like a moat of water. The level was approaching half a metre up the new plate glass doors. On closer inspection, he saw that inside the water was even higher. Suddenly, Renata was at the door up past her waist in water. She had a look of terror on her face as she pulled at the handle to try and open it. Tom realised that with the water inside so much higher than that outside, the weight and pressure held the door firmly shut. He pushed at it with his shoulder but without causing any movement at all.

Looking around for something to break the door with, Tom saw a large terracotta plant pot. Waving to Renata to stand back, he threw the pot with all the force he could muster at the door. It shattered into pieces, making no impression on the plate glass. Then he remembered that he and the others had been working just around the corner on the reception for the Albergo Diffuso.

He ran the thirty metres as fast as he could, returning a minute later with his sledgehammer.

Renata was now at the door again, banging on it with both fists in desperation. The water had risen past her waist, and she was beginning to panic. Tom could just hear her calling out for help. He pointed to the hammer he was holding and waved her to stand well out of the way. Standing on the steps leading down to the door gave him a good swing at a point around the door handle. The blow struck where he had planned it to and the whole door shattered into a million pieces, allowing a tsunami of water to surge out into the piazza.

The water flowing out of the building joined with the rain still washing down from the streets all around. The swollen flow searched out the lowest-lying outlet to relieve its pressure. A set of steep stone steps, barely wide enough for one person, dropped some ten metres before turning through ninety degrees and exiting on the road below. It was no longer possible to see the steps as this was now a full-blown waterfall spewing tons of water and detritus onto the street far below, making the main access to the village impassable.

In her rush to get out of the building before the water levels equalised, Renata was knocked off her feet by the force of the flow. She was washed, floundering out of the doorway and banged her head on the stone steps, losing consciousness for a moment. Tom dropped the sledgehammer and scooped up the diminutive chef in his arms, wading across the piazza with her towards higher ground. By now people from nearby houses had realised something was going on and were coming out onto the streets. Placing Renata gently on the floor, her back resting against the wall, she quickly started to regain consciousness.

"Was anyone else in there with you?" Tom asked. "Where is Cristiano?" he urged.

Renata looked very dazed and scared but began to remember,

saying, "All of a sudden water burst through the temporary wall between the kitchen and the dining room. It was even coming up under the floors. Cristiano was in the restaurant next door earlier, writing menus."

Neighbours were bringing towels and blankets to wrap the injured chef in. Tom went looking for Cristiano, trying to remember the building's layout from his only visit. The restaurant was in the old monastery's ruins. They had built around remaining stonework and extended it to create the Cookery School. It had a separate entrance with yet another plate glass door, on the same level Renata had been working at. It was also over a metre deep in water and furniture was floating on the surface. There were no lights inside, but Tom realised that the water might have blown all the fuses. There was no sign of any movement inside, but he decided it was better to be safe than sorry and take a look.

Then Tom remembered that he'd dropped the sledgehammer somewhere outside. He waded back to where he had picked up Renata and started reaching down to see if he could feel the hammer. He could just touch the ground without submerging his head and found the hammer on the third attempt. Water was still issuing from the building as though its strongest source was, mysteriously, somewhere inside the former monastery.

There were now several villagers standing in the streets leading down to the small piazza. One of them had sent their neighbour to the Osteria to fetch Ben and Alessandra. Seeing the commotion, the Alpini had finally stirred from the dry of their barracks to check on the Holy relic. With more confidence, Tom swung the three-kilo hammer at the second glass door. Once again it turned to glass beads in an instant and another wave of water swept out. After chairs, tablecloths, and other restaurant fittings rushed by into the street, the flow slowed slightly across the piazza.

Thankfully upright and bobbing along in the torrent which

now flowed more steadily out of the building came an emerald, green glass bowl. Acting on some unknown instinct, Tom threw himself on it, as if it was a rugby ball exiting a scrum. Clutching the bowl to his chest but now off his feet, the water carried him away. Managing to free one hand, Tom turned himself onto his back. He struggled to keep his head above water while simultaneously holding onto the object. He managed to gain his bearings just in time to see that he was being swept across the piazza towards the steps. From there he knew there was a huge drop into the road far below.

His choices seemed clear: let go of the bowl and claw his way out of the main steam or be swept over a drop that would likely kill him. Instead, he chose an option which came to him in that instant. Using his spare arm, he managed to turn himself around in the flow so that he was feet first. As he reached the buildings between which the steps exited the piazza, he spread his legs wide and managed to get one foot on either side of the gap, stopping him almost dead. He took the shock and then the strain from the water flow behind on his now strong legs without too much trouble. However, he was now a human dam in the stream with pressure building on his shoulders and water pouring over his head into his eyes and ears. He had no plan for how to extract himself from there and the flow of water showed no sign of abating.

It seemed like minutes but was probably only a few seconds later when he felt something touch his waist, and heard a voice he vaguely recognised. "Are you wearing a good leather belt?"

"Yes," he managed to shout above the roar of water rushing around his ears.

Tom felt the hand grasp the belt and it became tighter around his waist. "I've got a good hold of you. When I say, I'm going to pull you towards me out of the main flow of water. Don't struggle or try to grab at anything, or I might lose you. Just stay limp. I have a rope around my waist; those behind me can use it to haul us both out."

The rescue took place precisely as the voice had said it would. Tom was dragged backwards, still clutching the green glass bowl tightly to his chest. When he was upright again, he saw that it was a sodden Marius who had stopped him from being washed over the edge. And who else but Vincenzo who had pulled them both back to safety using a rope. Ben came over, gently prised the Holy Grail from his grasp and handed it to Alessandra, who passed it to the Alpini. He hugged his son to his chest and said, "You were amazing. Just amazing. I'm so glad you are Ok."

Then Tom remembered he had not found Alessandra's son in the building and blurted out, "I looked, but there was no sign of Cristiano anywhere."

"He's fine, Tom. He'd left work to go home as soon as it started raining. Renata will also be OK; thanks to you, I hear."

Tom seemed to be in a kind of a trance. Everything had happened so fast, and all his reactions had been automatic. It was almost as though there was another force driving him, he would think later when he was alone. Walking back to the Osteria with his father's hand around his shoulder, Tom gradually regained all his senses. He became aware of all the people standing around in the rain, which was still falling, if not quite so heavily as it had done earlier. Some were clapping gently, and others were calling, "Bravo."

18. TAGLIOLINI CON TALEGGIO & TARTUFO

As soon as it was light, Vincenzo was in the Cookery School trying to understand why so much more of the water seemed to have been coming from either inside there or the connected Monastery. Inside the buildings, nearly all the floodwaters had drained away, leaving only a sodden mass of table linen and menus under piles of furniture and pans. He made his way to the cave opening at the rear of the monastery where the Grail had been on display. Inside the subterranean room, the plinth on which the Grail had rested was still fastened to the floor surrounded by rubble and large stone blocks.

One of the room's stone walls had collapsed, the falling blocks apparently just missing the Grail itself. The fall had exposed a void on the other side. It was too dark to see far inside, but from the collecting of debris it appeared that this had been the source of much of the water. Vincenzo surmised that an underground drain must have become overwhelmed with the volume of water and sought out new outlets.

The rain running off every roof and paved surface in the village had been channelled into one place. The walled-up section of the cave must have been a weak spot, and when the force was sufficient it had simply burst open. This explained why the pressure of water was greater inside the building than outside, forcing the doors plate glass shut.

Determined to discover why so much water had ended in the village itself, and why it had not flowed around and away down the mountains as it normally did, Vincenzo began to trace the flood's path backwards. Passing back through the piazza he bumped in Ben, also up early and similarly looking for answers.

"How is. . .," they both started to say, almost in unison. Ben deferred and said, "You first."

"How is Tom?" Vincenzo wanted to know.

"He's absolutely fine and having a late sleep. What about Renata – any ill effects from that knock on the head?"

"She's a tough one. It would take more than that to stop her going to work. But if your son had not acted quickly to release her from that goldfish bowl filling up with water, who knows?"

The two men shared a look that appeared to suggest that they were equally astonished by the turn of events that had seen Tom become the hero of the hour. Together they walked towards the road exiting the village in the direction of Negi, following the trail of rubbish left by the floodwater. They passed the new hotel and spa with its newly tarmacked car park and started walking along the Negi road. The outer edges of the temporary river were clearly defined by a line of flotsam from the forest. Leaves, sticks, pine needles, cones, acorns and chestnut husks all washed out of the land above the village. After a little while, the organic materials became scattered with white specks, which on closer inspection Vincenzo declared to be shards of plastic.

A few hundred metres before they reached the Passo del Bandito, they found more evidence of man-made material tracking back up the hill into the trees. Both men had begun to guess the source of this waste. Vincenzo dropped down from the tarmac road into the culvert running alongside the hill. It was nearly full to the brim with discarded rubbish. Then he crossed the road and dropped down on the opposite side where the land fell away steeply. He walked crouched, as though searching for something, and then suddenly announced, "Si. Bloccato. The storm drain is completely blocked."

Ben joined the big Italian who was bent down and shining a

torch into the concrete pipe, which was easily big enough for a man to fit though. All they could see in the distance was compressed plastic sheeting forming a seal in the other end of the black hole. Back on the other side of the road, Vincenzo used a branch to lever some of the leaves and branches from the entrance to the storm drain. He soon uncovered more building waste, including a lot of the lightweight foam insulation they had seen dumped earlier. Finally, in the concrete pit designed to feed water into the storm drain and under the road, was the uPVC window frame and more plastic sheeting. Together, they formed a perfect, almost watertight, dam.

"I hope that construction company has good insurance cover because we will be suing them," Ben threatened.

Standing back up on the road they could now both envisage the scenario as it had unfolded the previous night. The extraordinary storm had poured hundreds of gallons of water on the mountain. This had washed everything unsecured down the hillsides. The first barrier for the torrent was the roads criss-crossing its progress towards the river in the bottom of the valley. These tarmac strips had the potential to become rivers themselves unless they were relieved by man-made culverts and storm drains. This system had coped with all previous storms, but last night had been different.

"Si. I hope that lazy building foreman has a tough skin because he's going to get a visit from me early on Monday," Vincenzo added.

The blocking of the biggest storm drains on one of the steepest hillsides was the first broken link in the fateful chain of events. This event created a build-up of water that flowed along the conveniently- tarmacked road, the path of least resistance towards the village. On the outskirts, a previously permeable earth play area had been concreted over for new car parking, speeding the water's progress into the village. With water flowing both over, and it appeared under, the stone paved piazza, the twelfth century ancient drainage systems were simply overwhelmed by twenty-first century extreme weather.

Tom arrived at the Osteria around 10 am to find it empty except for Alessandra, who was making phone calls to people on a handwritten list in front of her. She stopped to make them both a coffee and get Tom some of her freshly baked focaccia, made with cinnamon-sugar.

"I'm calling insurers, contractors and suppliers. How are you feeling after your heroics last night?"

Tom thought for a minute and then answered, "A bit dazed, if I'm honest."

Alessandra gave him a puzzled look and asked him to explain. The young man confessed that he felt confused by what had happened and was struggling to rationalise his feelings.

"The only way I can explain it is that it genuinely felt like that was someone else out there, last night: not me. I instinctively knew that I had to help that woman get out of that flooded building but have no idea why I risked my life to save that glass bowl."

Tom explained that he had no time whatsoever for religion and thought those that did have a faith were either fools or fanatics. As far as he was concerned, the Holy Grail was a great plot device for Steven Spielberg and Monty Python but was otherwise completely mythical. He thought the idea that this glass bowl was used by Jesus Christ at a dinner in Galilee over two thousand years ago was the biggest con trick he had ever heard of.

"And yet, armed with that point of view, you can't explain why you dove into a foaming torrent to save it, and then clung to it like your life depended on it? Which, in fact, it almost did."

Tom could see the contradiction that he was asking Alessandra to accept but he also understood that this was what was confusing him so much. He had never acted so completely out of character or felt that he was not totally in control of his own actions before that day. For a young man used to being certain about everything, and one hundred percent sure that he was correct in all his beliefs, these unexplainable phenomena were deeply unsettling.

Alessandra said, "I have found that certainty about anything diminishes with the passing of years, until you reach that point where few things are unequivocal. Also, a certain amount of mystery means that hope is not entirely constrained by what we can prove," finding herself unintentionally sermonizing.

Changing the subject, Alessandra asked if he had heard from Selene or seen the news about Andrea, but he had not. She summarised the events of the previous evening in Rome, including the allegations that Selene and he had both benefited financially from public money through their father's connections.

As she spoke, Tom realised that this information could only have come from one source: the pretty journalist he had chatted to right there in the Osteria. To underline the significance of what she was telling him, Alessandra added, "These allegations and revelations from the same source about Selene's relationship with Andrea cost your sister her job and nearly forced the resignation of the prime minister."

Allowing this news to sink in, Alessandra went to get Tom another coffee. She knew that one small Italian cup was never enough to satisfy his northern European caffeine habit and so made him a large café Americano. When she returned, she added, "Those hurt by these allegations will doubtless be conducting a witch hunt for those responsible. While you are the hero of the hour and therefore likely to be judged more sympathetically, even by Selene, this might be a good to time to unburden yourself of anything you feel the need to."

This suggestion left Tom in no doubt that Alessandra knew

perfectly well that the information had come from him, but also suggested that she had not yet told his father or sister. Leaving Tom to contemplate his dilemma, Alessandra collected her papers and went back into her kitchen. Tom was sure that, if pushed, that journalist would not hesitate to name him as her source of her information. He also remembered that, in trying to impress her, he had greatly exaggerated his personal role in the reconstruction of Seborga. He recalled that he had strongly suggested that it was his own construction company doing the work.

A little later, as Ben and Vincenzo re-entered the village, they could see something going on outside the Osteria. When they got closer, they could see Tom sat at a table almost surrounded by people. Other groups of villagers were milling around, chatting in the piazza. As they approached it became clear that the villagers had come to thank the young Englishman for the bravery and selflessness that many of them had witnessed first-hand. He had saved not only a life, but also possibly the most cherished relic of Christianity. Vincenzo pushed past his neighbours and grabbed Tom's hand, shaking it vigorously. He said only, "Grazie," but with more conviction than Ben had heard put into any previous thank you, before leaving and heading home to check on Renata.

Ben went out back to ask his wife for a coffee and slice of focaccia before taking a seat next to his son. Recognising that this was now a family discussion, the villagers evaporated into groups with their neighbours to continue their post-flood analysis.

Tom looked confused. "I have no idea what any of them were saying to me. At first they looked angry but then they started shaking my hand and patting me on the back. They do seem to be angry at someone or something else." The young man had got this impression from them.

Ben realised that his son was unsettled by all this attention, even more so than he had been about the events of the night before. It was as if he would like to pretend that none of these things had taken place: to just go back to how things were before the flood. Maybe having found some solidity and natural rhythm in his life, Tom resented what he saw as this being shaken up, Ben speculated.

Now it was Ben's turn to be puzzled. Tom had accused him of not paying him much attention for all the years and now he was the centre of Ben's, and everyone else's, focus. Added to that, his son was from the generation who, as far as Ben was concerned, seemed to live their lives under a social media lens. He assumed he would love being hailed the hero and having his photograph in the paper; yet it seemed not.

The better Ben got to know the relative stranger in front of him, the less he reminded him of the teenager he had left behind with his sister and Ben's ex-wife more than a decade earlier. He had seemed more self-assured at thirteen than he had been when he'd arrived in Seborga at age twenty-five. Although, his self-confidence had grown rapidly since he had started working with Vincenzo. The tough Italian treated him like an equal and that meant he expected him to do everything that he could at that age. He made no concession for Tom being the pampered product of an English, middle-class school system. Tom had also learned to expect no favours if he wanted to earn respect, and he did want that very much.

"Have you spoken to Marius to thank him? And, to apologise for judging him?" Ben asked.

"No, not yet. I will go and find him and do that when I leave here. But first, there is something I need to confess to you." Tom told his father about the young female journalist coming to the Osteria and asking questions, his answers to which might not have all been entirely accurate, he admitted.

Tom messaged Marius saying that he wanted to meet, and he responded straight away to say he and Cristiano had plans today but that Tom was welcome to join them. On the one hand, Tom thought the prospect of apologising to both men at once was just too daunting. However, he also realised that this would get both necessary, unpalatable discussions out of the way in one go. When he asked where he should meet them, Marius messaged him to say that they would call and collect him from the Osteria, but to dress for a walk in the forest.

Tom had spent the intervening hours thinking about what he was going to say to Marius, but the words did not come easy to him. By the time they were due to arrive, the regretful Englishman was no closer to an answer. As it turned out, any planned speech he had devised would have been useless because Marius and Cristiano turned the corner into the piazza accompanied by three girls and another young man. Tom guessed that the strangers, in their late teens, were probably newly arrived students from the Slow Food university.

"A foraging lesson," Cristiano offered by way of explanation for the group outing. The young chef offered his hand to shake, and this time Tom took it and shook it warmly.

Marius did the same and added, "No need for more words."

Tom could not have been more surprised and relieved. Although it had been disconcerting to realise that while he had been sitting in moral judgement on strangers, they had been universally magnanimous toward him. He had arrived here, the outsider, with all his prejudices, preconceptions and bad attitudes. Despite this, since the day he had arrived everyone had treated him with kindness and tolerance. He was, to say the least, contrite and more than slightly ashamed.

Tom was introduced to the students, who all spoke English to a greater or lesser extent and were keen to practice it. The cheerful and vocal party headed off on the road out of town. They took a track heading off east, marked with a hiking sign pointing to Perinaldo. Tom discovered that Marius had grown up a in rural Romania, in an agricultural community that was not so different from the one he now found himself in. His parents had taught him how to reap nature's harvest to supplement what they could grow. The chef and the MSc graduate in agriculture made for a formidable team spotting free food in the hills.

"The first lesson about foraging," Cristiano began, "is that the dish begins with the ingredients. It is the converse of deciding what you want to cook, and then going shopping for what is needed. If you apply conventional thinking, chances are that you will not find everything you want in nature's larder. That could be because of the weather, time of day, the season or just bad luck in finding it. Taking what you find on any day as the starting point, you start to build your dish. If you are lucky and your dog digs up a truffle, and you have some cheese at home, then there's your pasta dish – Tagliolini with Taleggio and Tartufo."

This was a lesson Tom's father had learned early on his relationship with Alessandra. Regional Italian menus are determined by location and season and not the whim of the chef, or indeed, the customer. This is also why Italian food is so varied depending on where you eat it and when. What is available in the cool mountains of the far north, the warm, damp rice fields of the west, and the dry heat of the south, is vastly different. It is a cuisine designed by nature and merely embellished by man.

The spell cast by the region of Liguria, and of Seborga in particular, was beginning to work its magic on Tom. At his lowest ebb during the recent financial mess of his own making, he had begun to realise just how vulnerable he had become. Prior to this, his only battles had been on the rugby field where there were clear rules, and a referee was there to enforce them. Afterwards everyone shook hands like gentlemen and went to the bar for a drink together. The world was a less forgiving place in adulthood, he had learned the hard way.

Faced with no income, no home and no one left he could turn to for help, his childhood shield of invulnerability quickly evaporated. These were foes he could not tackle just with muscle and bravado. If you fall out of the mainstream in a modern westernised society, it is a very long way down. Safety nets are few and wolves are waiting for the weak and unwary. For Tom, finally realising that he still needed people like his estranged father to bail him out was a wakeup call to the realities of what being a man really meant.

Tom had also begun to understand why life was gentler here in Seborga. Most people were part of an extended family support network, who were also in easy reach. As it was most often desperate people who committed petty crime and violence, there was little real need for this to be found here. Even the poorest farmer was a property owner who could provide shelter, eat reasonably well, drink their own wine and look after their families, including their elderly relatives. Foraging for them was not a fashionable hobby. It was part of a cycle of life that had gone on for as long as anyone could remember. The Englishman could not help but think that being penniless in Liguria was not quite as terrifying a prospect as being down on your luck in London.

Marius pointed to a plant growing in the rocks which had leaves shaped like lilies and floral stems like tiny fox gloves, "Ombilicus Rupestris, also known as navelwort, or even, Venus Belly Button. It can be used in a salad or to add flavour to an omelette."

The students bent down to get a closer look and take photographs on their mobile phones. It was Cristiano's turn to spot the next potential ingredient, "Rumex Acetosa, or Common Sorrel, which makes a delicious soup with some potato and onion. It's also good in a salad giving a lemony, acidic zing to otherwise bland leaves."

A few hours passed with the discovery and collection of several edible plants, many of which also had wide ranging medicinal properties. They learned that Malva Sylvestris, better known as mallow, could be used to make a pasta sauce but could also heal a cut wound or treat eczema. Cristiano pointed out, "If you've ever had marshmallows, then that distinct flavour comes from the root of the mallow."

Both Tom and the students were impressed with the pair's knowledge of the countryside larder all around them. They invited Tom to the Cookery School that evening to try some of what they would cook with their haul from the forest, and he agreed without hesitation.

19. TORTA DE CARCIOFI

Following the PM's impromptu press conference and adlib speech, his press secretary was now in awe of his boss. All normal rules of engagement with the media had been thrown out of the window. Nothing had been discussed, analysed or shared with government colleagues beforehand. He had begun by admitting his own errors of judgement, had offered his resignation without anyone calling for it, and had revealed a long-term, risk-laden strategy to his enemies. Any one of these tactics could be fatal for a leader. However, so heartfelt had been his appeal, so sincere his candidness and so breathtakingly bold his plans, that he had rendered the usually baying press pack almost questionless.

Although the initial public reaction online was only slightly more positive than negative, that was only for the first few hours of social media activity. Early online chatter had been taken up with discussion and digestion of all the issues raised. These included topics such as: did he really deceive the public by keeping his relationship with a foreign journalist a secret? Was his intervention in Seborga self-serving or part of a bold plan for a greener, more sustainable Italy? Had he demonstrated poor judgement? Should he resign as a consequence of any of these things?

As no further allegations appeared and most of those previously made were debunked after fact checks, the tide in the PM's favour turned into a tsunami. By the time the late evening TV news was broadcast, the Italian public had made up their collective minds, and the verdict of the jury of public opinion was not guilty.

The consensus was that Andrea was judged to be incredibly brave to have put his love for Selene before his position of power and personal ambition. So convincing had been his argument, that voters also believed his justification for the Seborga projects. What was more, they admired his vision for a sustainable Italy based on traditional values. According to the press secretary, if he had delivered this speech before the election, his party would have gained an even bigger majority. It was clear that the voters had almost unanimously declined Andrea's offer to resign from his post as PM.

Seeing the unbridled enthusiasm of public opinion, even the doubters and schemers amongst his party were queuing up to align themselves with his stance and his newly revealed policies. All except Amara, that was. Her leaked press release had seen her hounded relentlessly by the media all evening, as the only apparent voice of dissent. She had decided to go to ground until the dust settled and was holed up in an obscure hotel drinking her way through the contents of the minibar.

When he finally got some time to himself, Andrea called Selene in London. They eagerly shared their respective good news, although the PM's story had already been broadcast live online for all to see. Selene's sudden career change from journalist to author had been even more rapid than Andrea's recent rise to power. It was undoubtedly as unexpected, she revealed. Although they agreed that it was all too soon to start making plans, they both knew that things had turned out far better than either could have dared to hope.

"Getting our relationship out in the open feels like a huge weight has been lifted off my shoulders," Andrea sighed.

"All the women in our office were in tears watching you speak, myself included," Selene told him. However, the journalist in her could not help asking, "Have you given any thought to who was behind those initial Instagram photo posts?"

"Yes. It has the feeling of an orchestrated attempt to unseat me, and I have a good idea who would like to sit in the PM's chair. For now, I am going to let them stew in the discomfort of the unravelling of their plan."

"But how did they know all that detail about my house in Seborga? And that my brother Tom was working in the village as a builder? Someone has gone to a great deal of trouble to make enquiries on the ground," Selene concluded.

As they chatted, over the TV in the London newsroom came a breaking news story from Reuters about events taking place in Seborga. Mobile phone footage showed a drenched young man with blonde hair wading out of a flooded building carrying an unconscious woman wearing chef's whites.

"Turn on the TV news," Selene urged Andrea. Minutes later, the same young man was pictured swinging a sledgehammer to break a large plate glass door before scooping the famous Sacro Cantina from a torrent of water pouring out of the building, nearly drowning in the process. The floodwater swept him away, with him still clutching firmly onto the priceless relic. Only another dramatic rescue by others saved the young man from being plunged over a ledge to his near-certain death.

"That's Tom!" Selene exclaimed in shock.

"Are you sure? It's dark and the images are blurred by rain on the camera lens."

"It's Tom. I'd recognise that mop of fair hair anywhere. I'll have to hang-up, Andrea. I need to call Dad. I'll call you back when I know he's Ok."

Andrea continued watching and learned for himself that Tom was no longer in any danger. He was pictured walking away from the scene with Ben's arm around his broad shoulders. The PM instinctively knew he needed to get to Seborga by morning. He sent out messages to his staff to make the arrangements. He also messaged Selene to suggest that she meet him there if she could.

Gatwick's early flight would get her there by just after nine in the morning.

Being driven overnight from Rome allowed Andrea to gain a few hours of much-needed sleep. He'd arranged with Cecily to shower and breakfast on their boat. From there he would carry on to Nice Airport in time for Selene's flight arriving from London. As the pair drove up the mountain towards Seborga, Andrea outlined his plan to use the publicity from the flood in Seborga to justify his new green strategy and underline his plans.

"Now that we know no one was harmed, the timing could not have been better," he said, looking pleased with himself.

"It is almost like there was an unseen hand at work here," Selene quipped about the legendary effects of the Holy Grail.

"I will take help wherever I can get it," Andrea said, laughing.

The previous night's news had every Italian citizen and many other Europeans glued to their chosen media for further revelations. By cleverly tying his story to the near destruction of the Holy Grail, the newly empowered prime minister was now set to increase that audience to include the more than one billion Catholics in the rest of the world.

Selene explained that she had spoken to her younger brother the previous night and established that he was fine. Physically, at least, as she was sensing that he was not comfortable with how he was already being portrayed in the media and was dreading what seemed likely to follow. Tom explained that he had already endured a brief period of notoriety after posting an unintentionally misogynistic comment online whilst drunk one night.

He had not been prepared for the barrage of abuse that came back at him. He became on overnight pariah, with even his rugby mates avoiding him. Finally, he had cancelled all his social media accounts and since then had led a mostly offline existence. He had found out the hard way that he did not have the self-confidence to be in the limelight, in any capacity.

Andrea listened to what Selene had to say with some sympathy. They both knew that some people would not like what you wrote or said if you operated in the public arena. And some of those who vehemently disagree would cross the line of what is considered reasonable debate, and turn very nasty, abusive, and even threatening.

"You need a thick skin, and it is not for everyone," Andrea agreed.

Selene told him, "Tom does not want to speak to the press. Indeed, he would rather not be mentioned in the media at all, but I fear that particular boat has already sailed."

Andrea thought for a while. "The truth is usually the best default position. Let's tell them that, while he is happy that the lady was not badly hurt and the Grail not damaged, he does not want any publicity and has left the area. Vincenzo or Ben will have to find him somewhere to stay away from the village while things cool down."

"OK. But Tom will have to get all his hair cropped off and buy a baseball cap because he stands out like a sore thumb around here," Selene added, thinking aloud.

Having been briefed overnight by his press secretary, there was a good turnout of journalists and film crews to witness Andrea arrive in Seborga, now very publicly hand-in-hand with Selene. Selene was wearing a cashmere suit by an Italian designer, rather than her usual British label of choice. She looked every inch the perfect politician's partner. The couple went first to the barracks of the Alpini. Andrea wanted to check on the Grail in its temporary resting place and inspect the damage inside the monastery. The prime minister refrained from comment, saying that he would announce his thoughts when he had assessed the whole situation.

Alessandra and Ben joined them in the main piazza for a public display of unity to underline that they had nothing to hide following the previous night's allegations. Together the four walked side-by-side out of the village towards the Passo del Bandito, trailing a gang of media and a few curious villagers behind them. Ben showed them where the floodwater had descended from the mountain, and where its progress had been blocked by discarded plastic. Despite his fine blue wool suit and shiny black shoes, Andrea dropped down into the ditch and started pulling out bits of uPVC, a plastic sheet big enough to wrap a van in, and finally, one of the ubiquitous plastic drinks' bottles.

Using the cola bottle with its red cap as a baton, he began conducting his address to the media, "Look what we are doing to our countryside and our planet. Last night we nearly lost the most precious holy relic in the world. Not to the forces of nature, but because of our irresponsibility. We have overheated the planet by burning carbon, causing these extreme weather events. Not content with that, we have concreted over much of our land and forced our rivers through manmade gaps. Then, to make doubly sure disaster will befall us, we throw away millions of tons of non-biodegradable plastics to block the gaps the rainwater is trying to get through. And the tons of plastic that do get through wash into our seas, choking our wildlife and poisoning our fish." The PM was now pointing his plastic cola bottle out to sea while the camera panned around him to get the full perspective.

"This has to stop. And there is nowhere better than Seborga to start the revolution. From where we are standing, you can see the full cycle of this environmental insanity. Every discarded object, litre of pesticide, and bottle of chemical toiletry that we despoil this land with will eventually end up out there in the Mediterranean. In the same sea where our children play and the fish that we eat swim. Those of us who don't live in places like Seborga have lost sight of that connection between human actions and their consequences for the planet. But by prioritising price and convenience, we have passed on the cost to our environment and the inconvenience to future generations who will have to clean it up. We must take back that responsibility."

Andrea paused, holding his bottle pointed out to sea to allow notetaking and filming.

"This is not only environmental madness; it is economic suicide. We're all paying for these plastic products to be made using what's left of the world's oil, only to throw them away. My government must then use your taxpayers' cash to collect what we can of the plastic and dump it in landfill for future generations to deal with. As I cautioned last night, I can't say for sure that all our new initiatives here in Seborga will work, but we must start somewhere. And, for those that are not completely successful, we must find better alternatives. So, we should support Seborga's efforts to become a low carbon, plastic-free, sustainable economy, and learn from the trials that will be carried out here."

There was an outcry when the journalists learned that they were not going to get a photo opportunity with the PM, his new girlfriend and her heroic brother. Tom was now being tagged 'The Angel of Seborga,' presumably because the Holy Grail's saviour had almost white hair and was angelic in appearance. However disappointed, the media had no choice but to accept that Tom would not be making an appearance. For many, his reluctance to be recognised made his story even more intriguing. They would read all manner of things into his reticence. Still, there was more than enough material to keep them in headline-making copy for several days, so they departed reasonably content.

Andrea and Selene returned to the Osteria where Alessandra had made torta de carciofi (artichoke pie) with local black tomato salad for lunch. Ben had returned from the hairdresser in Bordighera where Tom had his hair cropped close to his scalp, a style he decided he quite liked. He had found his long, fair locks uncomfortable when he was working in the heat and dust. This military cut would be much more comfortable and he agreed with his father that it did make him look quite different, even without the baseball cap they had chosen from a newsstand by the railway station.

Whilst at the station, they both could see that all the newspapers for sale carried blurred photographs of the flood in Seborga. Meanwhile, Vincenzo had arranged for Tom to use a small holiday home in the hills above the village. It belonged to a family from Turin for whom he looked after the property and its gardens. It was Tom's for as long as he needed it, Vincenzo told Ben, dismissing his question about the cost with a wave of his hand.

"The family won't be back here until August."

20. PORCINI

When Andrea and Selene finally departed the village, Ben decided that he needed a walk in the country on his own to clear his head. The land smelled different after the rain. The sky was clear. The air felt fresher than usual, but the odour of damp organic matter and vegetation was strong. The sun was heating the ground and causing steam to rise from the valley.

As he approached the groves where the orange trees had been planted just a few years ago, he could see that there was something not right. The ground below the branches was covered in a carpet of the white petals of orange blossom. Ben realised that these fat, surfboard-shaped petals must have been beaten from their flower stems by the previous night's pounding rain.

Despite the bright sunshine, a dark cloud of despair descended upon Ben on learning that the village's precious blood orange crop appeared to be ruined. How many more disasters could be heaped upon them; could the Grail be cursed, he wondered? He called Vincenzo on his mobile phone to ask if he had seen this latest victim of the storm, and he confirmed that he had. The experienced farmer was, however, not so pessimistic that the entire crop would be lost.

"Many of the flowers will already have been pollinated and should be fine. The flowers and their petals could have already done their job. We might see a reduced crop, but not a total disaster. In a few weeks, we will know how many fruits are likely to come. I'm more worried that some of our terrace stonework at the vineyard might have been washed away. Want to come with me to check?"

Ben had agreed and waited for Vincenzo arriving in his Ape to give him a lift for the short ride to the slopes where his vines were growing. The Ape suddenly drew to a halt, the door was flung open and the sharp-eyed Italian strode a few yards into the forest while removing his penknife from his pocket. Stooping down he cut off three large porcini mushrooms, the first of which was bigger than his splayed hand. Returning to the Ape, Ben had also opened his door and stepped out so as not to be choked by the fumes from the idling old two-stroke engine.

"Lunch?" Ben suggested.

"Si. Gratuita (free)."

As they continued, along the roadside on both sides were piles of leaves and debris, all washed down from the hills by the previous night's storm. Earlier passers-by had cleared many blockages from the single-track road, sometimes only after cutting them up with a chainsaw. Some of the resulting logs were neatly stacked by the roadside, suggesting that someone was coming back to collect them for firewood. Piles of sawdust on the tarmac were evidence of this recycling.

"Only the olive and oak wood are worth saving," Vincenzo said, explaining that the pinewood was open-grained and burnt too quickly but the others grew slower, had greater density and so lasted longer.

When they reached the foot of the hill from where the vine terraces stepped up and clung to the hillside above them, they could see that most of it was intact. Only one small section of stone wall right at the top had slipped down onto the terrace below.

"The first section that Tom built on his own," Vincenzo offered to Ben as an explanation.

"In the light of recent events, I think today we can forgive him that small shortcoming," Ben replied in resignation.

"The many metres of wall that he built later have held firm, which is good," the Italian said, trying to reassure his friend.

Ben told Vincenzo the other thing that he had noticed in the orange groves earlier as they walked. When incentivised by EU grants, many of the farmers had agreed to try changing from olive to orange production, but it had meant clearing the terraces of olive trees ready for planting. Ben had watched in horror and uncertainty as they took chainsaws to their precious olive trees, many well over a hundred years old. As certain as he was that blood oranges offered better economic prospects for the farmers, he could not help fearing the consequences if he had got it wrong. As felled olive trunks began piling up on the ends of the terraces to be recycled into firewood, Ben departed the groves, unable to watch the slaughter any longer.

This morning he had seen that all the stumps left in the ground after the felling were now sprouting vigorous new branches from their sides. Some of these were already a metre high and carried their parent plants' distinctive silver-greens. Ben has always assumed that the trees' felling was the end of the line for them, but here before his eyes, they appeared to be regrowing. Was that anticipated, he wondered? If it was, no one had said so at the time.

"Of course, we knew they would grow back after a few years. You didn't believe we would cut down perfectly good olive trees if there was no way of reviving them? That would be madness. And no one said anything because those EU bureaucrats would have paid us less compensation if they knew the trees could eventually be restored back to production. They are our insurance in case your blood orange experiment doesn't work out."

Ben was unsure whether to be relieved that some of the pressure for his plan to succeed had been removed from him or insulted that he had been kept in the dark that olives trees were apparently almost indestructible. Vincenzo went on to tell him that even wildfires would not completely destroy most forest trees. Given time, olive trees were eventually able to restore themselves. Ben told Vincenzo he would stay awhile in the vineyard and walk back to Seborga later.

In the five years since arriving in rural Italy, Ben felt as though he had learned more of value than in the previous five decades of his life. This micro-nation had all the elements of a larger community, but in miniature. Here, the cycle of production, consumption and waste disposal was transparent. It was not hidden behind a complex food chain and utility infrastructure system. It was all on view for anyone to see and, eventually, to understand, as he had.

His ongoing education in understanding the natural world's workings had caused him to rethink much of what he had previously believed was important. His epiphany had come when he understood the connection between his own small, everyday actions and the environment. This had changed many of his habits for good. He had not bought a disposable plastic razor or shaving foam in five years.

He discovered that, in a largely off-grid community, everything that went down his shower, sink and toilet drain ended up on the land around him. From there it passed into the rivers flowing through the land and finally out into the ocean. Suddenly the purchases of shampoo, soap and toilet cleaner took on a new importance. He would not want to eat food or drink wine grown in the chemical residue of the products he used to buy and throw down the sink. Olives were surely the perfect example of sustainability. They grew without the addition of anything but natural fertiliser, and their fruits could be eaten, drunk and used as soap before ending up back in the soil where they came from with no harm done.

Andrea's speech the previous night and the public's reaction to it proved to him that attitudes were changing. Also, that the village's strategy to create a sustainable economy based on biodiversity and organic methods was the right one. The resulting produce would be increasingly sought after and of higher value than their mass-producing competitors. Ben knew that it was all very commendable being 'green' and sustainable, but farmers still had bills to pay and children to bring up. Their business model also had to make commercial sense. It was his task to see that it did.

21. RAVIORE

In an unexpected response to the near tragedy in Seborga, more visitors than usual arrived in the village on what otherwise would have been a quiet weekday. Alessandra busied herself, making pasta to take her mind off things and to have something to serve the influx of customers. Cristiano had dropped off some foraged greens that he had collected but now couldn't use because the Cookery School was out of action. Alessandra used them to make a batch of Raviore, a half-moon shaped dumpling to be filled with the wild herbs.

While she was working, Cecily called Alessandra's mobile.

"While you wait for everything to dry out and for the insurance assessors to do their work, why don't we take a short trip?"

Cecily suggested to Alessandra at the end of their somewhat depressing update on the situation following the flood.

"It's a lovely idea, Cecily, and a break from all this would be welcome, but there's just too much to do here."

Her friend reiterated that there would be little that could be done at the Cookery School until the insurance gave the go ahead. That was very unlikely to happen in the next few days. Cecily also admitted that she had an ulterior motive in offering to take Ben and Alessandra sailing. An issue had arisen that she and Roman would welcome their advice on.

"I'm thinking of an overnight sail to Corsica. There's a wonderful fish restaurant in Saint-Florent that does the most incredible Azziminu (fish soup). Two, or maybe three days max.

The last time we made this trip we had dolphins visit us on both the outbound and return journeys," Cecily added for extra appeal.

Alessandra had gone quiet, suggesting to her friend that she was now thinking about her offer. Cecily knew that Ben would go in an instant; it was always Alessandra who did not like to be too far away from the comfort of her kitchen.

"Two days, you say?"

The savvy businesswoman knew it was best to have some scope for negotiation, "Two. Three at most, if the wind is not with us. Pack a weekend bag and be at the dock at six tomorrow night. Bring sweaters. It can be cool out in the open sea in the evening. We'll have supper and then set sail. Fresh croissants in Corsica by morning."

Ben was delighted when Alessandra told him the news. He was only too ready to leave behind all his family, agricultural and construction worries for a few days. Sailing was a new passion for him, and the idea of visiting the not-so-well-known French Island in the Mediterranean was appealing.

"With its French heritage and unique geographical location, there must be some interesting and slightly different food and wine on Corsica," he speculated.

Alessandra had already done a little surfing of the Internet and learned that the cuisine of Corsica had a little more in common with that of Italy than the south of France. There was little sign of the North African ingredients found on the Côte d'Azur. Pasta, gnocchi and polenta were commonly used as the base of dishes.

"I'm sure Cecily will see to it that we taste the best there is," his wife laughed, now feeling a bit brighter about her decision to go, having done a little food research of her own.

Ben's mobile phone vibrated to tell him he had a message. It was from Vincenzo, asking him to come outside the house. In the street, the big man's tanned head was protruding above the windscreen of the Crazy Dutchman's old Kübelwagen. The almost fifty year old, open-top VW-based Jeep was ticking over quietly with a distinctive air-cooled Beetle engine note. Vincenzo had rescued it from its premature gave and revived it.

Every time Ben, and indeed most people saw it, it made them smile. The strange, bright orange, corrugated-panelled, vehicle, had been bequeathed to Selene, along with its late owner's other property in Seborga. It had not run for nearly two years and had been under a tarpaulin outside the back of his shop. Two summers of dust would need washing off to reveal the full glory of its faded satsuma shade.

"Selene asked me if I could get it going so the Tom could use it. Now that he is living up in the hills, he will need some transport. It only needed some new spark plugs and the brakes freeing-off. Want to come with me to surprise him?"

"I can't wait to see his face," Ben said, smiling broadly and stepping into the cab next to Vincenzo.

Tom could hardly get over the shock at his sister's unexpected generosity, especially surprising in the light of his latest folly. Ben told him that he and Alessandra were going sailing for a couple of days. The young man was still too ecstatic about his transport to pay much attention and said, "Enjoy." Tom was thinking about turning up at the beach on Saturday mornings in his quirky retro convertible.

"When you call your sister to thank her, tell her we are sailing to Corsica tomorrow but will be back in a couple of days."

Tom really wanted to hug both men, so grateful was he for what they had done for him in recent weeks, but his false pride still prevented him doing so. His circumstances had turned from having no male figure that he could look up to, to having two quite different role models. They had in common an inner strength that he was yet to acquire, but at least he now knew what it looked like. He was also aware that he had been given another chance at life and was determined to get it right this time.

Discovering that his friend Marius was homosexual, and that

Cristiano was his partner, had been a catalyst for change in Tom's thinking. The events on the night of the flood had made him re-evaluate all the stereotypes he had acquired over the years. Tom was finally learning to judge people by their actions, and not by their words or the labels that society hung on them. Alessandra's and Selene's recent kindness, even in the face of his rudeness and stupidity, were more examples of how wrong he had been about people. He even began to question whether he had been wrong about his mother and his stepfather. Had they been so awful to him, he now wondered?

22. RAVIOLI DI CARCIOFI

"We are far from the first Italians to set our sails for Corsica," Roman said to Alessandra, cryptically.

"Or the first Brits," Ben said, looking over at Cecily, having done some basic Google research into their destination island of over three hundred thousand fiercely independent people.

Alessandra responded, "Yes, colonialists seem to like collecting islands. Originally Italian, before you British took it then traded it to the French, but then Mussolini briefly reclaimed it, only later to be forced to hand it over to the Nazis. Finally, the Moroccans took it back on behalf of the Allies before it was eventually gifted back to France."

"No wonder some say that their food and people have something of an identity crisis," Ben joked.

There was a good breeze pushing the big old wooden yacht south away from the coast and out into open sea. The sun was sinking down into the hills behind the glimmering lights along the coastline. They were now too far out to distinguish between Monaco, Nice or Cannes, which had merged into one long, narrow strip of light. Only the landing lights and vapor trail of jet planes gave away Nice's Côte d'Azur Airport's location.

Ben loved this part of these trips, feeling the excitement build as the coastline faded from view. Sailing was the closest thing to a genuine adventure that Ben had experienced. When he first stepped onto the boat deck, he left his comfort zone behind on the quay. Once away from the shore, he quickly realised that there was only a veneer of wood between him and the incredible power of the ocean. It was simultaneously exhilarating and frightening, and that combination always gave him an adrenaline rush. It also instilled in him the value of a team, where each individual relied upon those around him, in this case for their very survival. The skipper instantly earned respect and became everyone's best friend.

Only a mile or so from the coast, Cecily and her guests had enjoyed a digestivo on the deck watching the sun go down after a supper of some early season ravioli di carciofi al pofumo di timo (artichoke ravioli with thyme). Claude, the skipper, suddenly barked orders to the two crew on deck. Both went below and one returned with a powerful searchlight connected to the power circuit. He pointed the beam out into the sea to the east where other lights could be seen above a line of white water. The other crew member could be heard speaking loudly and deliberately, very clearly into the radio microphone, first in English and then in French. No reply seemed to be forthcoming over the speaker, so he repeated his message.

The distant rising and falling note of an engine could now be heard, its low pitch drone getting slightly louder with each passing minute. Roman went to speak to Claude, who was at the helm. He explained that this boat was travelling at high speed according to the radar, and due to cross their path in just a few minutes.

"Nautical etiquette says that they should change course because we are under sail and they have engines powering them, but you never know these days. There are so many rich idiots around here with huge, high-powered boats but little or no experience, or nautical qualifications. They navigate as they drive on the roads, without care or respect for anyone but themselves. Or they could easily be on drink or drugs, or both. I can't take the chance they will see us at the last minute. Even if they do, they could still panic and turn the wrong way into us."

The crew member came up from below and confirmed there

was no answer to his messages on the emergency channel, speculating whether the approaching boat even had their radio turned on, as was required by international law.

Claude waited for a moment to see if there was any response to their flashing spotlight or radio message and then barked more orders, "I need everyone on deck to get ready to come-about and then drop all sails. There is what could be a big boat approaching at extremely high speed and I don't think he knows we are here in his path."

Having just got all the sails up and beginning to make good time in the fresh wind, Cecily knew that this was a real inconvenience that could cost them as much as an hour on their journey. She also knew better than to question the skipper's decision. Everyone, including Roman and Ben, got to the ropes they were assigned and readied themselves. Alessandra and Cecily were poised to coil spare rope as it became free from the cleats. In what seemed like a seamless movement, the skipper started the diesel engine, gave the command to drop the sails and then spun the wheel hard to port, so it was facing into the wind.

The big boat slowly turned ninety degrees, pitching quite considerably while everyone scrabbled about roughly folding the now collapsed sails and gathering rope tails. The boat quickly returned to a level once the sail was down. The diesel engine now pushed the yacht slowly forward in an easterly direction, directly toward the approaching motorboat. Ben looked concerned at this choice of course and turned to Roman and Cecily to ask them to explain what seemed like a counter-intuitive decision.

Cecily told them that Claude had no way of knowing exactly what path the approaching boat would take, and that the diesel engine was too slow to steer completely away from danger. The best strategy was to make the boat as thin a target as possible.

Ben could see the logic in this but asked, "Why motor toward him, when we could steer away?"

Cecily explained, "In terms of the time to contact, it will make little difference, but we can be more manoeuvrable if we are steering toward them. Also, in the worst case, the bow is higher and thinner so more likely to deflect the worst of a collision than the stern. Finally, if they miss us but pass by awfully close, we want the prow to cut through the huge bow wave that will be created. The stern would be swamped."

All of this made perfect sense when explained, Ben realised, but did little to remove the sense of foreboding he was now feeling. He sought out Alessandra and gave her hand a reassuring squeeze.

"Everyone put on their life jackets, and crew prepare to abandon ship if we need to," was the skipper's next commend.

The crew, who were already wearing their life jackets, untied the small inflatable boat and loaded it with two packs of emergency kit, fastening them down with Velcro straps. Then they all waited, as it began to look increasingly like Claude's suspicion had been correct. The droning engine was now much louder and the earlier peaks and troughs in volume had flattened to a more constant note. They could now see the boat's shape quite clearly as it ploughed through the swell, its lights rising and falling slightly with each white-capped wave it cut through.

"I'd say that boat is about fifty metres, Skipper, and doing as much as twenty-five knots," the crewman at the bow shouted back. "But it looks as though it is under a manual helm, as it's not keeping a completely straight line. I think we are slightly on its starboard side at the moment and so should be Ok. Maybe steer another couple of degrees to port and then straighten up."

Hearing this was the worst possible news to Claude. A boat steered by autopilot was at least on a predictable trajectory. It would keep its course no matter what, and they could at least try to manoeuvre out of its way. A boat being steered by hand, possibly by someone not in full control, could do anything. Even a slight inadvertent movement of the helm could change the boat's position by tens of metres by the time it reached them.

The skipper did as was suggested and then throttled back the engine to move steadily forwards. The black hull now appeared bigger, and the noise was louder. They could also hear another faint sound. It was a booming bassline of rap music. It sounded as if a party was in full swing on that boat while it ploughed through some of the busiest waterways for small pleasure and fishing boats anywhere in the world.

"Ben and Roman, please get as much video and as many photographs as you can when it passes but keep one hand with a firm grip on something, because all hell is going to break loose in a minute. We need to trace and report this lunatic to the coastguard." Now, talking only to the two men nearest to him, Claude added, "The best thing that can happen now is that they don't see us and just blast by. If someone spots our lights at the last minute and the helm turns even slightly, we're in trouble. That thing is the weight of two trucks and it's doing thirty miles per hour towards our fragile wooden barrel."

The crewman with the spotlight was now able to illuminate the black hull with the beam but could not yet make out a name on it. All those onboard looked relieved to see that the boat was about to pass on their starboard side at about twenty metres' distance, which only left its bow wave to deal with. The combination of noise coming from its engines, loud rap music, and rushing water drowned out a crew member's reassuring voice on the yacht.

Claude had one hand on the throttle and the other on the top of the helm. As the big black boat drew parallel, he thrust the throttle forwards and span the wheel to starboard toward the passing boat.

"Hold very tight," he bellowed at the top of his voice.

Within seconds the wake wave hit them, washing over their bow and lifting the whole boat a couple of metres higher. A small wall of water rushed down the teak decks as the yacht bucked like a wild horse. The diesel engine pitch raised as the propeller was lifted from the water by the rocking motion of the boat and the prop was allowed to spin briefly without the water's resistance. The skipper throttled back the engine and allowed the yacht to settle into the calmer water inside the V-shape the wake had left behind. They watched the brightly lit powerboat gradually getting smaller as it continued on its journey, unaware of the fear it had caused.

The water in the wake appeared phosphorescent, having been churned and oxygenated by the huge dual propellers of the big boat. It was suddenly incredibly quiet, with only the diesel's gentle burble on tick over and the gentle lapping of waves on the hull.

They all looked at each other, but only one of the French crew felt the need to say anything, "C'était proche."

"Far too close," Claude agreed. "Anyone see the name?"

"Zeno, registered in the Bahamas," the crewman on the stern shouted back before going below to check it on the Internet. "It is a brand-new boat. Built for the Ukrainian rapper, Zeno V, and launched in Genoa very recently. Its twin turbo-charged engines burn two hundred and fifty litres of fuel per hour at full throttle."

"That's roughly a thousand litres of fuel from Genoa to here," calculated Claude.

Alessandra shook her head and sighed, "Tons of plastic, annually burning fuel equivalent of the entire population of our principality. It's a one-man ecological disaster."

"While we can sail from here to Corsica and back on nothing but wind power. Or could have, if we hadn't had to run our engine for five minutes to avoid that idiot," Cecily observed.

"OK. Let's get the sails back up and get underway," Claude ordered.

**The terrace at Bordighera Alta
is perfect for enjoying a glass of wine
watching the sun, going down on the Mediterranean.**

Drawing by Linda McCluskey

23. AZZIMINU

Despite the delay caused by the previous night's events, as they were eating breakfast the next morning, the mountainous outline of Corsica slowly crept onto the horizon. Claude went below to check his charts and make a course to take them along the western side of the island's northern peninsula into the Gulf de Saint Florent.

Ben and Alessandra had found it difficult to get to sleep, now both acutely aware of potential perils of sailing at night on the open ocean. There were also strange noises on a boat, particularly an old wooden one. Creaks and groans from the timbers and the sloshing of water in the bilges took on sinister new possibilities. They had both been glad to be greeted on deck by daylight and the sight of dry land.

Most sea traffic from mainland Europe took the route to the east of the island, where the main port of Bastia was to be found. Much of the coastal waters around Corsica are protected by strict marine conservation laws, preventing boats anchoring in many places, so Claude had phoned ahead to book a place in the small harbour at Saint-Florent.

However, along the coastline, there was one stunning cove close to Punta Di Saeta where boats were allowed to drop anchor on the sandy bottom without any danger of damaging the seabed. It was possible to swim in the crystal-clear waters and explore caves eroded into the rocky coastline by centuries of storms. This was to be their pre-lunch destination before sailing the last few miles into port.

The old fishing town on Saint-Florent had, like many other similar places, lost most of its fishing boat fleet. The few that remained served only the local restaurants, whose customers were mainly visiting pleasure boat owners, and who were incapable of, or disinclined to, catch their own fish. The dish they all came for was the famous Corsicanve Azziminu. Although this French island may have retained several dishes from its Italian history, this unique fish stew contained ingredients which may have had their origins in Spain. Star anise and aniseed accompany the saffron, fennel, thyme and tomatoes in this feisty interpretation. The fish can be almost anything but almost always includes lots of shellfish.

Ben had learned that the Saint-Florent-Agriates region's red wines are world-renowned, with grenache being the most widely planted grape, and those grown around nearby Patrimonio seen as the best of breed. Less than twenty per cent of the wines produced in this small region are white. The only grape variety for white wine within the Patrimonio appellation is Malvoisie de Corse. It was this that Cecily recommended as the perfect accompaniment to their lunch.

Food and wine organised, Cecily began to explain the dilemma that she and Roman had been wrestling with. The one on which they wanted the opinion of their good friends. Roman's youngest daughter, Patsy, had been in touch to tell her father about a worrying development. No sooner had her elder sister, Caroline, got back to New York after their recent visit, she had informed Patsy that she planned to mortgage her half of the farm to release cash. Ross, her American broker husband, had previously tried to sell off part of the land to a developer. This plan had come up against local Sicilian opposition of a nature that he had not bargained for. Roman had left the orange farm in trust to the sisters and Patsy had since moved there to run it, hoping her American musician boyfriend would follow her home where they could start a new life together.

Roman and Cecily had been told that there was a property scheme that Caroline's husband was desperate to invest in, but he needed another quarter of a million dollars cash to make his stake up to that of his partners. The young couple had borrowed and cashed in everything they could but were still short and were running out of time. Roman was horrified at the idea of the land he'd inherited from his father being mortgaged to some mercenary American lender. He knew that if Ross's scheme failed or he could not keep up the repayments, the bank would try and foreclose on the farm. Roman neither liked nor trusted his son-in-law, thought he was a poor businessman and a thoroughly untrustworthy individual.

Cecily had met Roman when she first went to buy the blood oranges grown on his farm for her cosmetic products. She still took every orange grown on the farm under a supply contract that suited both parties very well.

"This is where things get tricky for me. I have cash sitting there in the bank earning virtually no interest. Investing in a trusted supplier would normally be sensible vertical integration for me. I have no wish to see an essential supply chain interrupted by introducing a potentially aggressive and disinterested third party lender. I would normally say, let me buy out one half and thereby safeguard my supply. However, these are Roman's daughters, and this situation is not the outcome he'd envisaged for his legacy. Nor is it an intervention in his family affairs that either of us is especially comfortable with."

Ben looked at Alessandra and screwed up his face, feigning pain. He could see his friend's dilemma. Like them, but for different reasons, he was uncomfortable crossing the boundary from friendship into personal family matters. To be sure she understood exactly what they were being asked their opinion on, Alessandra tried to summarise; "Caroline is determined to borrow two hundred and fifty thousand dollars and can use her share of the land as collateral. There's nothing anyone can do to stop her. But that action potentially puts Patsy's share, Roman's legacy, and your supply chain at risk. You have the money, and your intervention could mitigate that risk, but that would leave you as an effective partner, a situation you would rather not be in because of the potential pitfalls."

"That's the crux of it," Cecily agreed. "Reinvesting in this way is also quite tax advantageous for me, but that's another matter," she added.

Ben looked thoughtful, but his worries were less about the validity of his conclusion than whether he should voice it all. His English sensibilities were inclined to avoid expressing any opinion of private money or family matters. Finally, he offered, "Caroline is a grown woman entering into, what is, after all, a business decision with her eyes wide open. We should also remember that she might also be right. For all we know, her husband could be a property genius. He might treble their money with his plans and set them both up for life. The emotional connection to the land shared by Roman and Patsy is not something Caroline feels so deeply. She sees it merely as an asset to leverage as she sees fit."

Roman nodded whilst simultaneously grimacing, believing his friend had also summarised the unfortunate situation with uncanny clarity.

Ben looked directly at Cecily and offered, "So, as your motives cannot be misconstrued, why don't you offer to facilitate Caroline's immediate wish by buying her half of the land? But importantly, also offer her the option to repurchase it within– say–two years, for the same price plus bank rate interest and any transaction costs. That way if her husband's project succeeds, and she feels some remorse about giving up her father's land, she can reclaim it without anyone having lost out. This would mean that Caroline has got what she wanted but Patsy's, and your, position, are safeguarded in the event of their deal in America going wrong."

Aware of both daughters' previously tricky relationship with their father's lover, Alessandra cautioned, "But only if Patsy is completely comfortable with you as her silent partner, of course."

"Better Cecily than a New York banker," observed Roman, horrified by that thought.

Cecily smiled at the simple logic of Ben's suggestion, placing the onus on Caroline to undo the arrangement if their gamble paid off, but at the same time reasonably sure that a buy-back seemed unlikely to happen, whatever the outcome.

"Thanks, you two. Sound advice. I know we were asking the right people. We'll sleep on your suggestion before deciding. Patsy's coming to visit next week to talk to her father and to see where we plan to build our house."

By the time they had unravelled the problem of Roman's farm and talked through potential solutions, the enormous steel kettle dish of spicy fish stew had been and gone in a shower of crumbs from the fresh crispy bread, all washed down with the earthy white local wine. They agreed to forgo a dolce and go straight to coffee, saving their appetite for dinner at another eaterie in the small fishing town.

They had also arranged an appointment with the architect of a house, similar in design to the plan they had for theirs. It had been designed for some friends of Cecily's who lived part of the year here on Corsica. The owners were not there right now. They had arranged for the architect, who had a set of keys, to go with the couples on the visit. That way, he could also answer any technical questions that they might have.

They had booked a local taxi to take them a couple of kilometres to the hillside where the now completed house was situated, set amongst the wine groves. The architect's green Land Rover was parked by the side of the road, exactly where he'd said it would be. When he saw them approaching, the young man waved his arm from the open window for the taxi to follow him off onto a dirt road, which then began climbing up the hillside. After just a few minutes he stopped and got out, leaving the door open and the engine running. The four of them also got out of the airconditioned taxi into the mid-afternoon heat and a settling cloud of dust made by their own vehicles.

"There it is," said the young Corsican.

They all scanned the hillside looking for signs of a building, but there was nothing obvious to be seen.

"Where?" Roman asked impatiently.

"Right there, three hundred metres away in the centre of that hillside, a little higher than our elevation."

They all concentrated on the area where the architect was pointing. Ben was the first to pick out some faint vertical straight lines amongst the vineyard terraces' otherwise irregular surfaces. The hillside's undulating contours were scored through with two-metre-high stone walls retaining the soil in which the vines grew. A thirty metre section of terrace appeared like it had been fenced with planks of wood.

"They could be scaffolding boards," Ben suggested, as they were all equal width and length but slightly different shades of brown, which made them blend well into the stone terrace walls around them.

"Louvre shutters," the architect said, pulling out his mobile phone and selecting an app. He pressed a few links, and all the louvres began to turn simultaneously, revealing the wall of glass windows they had been shielding. "When the house is occupied in the summer, they can be programmed to track the sun, keeping the direct rays out. In the winter they can all be folded back to let in the light and heat."

Ben and Alessandra now understood what Cecily and Roman had been trying to explain about their plans for their proposed new house. This building sat so sympathetically in the landscape that it was almost invisible until any visitor got up close to it. Only from above could you see the straight lines of the structure.

"It's a stealth house," Ben joked. "Perfect if you like privacy and don't want any callers."

The architect elaborated, "Much of the house is underground. It's been dug into the hillside behind, which helps keep the temperature even all year round. It requires virtually no heating, and little cooling."

The visitors drove the remaining few hundred metres to a parking place above the house where they could then see the layout of those parts above ground level. The house still looked relatively modest in size, the pool reaching the terrace's very edge on the ocean side. Its designer was explaining that a barely submerged oxidised steel rim gave the impression of an infinity pool, without the need for an exposed glass wall on the other side. From below, they had seen for themselves that this rusted steel could not be seen protruding from the traditional stone wall terracing.

While the others went inside to look around, Ben checked out the vines growing all around the house. He noted that the planting on the narrow terrace in front of the house and behind the pool was also of vines, further helping the man-made structure blend into its environment.

Ben stooped to pick up a handful of the soil, noting how similar in colour and texture it appeared to that on his land in Seborga. Their taxi driver would later confirm that it was chalk and clay with high limestone levels, remarkably similar to that of western Liguria and its neighbouring region of Provence. Increasingly Ben realised that some of the most sought-after wines were grown on soil not so different from that of his vineyard in Seborga.

On the journey back down the hill after their tour of the house, Ben quizzed the driver, using Cecily as his interpreter.

He answered, "Oui. Patrimonio wines sell for good money in Corsica, some are even exported to mainland France and America," the local bragged with some pride. However, he also admitted that he never drank it, preferring a cheaper local variety from the south of the island that even Cecily could not repeat the name of.

Ben recalled that those on the menu at lunch earlier were all over forty euros a bottle, and some as much as one hundred euros, compared to imported French wine which was as little as ten euros for a carafe. The Patrimonio was bringing a big premium on the prices that were obtained for Rossese, also a local rustic wine with similar provenance. Ben's marketing mind was puzzled as to where perceived added value premium was in this obscure Corsican wine and who was willing to pay it. Was it better-off locals, visitors, or both, he wondered?

Claude briefed Cecily on the weather forecast for the coming days back at the boat, warning that some rough weather was due in between twenty four and thirty six hours. She explained that the winds blowing down from central France's hot plains could create high winds in the Mediterranean. The choices seemed to be leaving today in the clear weather window or risking a rough sail back, or worse, being stuck on Corsica for a few days until the storm passed. With Roman's daughter, Patsy, due to arrive in Menton a couple of days later and no one feeling up to a rough crossing, they universally agreed to leave later that day.

The weather was still beautiful, with little wind. Claude said there was plenty of time for a swim from the beach and pointed out that the sea would almost certainly be flat enough for a relaxing supper onboard once they had got underway. It was the calm before the storm so they should have a pleasant, quiet crossing overnight, and he would ask the chef to go ashore and get the ingredients.

"And a couple of bottles of Patrimonio red," Ben requested.

"My treat."

Roman countered, "You already filled up our wine cellar with your wonderful Rossese before we left Menton. These bottles will be my contribution."

Knowing that they were tasting red wines, the chef sought out a butcher to cut thin escallops of local veal to make his own fast version of the Corsican classic, veau aux olives. The same shop supplied him with some charcuterie to start, and some prized Calenzana goats' cheese to follow. The butcher even supplied the Patrimonio wine from his neighbour's vineyard. It would be the perfect end to a short but memorable first visit to Corsica for Ben and Alessandra. They would return, the couple agreed, as they slipped into their bed for a much-needed rest as the boat quietly cut through the swell, heading north.

24. TOAST DI FICHE E RICOTTA

Menton was like a picture postcard in the morning sun. Its painted houses were clambering up the hillside from the harbour in a patchwork of pastel shades between creamy yellow and brown. Dominating everything was the town's enormous church, a plain rectangular slab of primrose embellished only by its unusual belltower. Square at first, the tower becomes round halfway up, as if someone decided it was not grand enough and added a bit as an afterthought.

Ben and Alessandra had breakfast on board the boat in Menton harbour with Roman and Cecily. Alessandra had brought ripe figs from her garden and the chef had sliced these with ricotta cheese on toasted bread before dribbling on some Seborga orange blossom honey. They thanked their friends for the short trip, both saying that it had been a welcome distraction from the challenges of reviving the principality's fortunes.

"There is something about being separated from the land that makes it easier to empty one's head of day-to-day issues and so think more clearly," Ben observed.

Cecily looked at Roman, who seemed to nod his agreement and she announced, "The same for us. Having slept on your suggestion, we have decided to offer Caroline the money she wants for half the farm, with a buy-back clause. We are going to put the idea to Patsy when she arrives tomorrow."

Ben was crossing his fingers behind his back and hoping that going against his instincts in proffering that suggestion did not come back to haunt him. If it all went wrong, and any of their relationships were damaged, he would not forgive himself.

"I am also much more relaxed about things when we are sailing," Alessandra agreed, changing from the subject which she could see was making her husband uncomfortable. "Unfortunately, as soon as I am back on dry land my issues all come flooding back, apparently never having been too far away. I have been asked if I can suggest something special to mark the official launch of the Club's Albergo Diffuso. They tell me that they plan to invite some of their most prominent members. Then there is Vincenzo and Renata's wedding."

Alessandra said that she was worried that neither Vincenzo nor Renata had much money to do anything very extravagant for their wedding. It was too costly for most of Renata's family to fly over there from New York, and she was only able to pay for tickets for her mother and father.

"And yet, they are two of my favourite people in all the world, and they have both waited so long to find each other. I want to make this a special day for them."

As they sipped their coffee and ate croissants, Roman suddenly stopped mid-chew, swallowed the pastry and offered, "Why don't we make it two weddings, one feast, and an opening party?"

Now they all stopped eating and swallowed coffee while digesting what Roman had said.

The Sicilian continued, "There are two churches in Seborga. Am I not right? There is the tiny old Templar church of St Bernardo and the later, larger San Martino. Like Vincenzo and Renata, Cecily and I have few friends or family we would want to invite, but I would love to make a festival for all the villagers. It would also provide a spectacle for the guests of the Club's Albergo Diffuso who could join in the party. The village is used to catering for hundreds of people during the summer festivals. What's the difference?"

"Two Italian weddings in a beautiful old village. No matter

how well-off the Club members are, who would not want to be part of that party?" Alessandra acknowledged.

Cecily had only just begun to think about making wedding plans and had never envisaged anything other than a small, private affair for a dozen people, perhaps in a nice restaurant. Roman's proposition was far more ambitious than anything she had anticipated. However, an image of how such a day might look began to take shape in her mind, and it was not altogether unappealing.

"There's only one priest," Alessandra pointed out.

"He can bring in a colleague from Bordighera, or we could stagger the timing so one can preside over both," Ben put forward.

"Vincenzo is still a proud man. He would not be comfortable if he were not contributing equally," was the next obstacle spotted by Alessandra.

Roman thought for a while before saying, "I have now worked with Vincenzo in the orange groves. We understand each other. He's a farmer like me. He can provide good produce: some pigs, vegetables, olives, zucchini and so on. Cecily and I can pay for everything else. No one needs to know any numbers to compare the cost."

Suddenly very enthusiastic about Roman's wedding festival suggestion, Alessandra offered, "I could see if the Club will provide some good live music as their contribution."

The four of them talked over the remaining challenges and between them came up with solutions for every practical, emotional and ecclesiastical obstacle they could think of. They concluded that the idea seemed to provide everyone with what they wanted, whilst allowing no loss of face or denting of pride. They agreed to put it to Vincenzo and Renata-although not necessarily in that order, Alessandra contrived.

"If you are planning to show Patsy the land where you will be building your house, why don't you bring her to the Osteria for dinner? She can see the village, compare our orange groves and meet some of your new neighbours," Alessandra suggested.

"And meet the princess who is to be our head of state," Cecily added, grinning broadly.

"I doubt she will be very excited about meeting a has-been chef and ageing royal relic," Alessandra countered modestly.

"On the contrary." Roman joined in. "Having spent most of her life in American private schools, royalty and Michelin Starred chefs are top of the pecking order as far she and her friends are concerned. When will she ever meet a woman who can not only claim both those titles but who is also beautiful and successful in her own business? You will be her role model, I am sure," added the smiling Sicilian.

"That is just too much responsibility, Roman. Nevertheless, I am looking forward to meeting your daughter. Cecily tells me that she's stunning. I'll invite Tom, so she has someone her age to talk to."

After their guests had departed to return to Seborga, Cecily told Roman that she was driving over to Monaco for a few hours and would be back late afternoon. When she left in the Bentley, there was a bottle of Ben's unlabelled Rossese in her straw shoulder bag. She had read that a restaurant and wine club on the Monaco harbourside held an artisan wine event, and small growers from all over the south of France had entered produce into a tasting. These were predominantly white and Rosé wines, but there were some Grenache and Syrah blends which guests could blind taste and rate. Ribbons would be handed out to the taster's top three in each category and there was some vintage champagne for the winners.

Cecily entered Ben's unbranded wine, describing its origin as "northeast of Menton" which, although that suggested it was in France, was geographically accurate. Both she and Roman believed Ben was producing some excellent wine but wanted an independent view to confirm her instincts. She believed that this blind tasting would be attended by those who appreciated artisan wines. She did not consider wine snobs who stuck rigidly to the classic regions and producers to be her ideal audience. She had arranged to meet a couple of girlfriends for lunch while she awaited the event's outcome.

In Seborga, Tom, Marius and Vincenzo's structural work on the Albergo Diffuso properties was coming to an end. Teams of specialist contractors were now beginning to install plumbing and electrical infrastructure. With an opening deadline fast approaching, several different firms were awarded contacts and worked in parallel on the various buildings. Vincenzo's role continued as an overall site foreman, but Marius would soon be returning to the vineyards. After several months of enjoyable labour, work for Tom was running out.

The prospect of returning to London now filled Tom with dread. Like his father, he had grown to love this strange but beautiful place. Perhaps more importantly, he had found work that he enjoyed doing and was good at. Construction was physically and mentally rewarding. There was nothing better for Tom than standing back to admire some stonework he had completed. Vincenzo had taught him how to instinctively select the right shaped stone for each place in the wall. His speed had increased to almost that of a professional. He also understood structural woodwork and the basics of how a building was held together. The self-belief that he could perhaps one day build his own house was possibly the greatest achievement of his life so far, he decided.

As well as practical skills, the young Englishman's self-respect had returned. He knew that Vincenzo now valued him as a hard worker, and maybe even as a person. That meant a great deal to Tom. He had also noted that his father had begun to mention him and his achievements to people with a new sense of pride in his voice. He had decided that Alessandra was the kindest person, and latterly that her son was one of the strongest characters, he had ever met.

Tom was impressed by the tactful way Cristiano handled his gay relationship in this conservative society, which still had some way to go to accept such things readily. While he avoided any unnecessary public display that might offend older residents' sensibilities, he behaved with total honesty if confronted with direct questions about it. This matter-of-fact approach had disarmed the few people Tom had seen who had been stupid enough to make an issue of his sexuality, himself included. He suspected most of the villagers knew of Cristiano's living arrangements but simply chose not to mention it.

For the first time since school rugby, Tom felt like he belonged to something bigger than himself. He hesitated to admit it openly to anyone, but he felt his new family offered him more than his old one ever had. Also, he'd gone from living in a place where few people knew their neighbours, to having almost everyone in Seborga calling him by his first name. Indeed, since his actions during the flood, the easy-to-spot, blonde-haired Englishman had become something of a celebrity in the area.

Alessandra had asked Cristiano to prepare one of his now perfected Cappon Magro terrines to begin the lunch with Patsy, Cecily and Roman. She thought the light salad and fish dish would be a safe choice for a young woman who was possibly over-conscious of her diet. It was also a spectacular visual feast when all its contrasting colours were displayed on a long white serving dish. Two beautiful large, fresh sea bass, baked Ligurian style with olives and tomatoes, would be the main dish. There would also be sliced oven potatoes on the side, another shared platter that those with bigger appetites, like Tom and Roman, could eat heartily while others could do so sparingly.

Ben and Tom were already seated when Roman's classic Mercedes swung into the piazza with him sitting behind the huge, cream, Bakelite steering wheel.

"Cool," exclaimed Tom, who had never before seen the

Sicilian's nineteen-fifties model Ponton.

"Stylish, isn't it," agreed Ben.

"Wow. She looks very cool as well," added Tom, nodding in the direction of the young woman who was sitting forwards in the centre of the back seat, with her hand draped over her father's shoulder and her head swivelling around to take in the view. Patsy's hair was so thick and straight with a lustrous quality Cecily said she had never seen the equal of, even amongst all the professional models she had used in her cosmetics business. As she panned around the village, her hair swished back and forth and yet fell back exactly into place when she was at rest. Ben declared her to be, "Striking," but this seemed like an understatement to Tom with her deep tan and black sunglasses.

Alessandra walked forward into the piazza to greet them, exchanging hugs first with her friends and then Patsy, who looked decidedly uncertain of how she should behave. Despite her father's reassurances about the informality of the occasion, the young woman seemed ill-at-ease. Sensing some discomfort, Alessandra held onto the young woman's hand and guided her to the waiting table where she was introduced to Ben and Tom. She had removed her sunglasses, which Ben noticed was a sign of common courtesy that few people seemed to practice these days. One of his pet hates was strangers who believed it was acceptable to hide behind sunglasses indoors, or worse still, under baseball caps, especially when introduced to someone for the first time.

Ben asked Tom to open the prosecco and pour them all a drink. Ben then proposed a toast, "To our new neighbours and their beautiful daughter."

"And new business partner," added Cecily, while passing Ben a knowing look.

Tom looked confused, unaware of the background to this impromptu announcement, but Alessandra and Cecily both noticed that he seemed more interested in the younger partner's appearance. As the delicious courses passed by accompanied by friendly banter and talk of blood oranges, the merits or otherwise of Michelin Stars and even a little Seborgan history, it appeared that any remaining discomfort Patsy might have felt had drained entirely away.

By the time it came to dolce, Cecily and Alessandra, Ben and Roman, and Tom and Patsy held their own side conversations. Patsy's trials of learning to run a fruit farm, even with trusted staff left behind by her father, held Tom enthralled. He asked her to describe the setting of the land and the buildings. He declared it sounded "beautiful" with more volume and enthusiasm than he had intended, causing the others to all look around.

"The farm in Sicily," he offered, by way of explanation for his unintended outburst. Cecily looked at Alessandra, each knowing what the other was thinking.

When coffee was served, Ben told them that he had an announcement of his own. For a moment, he looked earnest.

"I am proud to say that my son Tom has reached the goal that we agreed on several months ago. He took on a big challenge to learn some entirely new skills, in a strange country, and save a substantial sum of money. He has exceeded our, and I suspect his own, expectations." Looking directly at his son, Ben added, "I am really proud, and I confess not a little surprised, by what you have achieved. Vincenzo has saved all the bonus money from meeting the construction deadlines. Your share is enough for you to take a break and have a holiday. Selene says you can use the Kübelwagen if you want to drive somewhere. You could go and explore Italy or France for a month or two, depending on how long you can make your money last."

They all raised their glasses and toasted, "Tom," while the subject of their good wishes looked extremely embarrassed by being put on the spot in this way. However, he was also very grateful that his father had pointedly not mentioned in front of the others the reason for his challenge to earn and save. Having his previous misdemeanours listed in front of Patsy would have been too much for the young man to endure. It also made him realise how foolish he had been back then. Had his father and Alessandra not helped him to change his ways, he knew that his prospects would almost certainly look a lot different at this moment.

By way of encouragement to explore, Roman said, "I drove up here from Sicily in that old Merc, following the coast all the way. Only took five days. I never got over sixty kilometres per hour."

"We're always short of fruit pickers if you're passing our way," Patsy chipped in.

Tom's head was now swimming with emotions and ideas. The sudden realisation that he was liberated of his obligations was both empowering and scary. Never before had he been in a situation where he had money in his pocket, a car, and easy access to places to go with it. However, after effectively setting him free, his father offered a final word of caution.

"In case you're labouring under the false impression that the Kübelwagen can run on fresh air, I have a little secret to share with you. Vincenzo has been regularly topping up your fuel tank from a spare can he keeps for the chainsaw," Ben laughed, "but I did not tell you that."

They all laughed aloud, except Tom, who looked a little embarrassed that he had not already guessed that something was not quite right with the mileage he appeared to be getting from the old jeep. He was once again deeply touched by yet another act of kindness from his supposed tough-guy boss. Tom was a little sad not to be going back to work on the construction site. Once he'd got used to it, he liked the physical work. He also like the camaraderie with his workmates. He was going to miss all of that, he realised.

25. TORTA PASQUALINA

In the days after the flood, in typical Seborga fashion, without any formal organisation or delegation of tasks, the villagers had set about clearing and cleaning the streets. Without waiting for local government help, they shovelled, swept and carried away several truckloads of material washed down off the hills behind the village. Wet rugs that had been stretched across some of the streets looked almost dry after only a day in the resurgent sun. Everyone capable was lending a hand, and those who were not watched on from their doorsteps, offering both encouragement and refreshment.

The clean-up and mostly superficial repairs resulting from the flood in Seborga had been completed in record time. Progress was given impetus by regular requests to the contractors for progress reports from the PM. Viola had from her doorstep scrutinised the operation. At each stage, as a new contractor arrived to begin work, the old lady raised her eyebrows and shook her head, before turning and disappearing back into the darkness of her house. Although she never said as much, Alessandra knew that was her way of saying 'you were warned' about bringing the Holy Grail back to Seborga.

There had been a notable increase in the number of visitors to the village. Not just all the contractors, but the publicity surrounding the flood and the daring rescue of the Grail had brought a steady flow of tourists. Some villagers were beginning to complain about parking problems and long waits to get their coffee from the cafes. However, every B&B room was full, and the tills were ringing at the shops and restaurants. Local produce was flying off the shelves as visitors wanted to take home something connected to the 'home' of the Holy Grail.

Never one to miss a marketing opportunity, Cecily had negotiated concession space in the largest souvenir shop. She arranged for this to be stocked with her blood orange beauty products. These expensive creams and lotions were displayed, along with smart marketing material explaining how the oranges packed with antioxidants were being grown all around Seborga. The first delivery had almost sold out within a week and a special delivery had been sent to restock the shelves.

Tom had set off on his road trip just as more people had started visiting. He had been supplied with a borrowed sleeping bag, rucksack and a cool box containing some beers, plus several days' supply of baked goods from Alessandra and Renata's kitchens, including a large Torta Pasqualina. Vincenzo had given him his two thousand euro bonus and discretely filled up the Kübelwagen with fuel again. He had also assembled a collection of essential tools which he had wrapped neatly in oily rags, fitted into a toolbox and packed in beside the spare wheel, just in case.

Some of the newly arriving visitors were asking at the Osteria if they could meet the 'Angel of Seborga' so it was as well that Tom was no longer around, Alessandra decided. Ben had received a message from Tom to say he had called briefly at Portofino but quickly left again when he found that a coffee cost seven euros and a beer twelve. He was last heard of heading for the Adriatic coast via Parma, where he had the offer of a room from the family of one of the girls enrolled at the Cookery School.

The fruits in Ben's vineyards were ripening nicely, and with all the other projects completed or remarkably close to being, the Englishman had a chance to concentrate on his new passion. He had also been researching the crowd-farming concept mentioned by the Slow Food guys, reading case studies and emailing some of those who had used the new online funding platforms. With the harvest approaching and the opportunity for some great photographs to back up his pitch, Ben decided the time was right to 'dabble his toe in the water' of online investment funding.

There had been no commercial winemaking in Seborga for as long as anyone could remember. However, many farmers with suitable land had grown enough grapes to make wine for themselves and their extended families. The nearest commercial winery was in Dolceaqua, and getting grapes there would require an hour-long journey in specialist transport. Ben wanted to process his own grapes on site and hoped to offer this service to his neighbours. He planned to encourage others in the village to grow more grapes and contribute them to a Seborga wine cooperative.

The former university lecturer in marketing believed that with changing customers tastes and priorities, there was now a fantastic opportunity to obtain premium prices for produce grown in Seborga. The principality had received global publicity in recent years because of its connections to the Knights Templar and the Holy Grail. A greatly raised public awareness of Seborga, combined with the legend surrounding the previously claimed 'health-benefits' of the wine from Ben's vineyard would form the basis of a marketing plan. There was a centuries-old tale told in the bars around the area about Lorenzo's healing wine. It was said that the old man's vines were irrigated by a spring that had miraculously appeared when the Holy Grail was removed from the cave in which it had been hidden. Crippled from birth, Lorenzo had been healed when he started drinking the wine as a teenager. There were other tales of cured snake bites, severe arthritis treated and even barren villagers made fertile again by Lorenzo's 'Holy Grail wine.' This was the very same vineyard that Ben had recently acquired and restored to health with the help of Vincenzo and Marius. The legend of Lorenzo's 'miraculous' wine would provide the basis of a marketing plan. Ben's would be the only commercially available wine made and bottled entirely by hand in Seborga, with all the positive associations that accompanied that provenance.

Ben's would be the only commercially available wine made and bottled entirely by hand in Seborga, with all the positive associations that accompanied that provenance.

Ben had learned that creating a basic winery was not too complicated nor was the equipment prohibitively expensive. Nevertheless, the seventy thousand euro cost was beyond his modest means. He knew that Cecily would invest without hesitating, but he was adamant that he would not mix business and pleasure with his good friends. Andrea had found out that agricultural grants could be obtained from the public sector, but these had to be matched with at least equal private funds.

Crowdfunding seemed like a possible answer, but Ben had narrowed it down to a hybrid version ideal for artisan growers, which was part auction of a share in future production. Those who bought into the concept would be looking for something more than just a financial investment. For the producer, this model was designed to raise maximum funds without equity ownership complication.

Investors would later be invited to come to Seborga to pick, produce and bottle their wine, followed by a harvest festival BBQ. The arrangement would last for five years, with an option to renew. Those who could not or did not want to make the trip would pay for the shipping of their wine but could still feel that they had been part of the process.

Ben believed that the type of investor would be people like him, who were interested in artisan wine growing but recognised that they would never be able to do anything on their own. This way, they could feel that they had part of a project and would later enjoy wine that they could genuinely call their own, having had a hand in its creation. Ben imagined that investors would probably serve their wine to friends at special celebrations or dinner parties and enthral guests with the harvest stories.

If his innovative marketing could achieve somewhere approaching twenty euros per bottle, Ben calculated that he only needed about fifteen small investors to raise the investment he needed. Potentially, if he reached his target figure, for giving up a little over ten percent of his estimated production output, he could do it. At his worst-case scenario of ten euros per bottle, he would be giving up twenty percent of his production for five years, and even that did not seem too high a price.

Before the crowdfunding offering, Selene instigated a highly targeted PR campaign on behalf of her father using the Slow Food Organisation channels. Marius had a friend with a drone camera who had taken aerial footage of the vineyard in which viewers could see the relationship between the land, the mountains and the sea. They had even been able to capture an evening when the mist rolled up from the sea below and enveloped the vines in the damp, salty air. Footage of Seborga was also included, along with images of the Holy Grail and Knights Templar iconography for context. When he felt ready, Ben set the minimum reserve bid at ten euros per bottle, clicked 'start campaign' and closed his laptop lid with his fingers crossed.

26. PINTXOS GILDA

Alessandra was in her Seborga Osteria patiently folding pasta into parcels around a spoonful of filling. She had prepared the traditional Preboggion stuffing by incorporating a dozen different wild herbs, which she had blanched in boiling water before adding a mix of local Prescinseua and Parmesan cheese, plus some breadcrumbs.

She had made only about half of the pasta parcels that she would need for an expected busy service when her phone rang. A vaguely recognisable voice from her distant past announced, slowly and very cautiously, "It's Matteo. Do you remember me?"

All of the blood suddenly drained from Alessandra's head. She became slightly dizzy, found a seat in the deserted Osteria and slumped onto it.

"Is that you, Alessandra? Are you still there?"

"Hello. Yes," was all Alessandra could think of to say.

"I'm sorry if I have shocked you. It's been a very long time," replied the still heavily-Basque-accented voice that strangely now sounded so familiar.

Alessandra had been at her uncle's New York restaurant for nearly two years when Matteo joined the team as a kitchen porter. He arrived as she had, an economic and social refugee, seeking employment, a future without boundaries and a taste for a culture not strangled by tradition. From the Bilbao area of northern Spain, the handsome Basque had grown up in a society even more matriarchal, structured and backwards looking than her own. The pair of young Europeans not only shared a similar background, but were both fiercely determined to become chefs at the highest level their talents would allow.

Both about the same age and working in a kitchen staffed mainly by more mature Puerto Ricans or Mexicans, Alessandra and Matteo were naturally drawn together. During service, the Italian head chef and his two Milanese assistants spoke in their native tongue, as did the Latinos. Matteo translated the bits of kitchen Spanish she had not already learned, and she did the same for the Italian. The pair conversed with each other in English, as both were keen to improve themselves in that language.

Matteo had also arrived armed with food preparation and presentation skills from childhood years working in a family pintxos bar. Alessandra was amazed at how the Spaniard could make something so visually appealing out of a few leftover ingredients from menu dishes. She was familiar with the rustic Italian version–bruschetta–which placed little emphasis on appearance: it was only about flavour and low cost.

In Spanish bars, Pintxos are marketed in an entirely different way. Basque drinkers are tempted to buy their Pintxos snacks for a few euros each from the beautifully displayed treats lined up behind glass counters. In Italy, bruschetta is most often served as a free of charge appetiser with an aperitivo in the early evening.

"Peen-toh" enunciated Matteo in his rough Basque accent.

"Pinto," tried Alessandra, not altogether convincingly.

Matteo laughed at her attempt, showing his immaculate white teeth contrasted against his almost black skin. Alessandra thought he had the colouring of a Gypsy, darker even than the other Latinos in the kitchen.

Working unsocial hours and living with her uncle's family in a strange city, Alessandra had no social life outside of the restaurant. She had got into the habit of staying back after service to practice her dishes and then eat the results. Keen to improve, Matteo asked if he could join her on some of these evenings, and they ended up sharing recipes and techniques. After a couple of weeks, they agreed to each cook the other a course from their home region one night. They drank a fine bottle of chilled Albarino with their respective dishes that Matteo had brought in with him. He'd also brought some Patxaran, sloe-based liqueur, for an after-dinner digestivo.

With his ink-black curly hair tied back in his whites, and his dark face unshaven, Matteo had all the makings of a future TV chef, the young Italian woman decided. After two years in New York starved of contact with anyone her age and heady with alcohol, it had been Alessandra who'd made the first move. She suddenly kissed him full on the lips with all the enthusiasm she could muster. The young man needed no further invitation, and within less than a minute, they were making love against the white tiled wall of the kitchen.

For Alessandra's part, the turn of events may have been unforeseen, but they were not in any way unwelcome. She thought Matteo extremely handsome, plus he seemed kind and honest. Also, she was beginning to think that she must be the only nineteen-year-old virgin in New York. If she later had any doubts, they were only about how she would deal with things when they went back to work the next morning. Matteo was technically her junior in the rigidly hierarchical pecking order of a kitchen. She knew that she would need to keep their liaison secret or cause problems.

Alessandra need not have worried about being in the kitchen with Matteo. When she arrived at work the next morning, her uncle was waiting for her in his office. The kitchen porters had found the Spanish liquor and wine bottle carelessly left on top of the garbage bin and informed their strict Italian boss. He had put two and two together, confronting Matteo when he turned up for work, early, as usual, the next morning. The young man immediately admitted his guilt. He was dismissed on the spot, told to collect his things and leave immediately.

Having collected her thoughts after the shock of hearing Matteo's voice on the phone after all, these years, Alessandra finally managed to say, "What a surprise. What have you been up to?"

Matteo filled in the events of the intervening three decades with a synopsis of his career, beginning with an unexpected and swift departure from New York. He told her that following his dismissal, a relative had sent him an offer of a job in Los Angeles and forty-eight hours later, he was working there. From there, he'd worked in San Francisco and eventually moved to London, from where he was calling now.

"But you could have called me then and explained," Alessandra said, suddenly feeling bafflingly emotional about what was effectively one date almost a lifetime ago.

"I can't repeat what your uncle said he would do to me if I called the restaurant or his house. I had no other way of contacting you. There were no mobile phones back then, remember. That Italian chef also warned me that he would have me blacklisted as a troublemaker in every New York kitchen. When I got the offer to go to LA, there seemed no choice but to go."

Alessandra said nothing; her silence conveyed her renewed sense of betrayal and sadness.

"To be honest, Alessandra, afterwards I thought that you were not only above my pay grade but also out of my league. You were so beautiful and talented and seemed to me so worldly. I could not believe what happened that night. I thought it was just the drink that made you kiss me and was not sure you would want to speak to me again, even if I had called."

Matteo was now sorry he had said what he just had. It had not been his intention to bring up the past in this way but now found himself surprised by Alessandra's reaction. From afar, he had watched her career with interest, picking up every snippet of kitchen gossip or industry media news that mentioned her name.

He was astonished when the story emerged a few years later that she was a princess of an obscure principality in Italy. This had convinced him that what had happened was a one off that would never be repeated. He'd moved on with his life but still kept an eye on her career as she scaled the ladder to the top.

Alessandra realised that her over-emotional reaction was ridiculous and the result of the shock of suddenly hearing Matteo's voice, like a ghost from her past. She composed herself and replied, "It's very nice to hear from you, Matteo, but I assume that you have not suddenly decided to make a call you should have made thirty years ago," while trying not to sound any more bitter than her choice of words made inevitable.

"No. You are right. That was not my intention. I too earned a Michelin Star eight years ago and have since gained another."

"Two-star chef. Congratulations. But again, I can assume that you had plenty of people in London to pat you on the back without ringing a former one-star like me in Italy."

"I'm ringing because the guy from the Michelin guide, who I am now quite friendly with, mentioned your name out of the blue recently. He is naturally very guarded when talking about other chefs or restaurants but in passing asked if I knew you or if I had heard anything about you since you'd departed New York. I told him that I was proud to have worked under you very briefly, thought that you were incredibly talented, and that you were working again in your native Seborga. He nodded as if he already knew that."

"And did your friend from Michelin say why he was asking?"

"Alas, he did not. However, I believe that he must have had a good reason to bring up your name after all these years. I would not be too surprised if you get a visit to Seborga, which is why I am calling. I wanted to give you a heads-up so that you're not caught unprepared."

"Well, thank you Matteo, but I don't think Seborga is quite ready for tiny portions of pretentious food dressed up with flowers foraged from a Norwegian fiord and flown halfway around the world because they're just the right shade of blue. That kind of cooking might still have a market in Copenhagen, San Francisco or London, but never took off in Italy and never will."

"You're angry, Alessandra. I get it, and frankly, I'm flattered. This call was a mistake. I am sorry. I wish you all the luck in the world, with whatever you do. Goodbye."

She sat in the chair for some time still holding the now silent phone to her ear, trying to work out her feelings. She was jealous; she concluded quickly. That could have been her in London with two stars. No, she changed her mind. She was angry. That loser ex-husband, who she had later clung to after Matteo left, had flushed their successful life down the pan with his drug habit. Finally, she felt ashamed. Ashamed that she had spoken to Matteo as she had, and now also sad that she had forgotten all the good things that had happened to her. It had been kind of him to call her, she acknowledged. She had no right to have spoken to him like that.

Her youthful encounter with the handsome Spaniard had been blissful while it lasted, and it had undoubtedly ended memorably in the kitchen that night: really without fault on either side, she now realised. She should have celebrated Matteo's success, rather than being churlish, and must have sounded mean-spirited and bitter. After all, she had made her own choice to return to Seborga to look after her father. The old prince had then seen her happily remarried and surrounded by his family when he later died. It was pointless and frustrating, wondering what might have been. Alessandra resolved to find the number for Matteo and call him back to apologise. She would do it this afternoon, when she had pulled herself together, she decided.

But the phone call had also stirred other old feelings. Although Alessandra had always tried to shy away from the spotlight and concentrate on her cooking, she admitted to herself that she had enjoyed her moments of fame. The glowing reviews and the flattering magazine features had made her proud. Mainly as these accolades were for achievements before anyone knew of her royal title. She never did find out who tipped off the press about her being a princess but always suspected it had been her then-husband and business partner. If it were him, trying to boost their restaurant's takings even further, his ploy had worked. The customers all wanted to be cooked for by, or even meet, the 'princess in the kitchen.'

There were times—not so many these days—when Alessandra missed New York. Matteo's call reminded her of her youth in the most exciting city in the world. A place that could not have been more different than the one she had grown up in. She could source almost any ingredient from anywhere on the planet, at any time of the year. Back then, she thought this was the most liberating thing for a young chef. What became known as 'nouvelle cuisine' was born back then out of the emerging globalisation of ingredients and cooking styles.

A new generation of chefs had now realised that they, and their children, might be the ones paying for their predecessors' excesses. The final irony for Alessandra was that now she had these young chefs coming to Seborga to learn about cooking, precisely because here they had always practised local, unpackaged and seasonal sourcing. Both her life and what she considered good practice had gone full circle.

27. AGNELLO AL PESTO DI FAVA

A handful of sun-weathered locals sat on two adjoining benches in the shade of a big old Ficus tree. There was much pointing and shaking their heads as they watched three young men erect state of the art solar panels. A week ago, a different team had arrived and built what looked like a wooden frame, like those used for growing vines, above six existing parking places on the edge of the village. When they had finished, a sign was erected announcing that this was an experimental project jointly funded by the European Union, FIAT and ENEF Energy.

Today, this team was installing two-metre by one metre black panels on top of the wooden frame already in place. These panels were facing south and would have sun for more than twelve hours each day. This design would provide electrical power from the sun and shade for the cars, reducing their need for fuel-consuming air-conditioning. Two days after the solar panel fitting, a car transporter navigated all the tight hairpin bends to reach the villages and unloaded six brand new Fiat electric cars. These cars had been custom painted in the azure blue of Seborga's flag. The truck driver parked the cars under the solar panels, plugged them into the new charging sockets and then dropped the electronic master keys with Alessandra at the Osteria.

She came out with Ben to admire their latest experiment, but by then the five older men were already running appreciative fingers over the cars' new paintwork and trying to peer into the cabins through the tinted glass.

"Bella, Principessa ma dureranno a lungo," said the boldest of the old farmers, expressing his prediction that they would be damaged or stolen before too long by people from the city.

Just then one of the men pressed a little too hard on the door to test the steel's thickness. An electronic voice emanated from somewhere inside the car, "Stop. Security alert. Possible intruder."

The old man let go of the metal as though he had received an electric shock, but was merely startled by the talking car. All his friends also backed away, looking disturbed by the idea that this car seemed alive with a mind and temper of its own.

Alessandra explained that only those residents who had registered with an account could book a slot to use the cars. The vehicles had satellite trackers, all-round CCTV and a remote disable mode programmed into their systems. A mobile phone application was needed as a key. The cost of hiring them would be debited based on the individual's insurance group, time used, mileage covered, and the number of people in the car. The number of passengers would be checked by CCTV and confirmed by a sensor under each seat. More occupancy would actually reduce the cost to the hirer. The aim was to promote car sharing.

The same mobile phone app could be used to build up transport credits from separating and recycling household waste into bar-coded bags, choosing plastic-free packaging at the store and refilling drinking water bottles at the central dispenser. This trial model was only designed to recover its operating costs and an element of depreciation. Although the cars had a petrol engine, that was only meant to be for emergency use, and any traditional-fuelled mileage was charged at a premium price.

"Good environmental practice will be rewarded with cheap transport," Alessandra tried to explain, but could see that this concept would take some getting used to amongst the older residents.

It was an experiment of as much interest to Fiat and ENEF as to the Italian Prime Minister and those in running the project in

Seborga. They had one year to see how well it worked or to discover what problems arose. They all understand that if it were successful, this was a model capable of being rolled out in similar communities all over Italy. It would take this afternoon in the sun to fully charge the cars and they would be available to use that night when Ben and Alessandra planned to drive to Bordighera to test one. Later the following day, the environmental group planned to meet to inspect the new cars and their solar charging point, before their progress review meeting.

When Ben arrived, the Osteria's kitchen smelled sweetly of rosemary, as Alessandra had been roasting lamb for the lunch they would have after the Environmental Committee meeting.

"What are we having?" Ben asked, rubbing his tummy in a circular motion.

"Oven-roasted lamb chops on broad bean pesto."

"A new twist on pork with white beans?" Ben suggested.

"Si, Signore Ben," replied his wife with a small curtsey, mimicking a stereotype of a servant's manner from an old movie.

Cecily arrived first, keen to exchange news with her friend before anyone else on the committee came, so Ben left them to chat alone. Within fifteen minutes a full turnout of members had arrived; only the prime minister was late, having messaged saying that he would join in later by video link from Rome. Before the meeting, each member had submitted to Ben a short, written summary of their progress on their allocated tasks, and he had sent an abridged version to Andrea.

Ben got things started by reporting that he had accessed an electric car after a brief struggle with the app technology and that he and Alessandra had enjoyed a comfortable, almost silent drive to Bordighera market to get the main ingredient for their lunch today. Less than five euros had been charged to his account for the round trip for two, which he considered good value. Having brought back fresh food in a car without air conditioning, as many people would do, he did have one suggestion—that a cool box or insulated bag could be left in the back of each car.

"I have some empty insulated boxes which the fish and meat delivery guys leave at the Osteria. I could clean and recycle these. They would easily fit in the back."

"Problem solved," said Ben.

The prime minister's face suddenly appeared on the laptop screen at the head of the table. The rest of the meeting passed at an astonishingly fast pace, as the young politician demonstrated his people management skills. He prompted speakers in turn, but then politely cut them off if they strayed off-topic or prevaricated. If he had the information on which to base them, his decisions came without hesitation. If no action was appropriate, Andrea made requests for further research directed to individuals with an exact deadline for reporting back to him. There was no ambiguity and no loose ends. He was generous with praise and sparing with admonishment, while at the same time making any disappointment with progress evident to all.

"Compared to most of the meetings I attend, this is a breath of fresh air," Cecily whispered to Alessandra. "These days, no one wants to make a decision or take responsibility. So, nothing gets done. Andrea's more like an entrepreneur than a politician," she added.

Whispering to her friend, Alessandra said, "Let's hope his willingness to take risks is not his undoing."

The initiatives put forward at the inaugural meeting nearly all seemed to have either been activated or progressed as far as possible. Only finding a practical organic fertiliser for the terraces was proving challenging. The suggestion to harvest seaweed had hit some barriers; ironically, mainly on environmental grounds. Because it had not previously been considered, there was insufficient research into the impact of what cutting large swathes of seaweed from the seabed might be on marine life.

Andrea had at once interrupted the scientist from the Monaco Oceanographic Institute. "That's something we will not resolve in an acceptable timescale. Here's what we will do instead. I will personally ask the fisherman's union at Ventimiglia to keep the seaweed which I know comes up every day in their nets, and which they normally throw back. We will get that delivered to Seborga every day for a week to run a proof of concept study on whatever area those seven loads will fertilise. If that is only a few hundred square metres – so be it. In a year we can see if that has improved the soil. In the meantime, you keep looking for a more sustainable supply source."

Reflecting after the meeting, Ben thought that they had made remarkable progress on a wide variety of issues in a truly short space of time. The take up of plastic-free packaging at the village food store was growing each week. He felt that this acceptance would accelerate with the school's initiative and now that villagers could also gain transport credits from using it. Andrea reported that the legislation on environmentally friendly building materials was underway, but would take a while longer. Only the sourcing of a local supply of organic fertiliser was preventing progress on all fronts.

"What about the organic matter filtered out during wine production? Stalks, leaves and skin etc," Ben offered.

"And the tonnes of stones removed from the olives during oil making. They could surely be crushed or ground down," Alessandra suggested.

Cecily then joined in with, "Then there's the skin and pulp left over after removing the juice from the blood oranges."

"Now we might be onto something, but more test sites are required to measure the benefits," Andrea quickly concluded. "The Slow Food students could surely run some simple tests. Also, get them to try one with a mix of the three sources of organic material to see if a blend works even better."

Andrea wrapped up the meeting by congratulating everyone on their achievements and thanking them for their time, before reminding each of what he was expecting them to do next. Before ending the video call, he asked, "What am I missing on the lunch menu today, Princess Alessandra?"

After hearing what she had prepared, Andrea sighed and quoted an old Italian proverb, "At the table, we do not grow old," to which Ben responded with another, "Age, like glasses of wine, should not be counted."

Andrea laughed. "Your grasp of Italian culture is getting better, Ben."

"It's understanding Italian women that I need help with," Ben joked.

"Ah, yes. I have a similar problem with English girls," the Italian sympathised.

Alessandra ended their private joke when she said, "I have a Seborgan proverb for you both: a husband who makes fun of his wife, often goes without lunch."

**Bordighera harbour overlooked
by the belle epoque Villa Garnier.**

Drawing by Linda McCluskey

28. TURLE

Roman and Cecily were due in Seborga for dinner with their friends at 7 pm. Cristiano was asked if he would cover for her in the Osteria that evening so that everyone, including Alessandra, could enjoy a relaxed dinner. Her son's agreement to cook that night also allowed Alessandra to dress up more than she would typically in her restaurant. She told Ben that he was to wear his linen suit. Cristiano had devised a special menu, different from that of the other guests in the Osteria. He had done most of the preparation for those dishes earlier in the day. Aware that Cecily and Roman's wedding was coming up, the young chef viewed tonight's dinner as an audition to cater for that event. Knowing that Cecily could easily afford to bring in caterers from Nice, San Remo or even Monaco, Cristiano was determined that would not happen.

Cecily arrived with Roman, who was carrying what looked like a wooden wine box. She was also carrying a small parcel, but neither handed these over when they arrived, as one would if they had been gifts. Instead, they greeted their friends as normal and placed the two items on the table. Ben poured prosecco, and on hearing the cork pop out of the bottle, Cristiano appeared with a plate of sardine fillets with soft white onions, raisins and pine nuts.

"I have a toast, which I will follow with a small confession," Cecily began. "My toast is congratulations to Ben Morton, the award-winning winegrower."

Alessandra raised her glass and looked to Ben for any hint of an explanation, but he seemed just as perplexed as she was. Everyone having chinked and then taken a drink from the glasses, Cecily explained how she had heard about a wine tasting for small artisan growers held in Monaco. She told them that she had taken one of the several unlabelled bottles of his own Rossese that Ben had brought onto the yacht to enjoy during their trip to Corsica and entered it in the competition.

It was the only Italian wine entered. All the others were French and were from established small wineries whose produce had previously been sold commercially. The event sponsors were looking for exceptional products that had greater commercial potential if they received sufficient investment or marketing support. Cecily now handed over the parcel she had brought to Ben, while Roman placed the wine box alongside it.

"Of the twelve entries, your beautiful Rossese wine won the bronze medal in the blind tasting," Cecily said with obvious glee.

Looking shocked and staying silent, Ben opened the brown paper package to discover a slim leather case. Inside that was a coloured ribbon sporting a large bronze medallion, embossed with a wreath of grapevines and inscribed in French. He looked at it, clearly not knowing quite what to say.

Alessandra stepped in to help him out by hugging Cecily, saying, "You little genius. What a great idea. Trust you to be so proactive."

"I'm only a genius because my hunch paid off. I am not sure what I would have done if the judges had declared Ben's wine undrinkable rubbish."

"Yes, that would have made us both look like fools," Ben finally joined in.

"Well, perhaps not you, Ben, because I don't think I would have had the heart to own up and tell you. I would just have kept my foolishness to myself," Cecily said, laughing.

Ben now opened the wine box to reveal an excellent bottle of vintage champagne which was the other prize.

"We took the liberty of keeping that chilled, in case you wanted to open it tonight," Cecily said, laughing.

"What a wonderful start to the evening," Ben said, still clutching his medal and now glowing with pride. "We have our own bit of good news to share. The deadline of my bid to obtain crowd-farming closes later this evening, but it is already past the minimum level that would give me the funds I need to complete the winery. My marketing message seems to have struck a chord with some people."

Roman and Cecily clapped gently, and they joined in with another toast proposed by Alessandra. "My husband, the winegrower and winemaker."

Roman patted Ben on the shoulder. He expressed his astonishment at how he had convinced people who he had never met, who had not visited Seborga, to pay upfront for a wine they had yet to taste, that they would not receive for another year.

"That's the power of marketing, Roman," was all Ben would say on the matter.

While they were chatting, a taxi pulled up outside the Osteria which, despite the recent tourism boom, was still an unfamiliar sight in Seborga. The lone passenger took some time to extract himself from the rear seat, as though they were not as agile as they might once have been. From his stature, skin tone, manner and dress, all four immediately guessed he was a foreigner, probably northern European and most likely English. He had the bearing of a man born to be significant or one who had made himself important through achievement. Perhaps an ex-military or naval man, Ben wondered.

The tourist trade at the Osteria had increased steadily in recent years. These diners were often pre-booked groups, or at least couples, who had made the trip specifically to eat there after reading or seeing some media coverage. There were few walk-in customers and virtually no single foreigners.

What these new customers all had in common was that they

were all devout foodies interested in what they saw as their discovery of the little-explored cuisine of the Ligurian Maritime Alps. They were looking for something different to taste, cook, or talk about at their dinner parties back home. They were good customers who ate heartily, drank good wine and tipped well. They would also often take away local produce and write lengthy positive reviews.

Cristiano greeted the stranger, beginning by speaking in Italian but being quickly interrupted by the man speaking in English. Switching languages mid-sentence, Cristiano confirmed his reservation and showed him to a small table set for two. Clearing the unwanted second place setting, the young chef quickly returned with a single sheet paper menu. Before he could rush back to the kitchen, as had been his intention, the man engaged him in a conversation that was unwelcome during this busy service. Cristiano kept turning his head and looking towards the kitchen door as he backed away from the table, but the man showed no sign of ending his apparent interrogation. In the end, Cristiano became more forceful. He apologised to the man but insisted that he had much work to do.

Turning reluctantly to the short menu, the stranger looked less than pleased, as though unused to anyone not paying him full attention. He glanced at the kitchen door every few moments as if expecting Cristiano returning to apologise and answer his questions. A few tables away, the newly-crowned bronze medal winemaker was too busy revelling in his new status to notice any of this. Cecily was also enjoying the smug feeling of having instigated Ben's award and seeing his delight at it. Roman was chatting to Alessandra about Patsy, telling her that he was still worried about her American boyfriend's commitment. The frustrated musician had moved into the farm with his daughter several weeks ago, but still spent much of his days writing songs, making video recordings and sending them to agents in the States.

"He has yet to pick up a shovel or some secateurs. My impression is that if someone rang him up and offered him a singing job, or even a support tour with a mediocre band, he'd pack his bags and go back," the savvy Sicilian told Alessandra. "That is no situation for my daughter, or for the farm, to be in. He's a nice enough kid, but he's chasing a dream. There's just no commitment. He's only in Sicily with Patsy because for the moment he has not got a better offer."

"I can't judge someone too harshly for chasing their dream," Roman said. "That's what I did, and I found mine. However, I agree that he's a fool if he walks away from Patsy and the farm. I had little to lose when I left, but she is beautiful and kind."

Wishing to change the subject to something more positive but without thinking about it too much, Alessandra asked, "How is your other daughter getting on? Caroline, isn't it? I assume that they will get over for the wedding." Even as she said it, she realised that this was probably not a safe assumption at all.

Roman pursed his lips in a false smile that looked more like a frown. "You would think that she would be happy, wouldn't you? Despite my advice not to, she has extracted the money she wanted out of the farm and let her idiot husband gamble with it. Instead of thanking Cecily, she now gives us the impression we have somehow conspired to side-line her to form a business partnership with Patsy. As for the wedding: frankly no, I am not sure that she will deem our wedding worth a transatlantic trip, no matter how much that pains me. She has not replied to our invitation."

Alessandra noticed that each time anything arrived at the Englishman's table, he tried instigating another conversation with the member of staff delivering it. She assumed that the man must be lonely. Perhaps a widower, she pondered, eating alone in a foreign country. Then she spotted a notepad on the table into which he kept making entries with a pencil which he withdrew from the spine of the book. A travel journal, she guessed.

When their pasta course arrived, talk moved to the wedding plans. Cecily revealed that they had received the agreement of Seborga's priest that his colleague from Bordighera would conduct a blessing for Cecily and Roman. It would be at the old Templar church of San Bernado, after their civil ceremony. The timing would be thirty minutes after Renata and Vincenzo's full wedding ceremony at the main church of San Lorenzo, to allow any guests who wanted to attend both.

Alessandra reported that Renata had told her that all her arrangements had been finalised. Her parents had now both received their passports, visas and plane tickets. While the women talked, Ben and Roman had begun eating their pasta with enthusiasm.

"Have you tried this?" Ben directed to his wife. "It's incredibly good."

"What is it?" enquired Cecily.

After tasting a forkful, Alessandra replied, "Turle. Shepherds' purse pasta made with homemade cheese and potato. The typical Cucina Bianca (white food) of this region."

"That sounds so stodgy, and yet it's so light," Cecily commented after tasting a forkful.

Alessandra explained that Toma was a soft cheese made by the mountain shepherds mostly for their own consumption. After the cheese is mixed with fluffy boiled potatoes, a little fresh mint is added to the pasta stuffing. The sauce is just butter and parmesan, with a bit of pasta water.

"Although the filling is not too heavy, it's the pasta that is so good. It's thin and slightly elastic and so does not hide all the flavour packed inside. I think this is Cristiano's suggestion as a pasta dish for the wedding feast. Cheese and potato are universal flavours which few people will not like."

The chef explained that when catering for larger numbers of people, the more of the skilled work that could be done well in advance, the better the final product.

"Only overcooking the pasta could spoil a course like this because all the preparation is done beforehand."

"But if this Toma cheese is so rare because it is only made for the shepherds and their families, how are we to source enough to feed two sets of wedding guests?" Cecily queried.

"That is where Vincenzo comes into his own," Alessandra said, smiling knowingly.

The elderly Englishman had finished his pasta and was making more notes, while keeping a watching eye for any staff member who might be willing to talk to him. Sure enough, when one of the young students came to take away his wiped-clean dish, he appeared to be bombarding her with questions. Alessandra decided that she would speak to the gentleman before he left and try to discover his story.

Cecily agreed that with the various backgrounds of the wedding guests, they would have to plan the menu quite carefully to please everyone. She acknowledged that Vincenzo's family and friends, being all local farmers, would surely be little challenge. However, Renata's parents had been poor Mexican immigrants, whilst her new American friends were chefs and foodies from several countries. Cecily's guests would be a mix of mainly wealthy internationals, including several British business associates. An only child with both his parents now deceased, Roman had only his daughters and their respective partners - if they accepted-plus some old farmer friends from Sicily.

Alessandra pulled a face and summarised the diverse tastes that they would have to satisfy with this menu, "So, there's a couple of Mexicans, some New Yorker caterers, your millionaire, international business associates and Roman's Sicilian Mafia connections. Have I forgotten anyone?" she joked.

"Yes, our VIP guest, the Prime Minister of Italy, oh and an Icelandic vegan, who works for me in Monaco," Cecily said, laughing. "Oh, and I nearly forgot, and the Princess of Seborga, who I hear is very choosy about what she eats. So, no pressure at all."

The two women laughed even louder at the absurdity of the situation they had just described. Hearing them laughing, the elderly Englishman looked over to their table and smiled when he caught their eye.

"At least the only journalist present will be Ben's daughter, and so no one will be writing a critical review of the food," Cecily assured her.

Hearing the mention of 'review' caused Alessandra to freeze. She looked around again towards the single Englishman who was once again writing in his notebook.

"No. It couldn't be!" she exclaimed, now looking horrified.

"Couldn't be what?" asked Cecily, their change in tone having now interrupted Ben and Roman's conversation.

"It's impossible," Alessandra continued, apparently speaking to herself and ignoring Cecily.

"What is so unlikely, darling?" Ben asked his wife, seeing the alarm on her face.

Alessandra collected her thoughts and then replied, "That could not be the inspector from Michelin?"

The other three all looked at each other in turn. Each was searching for any clue as to what their friend was referring to.

"You will have to explain, darling, because none of knows what you are talking about."

Alessandra explained about the phone call that she had received a while ago warning that a Michelin restaurant inspector had been making enquiries about her with a former colleague in London. And, that he thought that might be the prelude to an inspection visit to Seborga with a view to an entry in the guide.

"You didn't say anything about this," Ben said, both puzzled and slightly injured by her apparent secrecy.

Alessandra did not respond but quickly left her chair, threw her napkin onto the table and headed in the direction of the kitchen to speak to her son. Emerging a few moments later, she went to talk to the mysterious Englishman. He saw Alessandra approaching and rose from his chair to greet her.

"Have you enjoyed your dinner?" she asked him, smiling. Explaining, "I am the proprietor, and normally the cook, but tonight I am having a night off to dine with my friends."

"You look like you are having a wonderful time with your elegant friends. I have been very envious of your cheerful company. The owner of the establishment and the head chef, you say?" the man checked, trying to clarify her status and avoid her question.

"Si, Alessandra," she responded, leaving out her royal title to avoid having to explain that.

"And the man on the right is your husband?" he probed.

"Yes, a fellow Englishman, Ben Morton. My son is in the kitchen holding the reins for his mother. My son from my first marriage," Alessandra said instinctively, not knowing why she felt the need to explain this detail.

"A cooking dynasty. I must return when the queen is in her kitchen."

Alessandra now wondered if the word 'dynasty's' choice was deliberate and if this amiable stranger knew more than he was letting on. At this moment Cristiano emerged from the kitchen with the man's dolce. Beads of sweat had soaked into his bandana, and he looked more ill at ease than Cecily had ever seen him. Placing the dish on the Englishman's table, he wiped the edge with a clean cloth that he had draped over his arm.

"I will say goodnight before you leave. Enjoy your pudding."

As she left, Cristiano began explaining the dish in English, now eagerly volunteering the details that the guest had previously had to prise out of him. He described the Fruili Venezia Giulia as, "plum-filled potato dumplings with cinnamon and nutmeg."

Alessandra returned to her table where all three were eagerly awaiting her conclusion at the stranger's identity and any further explanation as to why he was here alone.

"And?" enquired Cecily, impatiently, when Alessandra returned to their table.

"I don't think so. He's just a lonely older guy who likes his food and keeps a journal of his travels. However, he has been asking lots of questions about the place and the staff," she added. "And yet, he won't be drawn into commenting on anything he has been served. He responds to every enquiry with another question."

"It doesn't sound like you are completely certain about him to me," Ben challenged. "You won a star in New York. Did you not meet the inspector from Michelin then and get some idea of what they were like?"

"The first we knew about the award of the star was a letter in the post, followed by a story in the New York Times the next day," Alessandra told them. "These people don't identify themselves when they book and they certainly don't visit the kitchen, where I would have been all night."

"What if he were a Michelin reviewer?" asked Roman. "Do you care about his opinion? You have nothing to prove that you have not already. Why bother about him?"

Alessandra knew that Roman was right to point this out. She had told her friends many times how she felt that this part of her life was behind her. Nevertheless, she found herself confused by her feelings about the evolving events. Seeking a Michelin Star at the Osteria had never even crossed her mind. Would she even want it if it were offered: probably not, she concluded? However, she knew that Cristiano wanted nothing more and had nearly fainted when his mother warned him of her suspicion about the man who had already consumed two of his courses. All the blood drained from his face as he tried to recall how well presented the dishes he had sent out had been.

Ben tried to rationalise the likelihood of this man being who Alessandra feared it might be by making one of his checklists and ticking off imaginary boxes: he was mature, a stranger, dining alone, inquisitive, apparently knowledgeable, and evasive.

"We either need to know the depth of his knowledge or the lengths he will go to not to give himself away. We will invite him to join us for a digestivo. Roman can divert him with Sicilian fishing tales while Cecily quizzes him about his favourite places to eat. Alessandra can ask him if he knows how a panna cotta is made and I will test his wine knowledge."

"Good plan," agreed Cecily, intrigued by the idea of secretly investigating the stranger with a devious interrogation of their suspect.

"What if he's found guilty?" Roman asked.

"Then you and Vincenzo will have to do away with him and dispose of the body before he gets away and writes his review," Ben joked.

The elderly Englishman enthusiastically accepted the invitation to join their table. They were all poured some of Cristiano's experimental blood orange version of their usual limoncello digestivo. The man was easy, agreeable company but with a politician's guile when it came to avoiding direct questions. After an hour of talking to the stranger, it felt like he had extracted more from the four of them than they had collectively learned from him.

Nevertheless, they had established that his name was Alistair, he was a well-travelled connoisseur of food and wine but they had no clue how he had made a living or paid for these indulgences. When he learned that Cecily lived on a yacht, he said he had once owned a Swan-a rare and expensive classic sailing boat, she informed them.

Although he was polite and engaged with everyone around the table, two things were evident; it was clear that Alessandra was the focus of his attentions, and there did seem to be a hidden agenda. He clung to her every word and encouraged her to elaborate on any comment she made on any subject. Afterwards,

Cecily said that she was surprised that he did not continue making notes, as he had been before he joined them.

"It has been an enchanting evening in fine company and a beautiful setting," was the stranger's parting assessment, apparently purposefully avoiding any specific reference to the food he had eaten. He had seemed unconcerned that his taxi had been standing in the piazza for at least twenty minutes with the meter running while they chatted. When it pulled away, all four friends looked at each other to see who would voice their opinion first.

It was Ben who broke the silence, "I am going to say no, I don't think he is from Michelin. Not because I think that he could not do the job well, but because I don't believe he would sit down with a chef-proprietor of a place he was evaluating, as he just did. However, if I am wrong, I would say we have nothing to worry about, because I think he has fallen in love with my wife and will award her three stars."

They all laughed, but Alessandra soon became serious again. "I'm now beginning to think he might just be an inspector."

Cecily agreed, saying, "His knowledge of relatively obscure but highly regarded restaurants around the world is impressive. He'd visited the little-known Petit Max in Hampton Wick in the early nineties when it was still opening as a greasy spoon café during the day, only to be transformed into a first-class rustic French bistro at night. After that, they moved further into London and won a Michelin Star. A coincidence?" she proposed.

Then Alessandra remembered, "And then there was The Cleveland Tontine, my chef-friend Eugene's family's place in Yorkshire. He said that he had also dined there, and Eugene acknowledged they could have easily earned a star if they had wanted it. But Eugene chose not to because they said it would bring what he saw as the wrong type of customer and put off all their regulars."

"He certainly knows his French wines, even if he'd never

before tried an Italian Rossese," Ben conceded, before qualifying any inferred shortcoming by acknowledging, "but then again, few people outside of Liguria have."

"And he immediately identified the merest hint of cinnamon in Cristiano's Quaresimali," Alessandra added.

With the jury still out on the English stranger's status, Cristiano burst out of the kitchen and almost ran across the Osteria to their table.

"Was it him? What did he say?" the young man quizzed breathlessly.

His mother answered, "We don't know. On the balance of probability, no. We don't think he would have joined us for a digestivo or been quite so amenable if he was here carrying out such important work."

"Unless that is just his way of looking under the skin of the restaurant. If he wanted to find out just how deep the commitment to quality and authenticity goes, he could not rely on just one meal," Cristiano argued, part of him hoping that the English stranger was from Michelin.

Roman as ever had the more measured view and framed his assessment in terms of advice for the young chef, "Whether he is or is not, if his approval is what you aspire to, the lesson is surely to assume any customer from now on could be the next Michelin inspector."

Cristiano mumbled goodnight and headed back to the kitchen with his head down, looking deflated, confused and concerned by the events of the evening, and with Roman's advice ringing in his ears and now burnt into his consciousness.

29. FARINATA

The day before the double weddings dawned damp and misty after an overnight shower, which everyone hoped was not a precursor to worse weather to come. Now that the morning sun had peeked over the roofs of the surrounding houses, the puddles in the piazza were evaporating and turning to steam. There was a frenzy of activity that would have looked like chaos to the outsider, but to the villagers was just like preparing for another festival: a weekly occurrence during the summer.

Vans were arriving, unloading and departing in a relentless stream, like ants delivering food to their nest. Local men were hanging lights on wires suspended over the piazza and another group were hanging Seborgan flags from any available upright. Despite the chaos, empty boxes, and vehicles, the setting for the wedding feast already looked impressive, Ben thought.

Later that day, when all the overhead work was complete, trestle tables and benches would be set out capable of seating four hundred guests. Amid the small army of people in the piazza, Vincenzo was directing operations; every now and then, his booming voice could be heard, "Si, si, si." and then moments later, "No, no, no."

As he approached to offer his help, Ben could detect some tension and urgency in the voice of the usually calm and measured Vincenzo. Ben was handed a bundle and asked to put up signs that would direct strangers to the village towards various facilities around the piazza. Armed with a stapler and a roll of gaffer tape he set about his task, happy to have avoided lifting anything too heavy or having to climb anything too high.

Ben was also relieved to be out of the house. Their home kitchen had been seconded as a pasta-making factory, while other food preparation was concentrated in the Cookery School. Ben had told Vincenzo that the collective chatter from all the village women while they kneaded dough was deafening. He had added that a choking cloud of double-zero flour was hanging in the air and had coated everything on the ground floor.

Ben was fastening the last sign pointing to the toilets when he heard the distinctive sound of an air-cooled VW engine climbing the last hill up the village. As he looked around, Selene's distinctive yellow Kübelwagen with its soft top down turned the corner. Tom's short hair looked almost white against his nut-brown skin. He spotted Ben and waved. Ben put down his tools and went to greet his son, who he had heard little from in the several weeks that he had been away. He did not know that he would be back for the wedding, so this was a great surprise.

"Why didn't you tell me you were coming?"

"I was afraid that you would line up lots of work for me," Tom answered with his famous disarming grin.

"You were right. As you mention it, I now have the funding to build the winery, so your return to Seborga could be good timing. You don't want too much time off, or you'll get flabby again." However, as he said this, Ben noticed that far from putting on weight, Tom looked even fitter than when he had left.

"I have been working. I travelled extensively throughout Italy as well. Me and this old Kübelwagen have visited three new seas— the Adriatic, Ionian and Tyrrhenian."

Ben quickly made a mental map of possible routes to take in these bodies of water and could see that his son must have traversed the full width and length of Italy.

"Alessandra will be delighted to see you, and your sister arrives later today. Andrea can't get here until morning. He's being driven overnight from Rome so that he can get some sleep on the way. Speaking of which, how tired are you, do you need to rest?"

Tom explained that he had spent the night before on Selene's journalist friend's sofa in Genoa, so he had only had a two-and-a-half hour drive this morning.

"I'm ready to help. I'll park the car and then go and see my site foreman and get instructions. By the way, I saw the solar electric car charging station on my way in. Very impressive. Somehow looks strange in this ancient place but I can't wait to try one."

Ben explained that the solar needed to be topped up with main power but that they were looking into the feasibility of siting some additional panels on the walls of the terraces below the car park.

"Oh, and the Albergo Diffuso has opened to visitors. Wait until you see it. It looks wonderful and is already full of wealthy guests."

The Albergo Diffuso had opened all fifteen of its letting rooms ten days earlier. They first had a dry run, when directors and managers from other locations and their partners were asked to try out and critique the rooms and facilities. Only then had they opened to invited VIP guests. Rightly anticipating being oversubscribed, the Club had chartered a large yacht in Monaco for any overspill. Members could book a few days at each location with shuttle transport laid on between them. It was an option proving really popular, meaning that both were now fully booked.

The recently appointed manager of the Albergo Diffuso was a Mancunian with a passion for motorbikes and live music. Kevin had arrived in Seborga two weeks earlier after using his annual leave to drive overland from London on a GS Adventure bike. He had sent his luggage ahead with a carrier. He had previously run the Club's country club offshoot, set in rural Kent, and so was deemed a safe pair of hands for this new Italian venture.

Tom returned from saying hello to Vincenzo, pulling a trolley loaded with aluminium rube frames and explained to his father that they had been asked to assemble these to form a stage. When it was erected, Vincenzo had told him that some plywood sheets were in the back of his Ape for them to fasten to the frame to make a floor. As they walked, Tom, pulling the trolley behind him, began filling in some of the details of his road trip. Ben brought his son up to date with events in Seborga.

"It's great to be back," Tom said with a genuine enthusiasm which was not lost on Ben.

"It's great to have you back," Ben answered with a sincerity not lost on Tom.

Ben reflected on the difference that just one summer had made to their relationship. After Tom arrived bringing with him so many problems, he was almost ready to give up on him, abandoning any hope of the boy changing his errant ways. What a mistake that would have been, he now realised. How much they both would have missed out on. Ben now felt guilty that he had even contemplated walking away from the then troubled soul.

Word quickly got round that Tom was back, and Alessandra brought two beers and a slice of farinata to welcome him back. Ben was also aware of Vincenzo and Alessandra's role in his son's turn around. This place had entirely changed Tom's mindset in the same way it had his several years earlier.

Existing in a small community somehow made it easier to put things into perspective and more challenging to avoid issues that needed to be dealt with. In the same way that Andrea had pointed out at his recent press conference on the environment, in a micronation, the citizens can't ignore the effects of their actions and must deal with them themselves.

Ben reflected that in modern urban society, it is too easy to distance oneself from difficulties to deal with issues. People can change groups of friends, ignore their neighbours, flush waste down a pipe and hand other rubbish over to a local authority. Ben now realised that being separated from the consequences of our actions makes humans lazy, both in their dealings with people and the world in which we all live. In threatening to send Tom back to London, he had nearly fallen back into that old trap of putting his problem aside for someone else to deal with.

30. CAVAGNETTI

The old horse belonging to the late Prince Claudio had some younger company in his stable for the night before the weddings. Vincenzo had arranged to borrow an open-topped landau and two colts from a nearby farmer in which Renata would ride to the church. Alessandra had suggested that the horses stay in the stables outside Seborga for the night before. She feared that they might be unnerved by a bumpy horsebox journey just before they were needed to be calm in their coach harnesses.

Alessandra had asked Tom to come and help get the horses ready. She thought dealing with animals would be yet another venture outside of his very narrow comfort zone. Having spent all of his life in cities, he'd had little or no contact with animals. Nervously he had agreed, but mainly because Alessandra had sweetened the request for help with the offer of breakfast afterwards. She had been up early and made some Cavagnetti, a sweet bread shaped in a crown around a boiled egg. Usually an Easter treat, it offered a more substantial and easily portable breakfast for a young man with a healthy appetite.

As they walked down the track through the olive grove leading to the stables, the sun was beginning to make its presence felt behind the hills. It had yet to show itself, but an orange glow could be seen in the otherwise pale blue sky where it was soon to breach the ridge. The mist that crept in off the sea sometimes at night was still lingering in the bottom of the river valley. It hung in pockets over a couple of the low-lying fields. Even as they walked, the first shards of sun crept over the mountain. These rays began to burn off the lingering mist and the air temperature seemed to rise noticeably. The real reason Tom had accepted this chance to be alone with Alessandra was that he wanted to ask her something, but so far, had not summoned up the courage to do so.

"I hear from your father that you've had a fun trip," Alessandra offered to kickstart the conversation.

"It was amazing. The best thing I've ever done." Realising that this opening gave him the opportunity to steer the conversation, he added, "I got as far as Sicily."

"Oh, wow. Speaking of which, Patsy is on her way from Sicily to attend the wedding."

Tom hesitated but then admitted, "I know. She arrived back with me yesterday. I dropped her at Cecily's yacht in Menton."

Alessandra looked astonished. "The pair of you drove from Sicily in that Kübelwagen? That's a long way," she added, inferring that it must have involved at least a couple of overnight stops.

Tom nodded and half-smiled, acknowledging that he understood what Alessandra was suggesting without directly asking.

"I spent a week travelling across Italy to the Adriatic and then another week driving south. For the last month, I have been working on Patsy's farm. I converted an old barn into a holiday letting room that she can also use to encourage fruit pickers in the busy season."

"And did her boyfriend help you with this project?" Alessandra probed, already guessing where this conversation was leading.

"At first he did, but he didn't know what he was doing and I don't think he liked taking direction on construction from me. He saw me as a hired labourer. One day he just stopped coming to help and sat playing his guitar indoors on the terrace. I didn't mind because he wasn't much help anyway. I spent much of my time redoing what he had not done properly."

"You mean just like Vincenzo did for you?" she replied, reminding him that it was not so very long ago that he needed such guidance.

"Point made," Tom conceded. "But it did get increasingly difficult after that. He and Patsy were always arguing, and if she invited me for dinner after work, the atmosphere was always tense. She didn't seem happy with their situation."

Tom told her how he had almost finished the barn and was fitting guttering to the roof when Patsy had begun decorating inside. This arrangement meant that they were working together for some days and chatting a lot.

"We just jelled. I don't know why. We don't have much in common. Anyway, when it came time for me to set off back to be here in time for the wedding, Patsy cooked a thank you supper. We all had a few drinks and then some things were said in anger. I walked away and went to bed; otherwise, I was going to lose it with him. I was certain if I did, that would spoil any chance I might ever have with Patsy.

"The next morning when I'd packed my bag, I was going to slip away unnoticed. However, when I got to the car, Patsy came out with a bag packed. She did not say a word but just got in the passenger seat. Her boyfriend was sleeping off a hangover. We drove off, and nothing was said between us until we reached Palermo."

Alessandra had been listening with a mixture of joy and fear, wondering just how all this was going to work out. Although Tom had matured enormously since he'd arrived, he was in so many ways still a boy with little confidence around women. On the other hand, Patsy seemed to know what she wanted, and with her looks, could get almost anything, Alessandra thought. Although she was numerically younger, she was emotionally his elder in so many ways. As handsome as Tom was, with his foolish, boyish behaviour still fresh in everyone's memory, was he ready for what Patsy was? was the question at the forefront of her mind.

"Why do you think Patsy and her boyfriend rowed, Tom? Because of you, or because he would not do any work on the farm?"

"Because he was lazy," Tom answered without hesitation.

"I can see that indolence is not an attractive feature in a man, but he might argue that he was working in his way, writing his music."

"Patsy didn't see it that way," Tom countered. "At least that is what she told me."

"So, you're clear about what Patsy's looking for in a partner?"

This threw Tom. He had not given a single thought to what it was that Patsy wanted. He had been totally preoccupied with what he wanted and how he could get it. Now that Alessandra had nudged him in that direction, he began to see what she was suggesting: that the woman of his dreams was looking for a man to share her life and the farm with. A husband, in fact.

Working on the farm had been idyllic and admiring Patsy at arm's length, she looked like a dream come true. Taking on the responsibility for both-probably for the rest of his life-was a prospect that had never even entered Tom's head. The thought of that liability looked like it had sent a shiver of fear down his spine. Alessandra could almost see the colour draining out of Tom's face as he came to terms with the reality she had brought to his attention. It now seemed so obvious.

"Through no fault of your own you've found yourself in the middle of an existing relationship, which even if flawed, had endured for some years before you came along. Before you break something from which there could be considerable fall out, you should know what you are doing. My father used to warn me that boys say: 'let's play it by ear,' but men say: 'get dressed I've made plans'."

Tom looked confused and concerned.

"Patsy made her position pretty clear when she got in your car to drive back here with you. I think now this is your time to put up or shut up."

They had arrived at the stable and Alessandra showed Tom how to make friends with the horses before grooming them. She had brought some small apples, two of which she gave to him to feed to the colts. They worked in silence for the next thirty minutes before Tom suddenly announced, "I think I love her, Alessandra."

There was a long pause during which Alessandra did not react.

"I've never felt anything like this before. I can't sleep. I feel sick. Even my appetite isn't what it was."

"Tom. It can't be a case of 'I think.' It would help if you were certain. If you really know that you love her, then maybe you need to tell her 'to get dressed because you've made plans.'"

31. LOUP DE MER A LA MENTON

Without a hint of wind, the water in the bay on Menton was glass-like. Inside the harbour all the boats were still on their moorings, creating perfect mirrored reflections of themselves in the water. Inside Cecily's lovely old ketch, things were not quite so calm. Roman walked into the cabin where Cecily was sat at her dresser, getting ready, and already feeling nervous.

"You won't believe it. I have just seen a message that arrived during the night to say that Caroline and Ross are now on a flight and on their way to Nice. They have finally responded to the wedding invitation."

His wife-to-be stood slowly and turned around.

"Bella sposa (beautiful bride)," exclaimed Roman, changing the subject at seeing Cecily in her wedding outfit. The long, cream, silk-crepe dress had a softly layered neckline, below which it was pin-tucked to show off her slim waist. The fabric rippled like liquid, just from the slight movement of her head.

"Wow. Looks expensive...but worth it," he qualified quickly.

"It was, and I am," she replied. "So, they have managed to fit us into their busy schedule," Cecily said, unable to hide her displeasure at this last-minute acceptance.

Cecily could tell that try as he might not to show it, her husband-to-be also had mixed feelings about this unexpected news. However, her own feeling was clear. As much as she knew how much it meant to Roman to have both his daughters at his wedding, she would have been quite happy not to have heard back from Caroline and Ross.

Roman's eldest daughter had made her feelings towards her soon-to-be stepmother obvious. Even after all these years she had still made no attempt to establish any kind of relationship with Cecily. Their most recent encounter over the farm funds had once again confirmed that peace was unlikely to break out anytime soon. Nevertheless, they had sent the invitation, and Cecily was determined its last-minute acceptance would not spoil her day.

In stark contrast of behaviour, his youngest daughter, Patsy, was going to be their driver and take them to the wedding in Cecily's Bentley. Cecily had picked up both their dresses from her seamstress in San Remo. While she had been out, Roman had seen his youngest daughter arrive at the harbour with Tom in his strange yellow car. He had been expecting to pick Patsy up from Nice airport and guessed that they must have been in touch and that Tom had volunteered to do it. Patsy did not offer any other comment on it and so he had left it at that. The day before their wedding, there were just too many other things to worry about.

Roman's few Sicilian guests stayed in a hotel in Menton, and he had enjoyed a local speciality of loup de mer a la Menton with a remoulade sauce, and a few bottles of wine with them the night before. Ben and Vincenzo had joined them earlier for dinner but had left before the night had ended with the Sicilians smoking cigars, drinking Gappa and fishing in the harbour at midnight. Alessandra and Cecily had both agreed that they were too busy for a pre-marital celebration, but they shared a thirty minute video chat over a glass of prosecco.

Renata had still been in the kitchen preparing food when her newly arrived parents came in. As she was too busy to go and meet them, Ben had agreed to collect them and bring them to Seborga. As Renata rushed to hug her parents, she saw over their shoulder her two younger sisters standing in the doorway waiting their turn. Her stream of tears turned to a flood at the realisation they were going to witness her wedding. As she rushed to hug them both at the same time all she could say was, "How? How? How?"

Renata's mother recounted that someone had called Cecily had phoned, saying that she was your friend and that she had thousands of unused airmiles. She said that they would expire soon if she didn't use them, and she would like to bring Renata's family to the wedding. But it was to be a secret. A wedding present to Renata and Vincenzo.

"A few days later seven business-class tickets arrived for the girls, their husbands and the children, and here we all are," her mother explained.

Tom and Alessandra had prepared the horses as much as they could before the newly inspired young man rushed back to the village, saying that he had an errand to run. When they were ready, she and Vincenzo would come and lead the now shining black horses up to the village at the last minute. As head of the Seborga guard, Vincenzo would typically act as master of ceremonies at any official event. As the groom, today he had another responsibility and so had conscripted Marius as his stand-in.

The piazza looked quite fantastic, Ben thought when he passed through mid-morning on his way to carry out one of the many jobs Alessandra had given him. The sun was shining, and there were already a couple of hundred people milling around admiring the scene. From their dress, Ben could see that these were a mixture of villagers adding last-minute touches to decorations, early arriving wedding guests, and tourists who had stumbled on the event by accident on their way to visit the Holy Grail.

At least twenty people were standing at the railings on the piazza's edge looking out at the view. After recent rain, below the valley was a verdant green, broken only by a scattering of terracotta roofs and the winding road up to Seborga from the coast. At this time of year it was a narrow corridor of outlined by coloured roadside flowers snaking through the landscape. The temperate climate of the south-facing coastline of Liguria was awash with exotic flora. Gardens and public spaces overflowed with bougainvillaea, alliums, geraniums and even orchids.

Above these blooms towered giant palms, Ficus trees and every now and then the extraordinary purple haze of a Jacaranda. It is a local tradition that every year palm leaves from Bordighera are sent to the Vatican as a gift for the Pope to use on Palm Sunday. As the road winds away from the coast toward Seborga, these garlands of colour follow until the altitude changes. Then, native species such as rosemary, lavender, broom, and early in the year, mimosa, become more prevalent.

From the piazza's valley edge, the distant Mediterranean glistened in the sunlight as though it knew this was a special day and it had to put on its best face. No visitor witnessing this scene for the first time could fail to be wowed, Ben thought.

Cristiano was running back and forth between the Cookery School, the Osteria and the charcoal braziers set up at one side of the piazza. Several whole porchetta on spits had been slowly cooking since very early morning and would take several more hours before being perfect. One of the students was there tending the charcoal and basting the skins, but the young chef knew these were too important an ingredient not to keep checking on. With Renata now getting ready for her big day, Cristiano was acting head chef and feeling responsible. Also, at the back of his mind almost constantly since his visit was the man who may or may not have been a Michelin restaurant inspector.

Ben said 'Buongiorno' to Viola as he passed her, sitting on her step wearing the same black smock dress, headscarf and mocking look she always wore, oblivious to the heat of the approaching midday. She acknowledged his greeting but shook her head as if in despair at all the strangers in her village. When one tourist asked if they could take a photograph of her, it all got too much for her. She waved them away with her hand, went inside into the darkness and closed the door.

By one o'clock every man and child in the village was scrubbed clean and wearing their best clothes. Most were dispatched to the piazza while their wives or mothers got ready. The result was that every bar seat and shady bench was overflowing with overdressed, perspiring males. The conversation was dominated by food, with everyone having an opinion on whether Cristiano was cooking the porchetta correctly. Their scepticism ranged from was there enough fennel in the stuffing, to whether the spits were too close the flames. Some even suggested he had used the wrong type of charcoal. When it came to food, every Italian had an opinion, and they were all different in some subtle way.

"It should be hardwood charcoal, but I can smell pine in that smoke," said one gnarled old farmer.

"That smell is that cheap tobacco that you smoke," his friend joked, all the others joining in laughing.

The Commander of the Alpini troops tasked with guarding the Holy Grail at the monastery had decided to inspect his forces two hours before the weddings. The soldiers had therefore been up since dawn polishing their boots and shining their weapons. Vincenzo's half-dozen Seborga guards were also looking their uniformed best. They were already performing crowd control at the piazza, which was filling up with wedding guests. When the time came, their main task was to clear a corridor for the carriage to drive through into the centre of the piazza.

Many of the wedding guests were also using this opportunity to visit the Holy Grail, most for the first time in their lives. For the devout, it was the first emotional experience of what should be a memorable day. As it passed midday, a slight breeze had got up, which had been welcomed by the overdressed villagers and guests who were beginning to overheat. This draft also wafted the smells from the roasting porchetta around the piazza, whetting appetites for those who would later enjoy it but causing consternation amongst the Italian soldiers who could only watch over the feast.

The residents of the Albergo Diffuso and all the other accommodation in the village had been invited to join the wedding feast. Almost every single one had accepted with enthusiasm. In keeping with tradition, the bride and groom would abandon any transport before they arrived at the church and walk through the crowds of guests so that everyone could admire them, cheer and clap. Today the crowd would get double the normal spectacle with two bridal processions.

Before they set off on the drive up to Seborga, Cecily said to Roman, "Have you seen what came into the harbour last night?" He shook his head. "Zeno V, the superyacht that nearly ran right over us on our way to Corsica."

"The rapper?" Roman questioned, screwing up his face in distaste. "On any other day, I would go over there right now to tell what I think of him and his music and his driving."

"Luckily for him, we've got a more pleasant task today. So, just keep calm, darling."

The couple planned to get there before Vincenzo and Renata but park on the village's outskirts and then discretely watch the first bride arrive along with everyone else. Marius had cordoned off a parking space for their Bentley. From there, they would walk to San Martino behind the procession. After their friend's wedding service, they would sneak around the back of the village using the narrow lanes to collect the Bentley and then drive up into the piazza as though they had just arrived. In the meantime, after their wedding, Vincenzo and Renata would have retraced their steps back to San Bernado for the second, much shorter, blessing ceremony of Cecily and Roman.

A couple of weeks earlier, Alessandra had given her late-father's dress uniform to Cecily, who took it to San Remo on her dress fittings. They had it altered to Ben's size using one of his suits to get the measurements. The seamstress had also made some much-needed repairs to the frayed fabric and had it dry cleaned. When it had been returned, Alessandra was crestfallen that Ben point-blank refused to wear the former prince's old uniform.

"I am not a prince. I see it as hugely disrespectful to Claudio, who I loved dearly. It would be like wearing his crown. I'm sorry but I can't do it."

"When you married a princess, you took on a role. Perhaps not an official role, but you have a position to uphold in the village. The citizens all look up to you. You know that."

"Alessandra, I'd do anything for you. You know that. But don't ask me to do this. I really would feel extremely uncomfortable. It's just not me."

She had expected some resistance but was surprised at how strongly he felt about what she saw as a small thing. There also seemed to be more than a hint of hypocrisy in his stance. When it had been suggested that she get a dress uniform made for formal occasions, Ben had enthused about the idea. Nevertheless, she let it go for a week and then tried broaching the subject again the day before the wedding, only to get the same reaction. However, her husband did have what sounded like a more valid reason.

"With Cecily, Renata, the Prime Minister of Italy and the Princess of Seborga, plus whoever the VIPs are staying at the Albergo Diffuso, there are already far too many stars for one show. The last thing today needs is an English peacock strutting around."

Then Ben received a text message from his daughter, Selene, confirming that Andrea had arrived at her house and they were ready to leave.

**Pétanque (like boules) played at Bordighera Alta,
an example of
the French influence on this area.**

Drawing by Linda McCluskey

32. PORCHETTA

The shiny, bible-black colts had been harnessed to the landau for fifteen minutes so they could get used to their leather restraints in the shade of some trees. The had been fitted with their embroidered white linen ear covers and looked resplendent, if slightly jittery. When the time came, the driver gave them a short test ride along the tarmac road from Negi to collect Renata.

Alessandra was already sat up on her father's old horse and waiting on a grassed area outside the village where the older men played petanque. The carriage came trotting along the road, but the horses were still acting nervously despite the careful preparation. One occasionally skipped a step causing the other to try to rear in its harness, and the driver had to rein them in, speaking to them reassuringly.

As soon as Alessandra trotted out to meet them, the colts seemed to calm down. Even wearing his own white linen headdress, the gentle old stallion was now a familiar friend in an otherwise strange place to the two young horses. Wearing her black dress uniform with its blue sash and her hair in a thick ponytail, Alessandra looked every inch the princess.

She mouthed to her old friend, Renata, to tell her that she looked beautiful before turning the reins to start their slow walk into the village. Renata had chosen a traditional white wedding dress with a veil. Her father wore a plain dark suit over a white shirt, embellished with Western-style silver collar tips, and the whole ensemble was topped with a wide-brimmed black Stetson - a nod to his Mexican cowboy roots.

A ripple of clapping started at the edge of the piazza amongst those who could hear the unfamiliar but distinctive sound of horses' hooves on the tarmac. The applause then rolled back into the crowd as the wedding party rounded the corner. When all of the four hundred or so people could see the princess sitting up high on her horse, then they began cheering as well as clapping. Alessandra's old horse remained unmoved by the noise and kept up his steady pace.

The colts were spooked again and both reared, restrained only by the straps of the harness. Alessandra quickly spun her horse around to face them, causing the youngsters to settle once again. This undiscipline may have been unwelcome to the landau's occupants but looked spectacular to the audience, who snapped hundred photographs.

The remainder of the procession was smooth as they rode gently up into the piazza and through the crowd until it could go no further. Alessandra slipped down from the saddle while Renata's father stepped out of the landau. Marius was there to take the reins and pat the horses reassuringly. They both helped the bride extract herself and the many layers of her dress from the carriage, and paused for people to take photographs. Renata's two nieces were last-minute bridesmaids and now the wedding party was ready for the walk to the church through the narrow streets of Seborga.

The people of Seborga were on every balcony and doorstep, some even on rooftops to get a better view. It took the best part of fifteen minutes to walk the distance that could normally be walked in a third of that. Everyone wanted a photograph or to offer their best wishes. Charcoal smoke from the braziers combined with the roasting porchetta and baking bread's aroma was getting everyone in a party mood. Weddings had been rare in Seborga in recent times, and two in one day was unheard of.

Meanwhile, Vincenzo waited, looking slightly nervous in contrast to the calm authority he usually exuded when wearing his uniform of Captain of the Seborga Guard. In front of the church, the tiny Piazza San Martino was packed, mainly with the groom's party and the small group of guests who could cram into the little church to witness the service. Roman and Cecily were there keeping well back in the shadows, but clapping wildly along with everyone else.

Ben and Tom were to act as best man and usher, respectively. When Vincenzo had asked him, Tom had said it was his proudest moment since being picked to captain the school team for a county cup match. Ben was typically reticent to accept the honour, feeling he might upset any number of more worthy locals as he saw it. But Vincenzo had been insistent, and Ben found him a difficult man to argue with.

To everyone's relief, especially Vincenzo's, the bride's party finally appeared out of the narrow alley opening into the Piazza San Martino. The party was heralded by the uniformed Marius, who walked ahead firmly parting the bystanders to make a way through for the bride. The priest, who had been standing waiting on the steps of San Martino, his bible in his hand, now turned to lead the guests into the dark, cool interior of the church.

Thirty five minutes later, the unlikely pairing had been made. A seemingly perpetual bachelor, farmer, hunter, soldier and all-round giant Italian tough-guy was joined in matrimony to the diminutive, Mexican, workaholic chef from the New York Bronx. Outside there was much cheering, along with the throwing of rice and confetti before a five minute break for photographs. Meanwhile, Patsy, Cecily and Roman slipped away down a side alley for a short stroll around the village back to the car. Roman walked in the middle with Patsy and Cecily looping their arms through his. Up until then, he had heard no more from Caroline and Ross.

As they reached a bend in the path from where they could see the Bentley parked below, they also saw a black Mercedes stretched limousine struggling to navigate the hairpin bends up to the village. The driver had stopped and was now performing a three-point manoeuvre to turn the six-and-a-half-metre motor around the corner. Cars behind them were hooting horns, and drivers who had now been stuck behind the slow-moving limousine for ten kilometres were gesticulating wildly out of their open windows.

"What kind of idiot would bring something like that to a mountain village like this?" Roman said.

As they continued walking, their path came parallel with the road coming up from the coast just at the point the limo was passing.

"It's Caroline," Patsy shrieked, in what seemed to Cecily like a mixture of pleasure, astonishment and embarrassment.

The rear window was down, and a passenger was making an unmistakable gesture with one finger to the drivers behind. They could now all see that it was Ross, and by his side was Caroline.

"What on earth is she wearing?" Cecily asked, more to herself than anyone else. "Are they going horse racing at Ascot after here?"

The driver of the long black Mercedes rental, now sweating in his uniform and cap from the stressful drive up from Monaco, did as he was directed by his passengers and drove up to the edge of the piazza to disembark them. Opening the rear door and stepping back, the chauffer watched as Caroline ducked down low to ensure she and her huge hat left the car intact. The headpiece had been pinned into place at the hotel and removing it for the journey had just not been an option.

Caroline was wearing a white organza, puff-sleeved dress with a giant bow tied at the waist. With the wide-brimmed hat and ultra-thin heels, all the excess of fabric made her appear top-heavy and unstable. Ross opened his own side door and stepped out, smoothing out the trousers of his pale blue suit. It was a size small, in the current style for a slimmer younger man, but just too tight and ill-fitting on a paunchy thirty-something.

The clapping began again, started by the nearest tourists but with others who would not recognise Cecily and Roman joining in. By their attire, the crowd assumed this was the second planned wedding and that this must be the bride and groom. Marius, who had now returned from San Martino to welcome Cecily and Roman, was the first on the scene. A furious Marius screamed, "Who the fuck are you? You can't park that here."

It was Caroline who responded, "How dare you speak to me like that, you little tin solider."

Without his mentor, Vincenzo, by his side, Marius was feeling the weight of responsibility. So far everything had gone like clockwork. He did not want to have a stranger's wedding party, who must have taken a wrong turn and ended up in a different village, spoil this day. Witnessing the whole scene was the sergeant of the Alpini troops. He was all too conscious that the prime minister was due any second. He began to worry that these unknown, and unwanted, strangers in this huge car might be some terrorist plot. He was moved to action; calling over his four nearest men, orders were barked and their weapons were unshouldered.

The troops quickly surrounded the couple and the car and ordered them back in at gunpoint. The driver had the engine running and it was in gear before Caroline got her hat back under the door frame. The limousine driver was reversing quickly out of the piazza just when Patsy drove around the corner. The Bentley's tyres screeched, as did those of the Mercedes, as they both stopped less than a metre apart. Marius ran toward them, still shouting and swearing at the limousine driver and waving him away: requiring a tight manoeuvre his huge car was incapable of achieving.

Patsy, now trying not to show that she was laughing at her big sister, reversed the Bently a few metres and then drove around the Mercedes and up into the piazza, much to the relief of a now highly stressed Marius. The timing was in fact perfect; Cecily was stepping out of the car just as Vincenzo and Renata entered the piazza from the other side. There was now a cacophony of cheering and clapping as the crowd welcomed both the newlyweds and soon-to-be-married couples. Meanwhile, Patsy had gone back to explain the situation to the Alpini and try to prevent her sister and her husband from being arrested or even shot.

She managed to contain her amusement and resisted asking why the show of ostentation. They hugged briefly, but she could tell Caroline was bristling with a mix of anger and discomfort. Ross only looked shamefaced. Patsy guessed that this would not have been his plan and that he had probably gone along with it to keep Caroline quiet. Although she knew him also to be a braggart, this was just too contrived to have been his idea. As sisters, Patsy knew this was Caroline's attempt to upstage Cecily and show how successful they had been in business.

"Wow. It looks like things are going well in the property development business," was Patsy's way of offering her sister a way out of explaining the gratuitous display of wealth.

"Very well," was her curt response. "You look well," she added, with what sounded somewhat like disappointment.

Cecily had helped choose Patsy's strapless, apricot, tulle mini dress. She had thought it a little frivolous and that it made her look even younger than she was, but it was Cecily's wedding and so she went along with it. It had not occurred to her that it also exaggerated the difference between her and her sister's ages, annoying Caroline even further.

"I think we have a wedding to go to. If you wanted to lose the ridiculous hat, this would be a good time while the car is here. I can help you fix your hair again."

While reluctant to admit that she had badly misjudged things, when Caroline had looked at the attire of the assembled crowd of wedding guests and saw all the trestle tables set up for an open-air wedding party, she knew they were both badly over-dressed.

She had assumed that with Cecily's fortune and guests, including a princess and the Prime Minister of Italy, that this would be like the weddings she had seen in glossy magazines taking place in Rome or Milan. The last thing she'd expected was a barbeque in a village full of Italian peasant farmers.

Fewer than twenty guests could squeeze into the old Templar church of San Bernado, but the doors were left wide open so many more could see and hear in from outside. The bare stone walls were punctured only by narrow slit windows. The dark interior had been lit with a hundred candles. It was stark, yet beautiful and timeless, those present agreed. Ben never ceased to be in awe of the fact that ancient knights had once stood on the same stone slabs that he was standing on, probably praying for deliverance from the battles they would face in far-away Palestine.

Alessandra was by her husband's side, wondering if this was the first time in the church's 'near thousand year' history that any woman in her wedding dress had stood watching another bride having her own marriage blessed. A single violinist played quietly in the background. It was the triumph of minimalism that she had come to expect from her friend, and which she was sure Roman would appreciate.

Patsy stood next to Tom, both of them trying not to look like a couple but failing because they kept glancing in each other's direction every few seconds. When Alessandra looked over, she saw a tear run down Patsy's cheek. She suspected that, as glad as she was for her father's newfound happiness, she was also being reminded of the loss of her mother. Whatever it was, the emotion of the occasion was apparent on her beautiful young face.

It was difficult to judge what Caroline's feelings were as her eyes gave away no clues at all. Her husband just looked like he wished that he was somewhere else. His previous experiences of Italy had all been bad ones and he still had nightmares about his last visit to Sicily. On his last visit, he had hoped to conclude a deal to develop some of his wife's land on Sicily for building but had been frightened off by local mobsters. He had only ever spoken to his wife about the events of that day, and even she only knew the half of it. He had concluded that country was populated by mobsters and criminals, just like all the TV movies he had seen. They had terrified him.

Finally, the extravagantly costumed Roman Catholic priest from Bordighera splashed some holy water, the groom kissed the bride, and they were all back out in the sunshine of the piazza. Roman appeared relieved. Cecily looked ecstatic and radiant. There would now be an hour before lunch when everyone could catch up with their guests, have yet more photographs taken, enjoy a glass of prosecco and try some of Renata's canapes.

A former banker from London, Drew had become a trusted advisor to Cecily's on her financial and corporate matters. He and his wife Kate-the best photographer in Monaco-had also become friends and were invited to the wedding. Kate had volunteered to take some informal, candid photographs before and after the ceremony and Cecily had eagerly accepted.

There was a carnival atmosphere in the village: more so even than for any of the numerous festivals held there each year. It was as if a double wedding had brought with it twice the joy, and indeed it had for many of those present who knew both couples and how well suited they were. The villagers were riding a wave of good fortune. The future looked brighter, mainly due to the innovative changes but also because of the new blood which had revitalised the village.

During this lull in the proceedings, Tom had arranged with Patsy to show her the Holy Grail. Most of the guests who wanted to had visited before the ceremonies, so there were only a few passing tourists filing past. As the man who had saved the holy relic from almost certain destruction, Tom had earned considerable respect from the Alpini guards looking after what they all called the Sacro Cantina. He had spoken to them earlier and arranged for the protective cover to be raised when he visited with Patsy.

As they entered the old Templar monastery, the guards closed the doors behind them and prevented anyone else from entering. There was then a short wait while the party of four pilgrims inside completed their visit, crossed themselves, and departed.

Now realising that Tom must have arranged this, Patsy said, "A private audience with the Angel of Seborga," teasing Tom with the nickname given to him by the press after the flood from which he'd rescued the ancient glass bowl.

Two of the four soldiers present put down their weapons, unlocked the lid, and carefully lifted the Perspex cover from the Holy Grail. As they approached the display case, one of the other Alpini dimmed the room's lights so that only the uplighter under the emerald green relic remained illuminated.

Patsy stared at the iridescent object in awe. "It looks almost like it's alive," she said, sounding slightly concerned.

"It does, doesn't it," Tom confirmed. "I think it's just the heat from that lamp below, heating the air and causing it to swirl around."

"You're such a cynic. "she admonished. "This is possibly the most important holy relic in Christendom. Even if you're not a believer, please show some deference."

"It's warm to the touch. Again, I think it's the light bulb," Tom argued. "Put your hand inside and feel it."

Patsy recoiled as though the very idea of touching something so holy and so old frightened her. The bowl was fixed at an angle of about thirty degrees so the visitors could see the hexagonal shape of the rim. The glass was so thick and such a deep green that it was impossible to see much though it.

"Go on, feel inside. It's now fixed on that frame so it can't fall off."

Part of her really wanted to be able to say that she was one of the few people in the world ever to have held the Holy Grail. On the other hand, her early convent school upbringing made her wary of showing any disrespect. After just a moment, the former instinct got the better of her, and she gingerly slid her hand over the rim and touched the glass. She let her fingertips savour the moment before moving them around. Suddenly she froze.

"Tom, there's something in here," Patsy said, looking frightened.

"No, that's simply not possible."

He turned and looked at the guards, who both shook their heads.

"What it is?" Tom asked.

"It's small and metal."

"Then get it out. It's not supposed to be there."

Patsy removed the object, and as she did so, realised what it was. Such was the level of her surprise and with the darkness all around, she became disorientated. Thinking that she might faint, Tom took hold of her and pulled her to him. She just stood there in silence, her face pressed against his shoulder, her fist tightly clenched around the object. The soldiers looked at each other for clues, as this was not the reaction that any of them had expected.

"Are you OK, Patsy?" Tom asked.

There was silence for a little while and then finally she said, "I think I need to sit down. Can they turn the lights back on, please?"

One guard dealt with the lighting while another brought a chair, which was kept ready usually for elderly visitors, who might be overcome at seeing the holy relic. Tom guided Patsy to a seated position and for the first time, she looked into his eyes. Then she looked down at her still-clenched first before opening it wide. Tom, who was already uncertain about his last-minute decision, was now close to panic. It was not going as he had hoped. Patsy looked ill, he thought. He wanted her to speak but also feared what she might say. Words that he had not prepared poured from his lips.

"It's all I could afford. I can take it back. I mean that I could change it." Then the words that Viola had said to him after the flood came back to him. She'd said, 'That Grail is cursed,' adding that it had brought 'nothing but bad luck.'

"I'm sorry, Patsy. You're right. This was a mistake."

Patsy now stood and pulled Tom close, like it was her turn to reassure him.

"Hush. You're talking gibberish," she said. "Give me a minute to catch my breath. I had absolutely no idea this was coming. I need a moment to think. Let's go outside where we can be on our own."

The couple apologised for alarming the guards and thanked them for the trouble they had gone to. Back in the sunshine Patsy finally looked at the tiny ring in her hand, but only briefly- apparently not with the slightest interest what it was made of, what stones it contained or indeed even if it fitted. This nonchalance confirmed Tom's worst fear that she was going to hand it back at any moment. What was he thinking of, he asked himself? He had caught her on the rebound from a row with her long-term boyfriend. She was way out of his league; he had embarrassed her and made a fool of himself, he concluded.

They stood in the alley, each with their head on the other's shoulder, attracting strange looks from passers-by. Finally, Patsy stood up straight. She used the hand without the ring to push Tom back a step.

"I have a proposition in response to your proposal. We have known each other just a couple of months and have met just a few times. We had our first kiss just four nights ago. I don't think anyone would disagree that this all seems somewhat hasty."

Seeing the disconsolate look on Tom's face, she added, "The last few weeks have been surprising and the last few days blissful. If I thought for a moment that the joy that we experienced on our short road trip could last forever, I would say yes in an instant."

Tom face changed to one of hope at hearing this, and Patsy's next few words rescued him from the black hole into which he had felt he was descending.

"Let me keep the ring with which I am overcome with happiness. Let's keep this conversation to ourselves and get on with building our relationship. If we both still feel the same in exactly six months from today, I will get down on my knee and beg you to marry me. Deal?"

33. FOCACCIA

Their faces glowing with barely concealed joy, Tom and Patsy returned to the piazza where the wedding guests were taking their seats for the feast. The tables were laid out in five rows forming a wide arc that covered most of the open area. Three long tables were at the focal point of the semi-circle, with the drop to the valley behind them and the Mediterranean in the far distance. Vincenzo and Renata sat with their guests at the centre table. Cecily and Roman were sitting to one side, with the Albergo Diffuso VIP guest seated with Ben and Alessandra, along with Andrea and Selene on the other side.

Patsy was still clutching the ring tightly in her right palm when the first course arrived, as she had no pockets or bag in which to keep it. Handing it back to Tom for safekeeping would send the wrong signal, she decided. Taking the napkin from the table in front of her, she carefully folded it around the ring, making a neat, flat parcel.

Turning to her father, she handed him the parcel and whispered in his ear, "Keep this very safe in your pocket; there is something precious inside this napkin, but do not open it. I'll explain later."

Roman was distracted. All the guests arriving to take their places congratulated him, shaking his hand and patting him on the back. On his left, Cecily was tugging on his sleeve because she had something to ask him. He nodded to Patsy that he had heard her instruction but had taken little notice, in truth. He took the parcel from her and slipped it inside his jacket pocket before turning back to Cecily, who said she wanted him to pass the prosecco down the table.

As she passed by on her way to her table, Alessandra bent and whispered over the shoulder of the seated Cecily, "Did you see him in the crowd at the church?"

"If you mean Alistair, the mysterious Englishman, yes, I did, and I asked him outright why he was here," Cecily replied, looking pleased with her initiative.

"And? And?" Alessandra said, barely able to contain herself.

Cecily paused, making her friend squirm with expectation before revealing, "He's a retired lecturer turned amateur author, carrying out research for a foodie romance set in Liguria."

"Thank God," Alessandra said, exhaling at the same time, with obvious relief at this news. She then confided in her friend that, whoever Alistair was, she had already decided that another star was the last thing she would want. If it had been offered, she was going to turn it down. However, Alessandra had been dreading telling Cristiano of her decision if it had come to that. This news would still be disappointing for him but nowhere near as bad as the alternative she had feared.

Before she continued to her seat, Alessandra added, "Let's hope he has now left Seborga and that we don't hear from him again."

Ben's Seborga wine had been decanted from the substantial green demijohns into one-litre bottles. Cecily had labels printed explaining their provenance. She had decided against buying French champagne and instead had cases of Roero, Sigillo Ducale sparkling Arneis sent from Piedmonte. Cecily's favourite bakers, San Antonio's in Bordighera, had brought up portable ovens and baked bread all morning leading up to the feast. This meant it was not only as fresh as it was possible for it to be, but it took the pressure off the commercial kitchens in Seborga which were all working at full capacity.

Andrea declared Cristiano's Turle pasta course a triumph,

adding it was, "A tribute to the teaching of his mother, Princess of Seborga, and queen of Ligurian pasta." Patting his tummy in satisfaction, the prime minister stood, and tapped his glass with his knife loudly enough to gain the other guests' attention on his table.

"Don't worry. It's not a political speech," the prime minister joked. "Roman, Vincenzo and I discussed the seating arrangements beforehand and agreed that these long benches mean we only get to meet two or three people. So, after each course, we men are going to move three places to our left, so we all make some new friends."

Andrea, who had been at the head of the Albergo Diffuso table, led by example by extracting himself from the bench, and moving past Selene to take a place between a man and woman he had never met. Looking around, the guests at the table could see that something similar was happening on Roman's and Vincenzo's tables. The volume of conversion rose markedly as new introductions were made. The Prime Minister of Italy now found himself sitting opposite his recent friend, Zeno, the Ukrainian rapper, and the two exchanged a knuckle bump and a big smile.

"So, you're a member of this Club in London who have opened Seborga's new Albergo Diffuso?" Andrea proposed, by way of the only likely explanation for the rapper's presence at a wedding in a small Italian village.

"I joined the Club in New York, but then started using the London venue when I was in England and met a lot of cool musicians there." The rapper gestured to the new manager of the hotel on his left, "This crazy guy from Manchester asked me if I wanted to come and try out his new place. I was in the area to meet up with my boat which has been brought here from Genoa, and so here I am. I love it! What a cool place. Have you seen the rooms? They're so chilled. My neighbour, a villager who I have never met, came around this morning with some freshly made focaccia for our breakfast. How cool is that?"

The man to his left offered his hand, "Nice to meet you—Marcus-out of work actor."

Zeno laughed, nearly spitting out his prosecco, "Out of work. Yeh, crazy."

Before the rapper could add anything to his contradiction, the attractive woman to his right proffered her hand. "Charlotte. Wife of Marcus. Also currently unemployed."

The Ukrainian laughed again, "You guys kill me."

Andrea ignored what he could see was a private joke and welcomed them both to Italy and the now semi-autonomous Principality of Seborga. Both his new acquaintances observed that the day so far had been more like being on a film set than attending a wedding, and said that they were really pleased that they had come, adding, "Everyone is so friendly and relaxed. It's been a wonderful spectacle."

"Yeh, no one has asked me to sign anything all morning," Zeno added. "People just say hi, or Buongiorno. They're totally cool. I've even given my bodyguards the day off."

Zeno leaned in toward Andrea and whispered, "Those two are only unemployed because they are resting between Hollywood movies. Don't you recognise them?"

They were interrupted by a beautiful young girl to Zeno's left. Andrea guessed she must be a model. She said, "No one's asked for your autograph because no one here knows who the fuc..." then realising the company that she was in, stopped mid-sentence, before continuing, "...you are. There are only a dozen people here under thirty. They all look like they have only heard of one Ice-T and that's the one you drink."

All those in earshot laughed, no one more so than Zeno. The as-yet-unnamed girl continued, "And I must say, it is such a refreshing change for me to be treated as an equal. If fact, better than equal; I have received more compliments from the Italian men here today than in a year anywhere in London. They make me feel great. Anyway, I am Anna, and I am especially pleased to meet you; can I call you Andrea, or is it Mr. Prime Minister?"

Now it was Andrea's turn to laugh, "You can call me anything you like; it can't be any worse than my political opponents' names for me. A pleasure to meet you, Anna. And may I say that you look stunning?"

Holding out her upturned palms in a questioning gesture, "totally charming," Anna replied, "There you are. I rest my case. I'm moving to live in Italy."

At Roman's and Cecily's table, Tom had initially sat across from Patsy but when they all moved seats, he ended up opposite Alessandra. She looked along the table to where Patsy was now chatting to Turi, who was making her laugh; probably with his inappropriate stories, she guessed. Just as she was beginning to think something had taken place between Tom and Patsy, he asked, "Why does Viola say the Sacro Cantina is cursed?"

Alessandra thought for second before answering, "Because it seems as though it has been a curse to her and so she believes it will be to others." Realising that this statement would need some explaining, she continued, "Her two teenage brothers fought with the partisans with my father as their leader. When the Nazis found out their names but couldn't catch them, the soldiers came to Seborga and executed their mother and father in front of the teenage Viola. They left her with absolutely no one to support her, except for the other villagers, who rallied around as best they could.

"The Italian partisans were not a single unified group, but faction-ravaged bands of poorly armed and mostly untrained young men separated by geography and ideology. They were communists, Nazis and even royalist supporters who took up arms to fight either the Italian forces, the Nazis or the Allies; and sometimes each other. Claudio's group fought against the occupying Nazi forces and were instrumental in a largely unopposed liberation of the Riviera towards the end of the Second World War.

"In the final hours before the Allied invasion, the two brothers were killed in action in which my father, Prince Claudio, was also wounded. Because of all the secrecy surrounding their activities, later all that Claudio would tell her was that her brothers died to save the Sacro Cantina from the Nazis so it could bring joy to others. No one understood what he meant, and the prince would not elaborate. It was Viola who cursed the Sacro Cantina."

"So only Viola believes it?"

"Exactly, and given Claudio's deliberate vagueness and what happened to her entire family, she has good reason to be a little crazy. But Claudio was right about one thing. The Sacro Cantina has since brought peace to many troubled souls. Did you know that the cathedral in Genoa where it was on display was shelled early in the war, but the bomb did not explode? They still have the huge, unexploded shell in the cathedral. A miracle, many believe. So, no, I do not believe the Grail is cursed, otherwise we would have never brought it to Seborga."

Although it had been sad to hear about Viola's experience, Tom looked very relieved at hearing the other information and his mood brightened. Alessandra resisted the temptation to ask him if anything had happened between him and Patsy, but she had her suspicions by their appearance.

The porchetta and oven potatoes were universally acclaimed by the English, Mexicans, Italians, and other Europeans. Only a couple of vegetarians and vegans amongst the hotel's guests needed to be provided with an alternative, which Renata had prepared the day before. Ben's wine received many compliments and several guests had asked where they might buy some to take home.

Roman had been the first to finish his main course. In the first change of seat, he had found himself sat next to his son-in-law and after only a few minutes looked uncomfortable to Cecily. Ross suggested to his father-in-law that Cecily might want to think about buying stock in their property company. As soon as he finished his course, Roman put down his cutlery and stood up again, ready to change seats with someone else.

When he sat down again between their friends from Monaco, Drew and Kate, he turned to them and said under his breath, "Thank the Lord I got away from that idiot. If I hear one more time how much money he stands to make from this property development, I swear I'll call him out as the crook he is. He and his Ivy League college mates are selling what he admits are badly made wooden box houses, at inflated prices, to poor young Americans and giving out dodgy mortgages to buy them so that they are getting ripped off twice. And he thinks that's clever. I can't listen to him gloat any longer."

Kate said, "That's terrible. Is it legal?"

"Barely legal," answered her former-banker husband, who knew a thing or two about mortgages.

Roman looked across to his new wife and saw that his eldest daughter had turned her attention to Cecily. She also looked less than pleased about the line of conversation. He guessed that she was now on the receiving end of Ross and Caroline's success story. Roman then realised that every time they changed places, a new set of guests would be subjected to what was in effect a sales pitch from one of them. It became clear that his daughter and son-in-law's attendance today and their ostentatious display was all part of a ploy to suck in more investors by making people think they were doing well from their dubious scheme.

The very idea of members of his own family blatantly using his wedding to canvas money from their friends was too much for Roman. As his blood pressure rose, an idea came to him. He excused himself by saying he needed the bathroom. Instead, he went over to the table where seated were a mixture of villagers from Seborga and Roman's visiting Sicilian neighbours. There was a whispered conversation between Roman and the tallest and youngest of the group.

The giant Sicilian then also rose to his feet and went with

Roman to where Cristiano was carving the last of the porchetta, where another whispered conversation took place. A minute later the long pointed blade of the chef's knife pierced the trestle tabletop directly in front of Ross, pinning his napkin to the timber.

The owner of the hand holding the knife then forced his bulk into the space next to Ross and said, "Per il formaggio," (for the cheese) as if that explained everything to the other guests. Even Ross, a food-savvy New Yorker, knew the Italian for cheese, but was unconvinced that was an explanation for the knife. The preppy American looked deeply concerned.

The Sicilian leaned into him and said something in English that appeared to supply the explanation he sought. Finally, he added out loud, "Capisci? You understand?"

Ross nodded vigorously. The man stood, said, "Gotiti il tuo formaggio, (enjoy your cheese)," before returning to his own table.

The American had to call out his wife's name to attract Caroline's attention, who was now sat several places down the table from him. He gestured with his thumb that they were leaving, and when she questioned this with shrugged shoulders and raised eyebrows, Ross showed his wrist and tapped a very shiny, gold Rolex with apparent urgency. Caroline was still puzzled when her husband came around the table and helped her up out of her seat.

"What's the rush? We haven't even had dessert."

"Plane to catch. Don't want to be late," was his curt response, but it seemed to be targeted at the other guests at the table rather than his wife, to whom he then whispered, "Just come with me, I'll explain later."

When they were stood on their own and out of earshot, a conversation took place between them. It involved a lot of hand gestures and some pointing to the table to which the Sicilian had returned. Caroline apparently then agreed to leave. She spoke very briefly to her father and kissed her sister, but merely waved to Cecily as they walked away. The guests all looked to Roman to see if he would offer an explanation, to which all he would say was, "Apparently, they don't like cheese."

Cecily rose and came around to her husband's side of the table for a better explanation. Roman stood and whispered to her, "Ross has been trying to sell shares in his dodgy scheme to our friends and neighbours, and I've had enough of the pair of them. The guy who just spoke to Ross is my former-neighbour's brother: the one who persuaded Ross to leave Sicily in a hurry last time when he'd been trying to develop my farmland. He has just reminded that fool that the Sicilians can find him anywhere- maybe even New York? Between you and I, he's a pussycat. A gentle giant of a farmer. But he does make a very convincing Mafia enforcer."

Cecily might have appeared concerned by the method, but she was relieved at the outcome and seemed to conclude that the end justified the means.

"Don't let their greed and foolishness spoil our day, darling."

"Cecily, nothing could spoil this day. It's their loss. Hopefully, one day she will see that."

Alessandra had found herself sitting next to guests of the Albergo Diffuso. To her left was a man who looked more than seventy years old, perhaps older, but had a physique of someone forty. He also dressed like a much younger man, in casual but expensive-looking clothes. He seemed somehow familiar. His glamorous and much younger partner introduced herself and seemed pleased to meet Alessandra. He was either rude or thought that he did not need an introduction; both amounted to the same thing in Alessandra's eyes. He shook her hand and smiled, as though any honour was all hers.

Alessandra asked them both what they thought of Seborga, to which she responded in glowing terms, but he made no comment. Opposite her were two more English women who seemed desperate to chat with Alessandra and had a barrage of questions, including what it was like to be a princess. She discovered that Emma did something highly technical in the movie business and Helen was an actress when she could get parts, but a yoga instructor when she couldn't. They both said they thought Seborga would make a fantastic film set.

While the undemonstrative older man was checking phone messages, Alessandra caught Ben looking over at her. She gestured a thumb in the man's direction and then held her palms open as if to ask, 'who is this guy?' Ben laughed and made a gesture like he was playing an air-guitar whilst shaking his white hair as best she could. Alessandra now guessed he was in a rock band but thought it must be an older one that she was unfamiliar with. She was a few years younger than Ben and her career in restaurants had left her little time for hobbies, including popular music. Ben took a pen from his inside pocket, scribbled something on a paper napkin and passed it down the table via Selene.

When unfolded, it read: rock legend who played at Woodstock, Live Aid and Glastonbury. Ask him about Jimi Hendrix, Bob Dylan or Freddie Mercury. He's met them all.

Alessandra decided to keep up the pretence of ignorance a little longer and turned to the ageing rocker, asking, "So, you're a musician. Are you in the band that are playing later?"

The time-worn musician guessed her game and went along with it, answering, "Yeah, I'm with the band."

"Are you going to get up and sing later?"

"Well, I've already played with Prince, as well as for a prince and a princess at Live Aid, but this is my first royal lunch date. So, yes, I'll sing you a song or two."

Overhearing this conversation, Zeno now joined in with, "That's a great idea. I haven't played for any royalty at all."

Alessandra was now intrigued. "You're both in this band? Together?"

"Yep. The crazy rocker and the Ukrainian rapper. We're known as Shrink-Rap," the old musician said, teasing her further.

Alessandra was now unsure who was kidding who and turned to Kevin, the manager of the Albergo Diffuso, looking for clarity.

"It's strange but true. These two met at our Club and just hit it off. It's the strangest, but possibly best supergroup ever formed and for one royal command performance only. A rock 'n' roll legend and rhyme artist extraordinaire."

"Well, we are indeed honoured. Intrigued and honoured," Alessandra said, laughing, the others around her now joining in.

The continuing game of musical chairs had finally allowed Cecily to take the seat opposite Zeno, a moment that she had been relishing. She was surprised when he stood to greet her with what seemed like genuine enthusiasm before complimenting her on her dress and her beauty. The rapper thanked her for allowing him and his girlfriend to join in her wedding celebration. He concluded by wishing the newly married couple a long and happy life together. Although somewhat disarmed by this unexpected charm offensive, Cecily was determined to reprimand Zeno for nearly cutting her yacht in two.

"That is your boat moored near mine in Menton Harbour?" she said in an accusatory tone.

Feeling the mood change to one of confrontation, the rapper appeared to be weighing up the possible consequences before answering, "I'm guessing yours in the classy wooden ketch with teak decks and polished brass fittings moored at the end of the quay?"

Again, this was not the response that Cecily was expecting and yet she pressed on with her reprimand. "Yes, and it's still all in one piece, no thanks to your reckless seamanship."

Zeno looked stunned by this unexpected turn of events. He could see that Cecily was furious about something; however, he had no idea what that was.

"You are saying that my boat nearly ran into yours?"

"Yes, at full speed, at night and out in the open ocean. You could have killed us all and left us in the water."

"And where and when did this take place?" the rapper asked, himself now looking a little angry.

"A few weeks ago, about two miles south of San Remo," she replied.

Zeno stood up once again and made a small bow before saying, "I apologise unreservedly, however, I was not onboard my boat. I was touring in America until a few days ago. A delivery crew brought the boat from Genoa to Antibes where I had found a permanent berth for it. The boatbuilder recommended the captain, but I promise you that they will not be doing any more work for them or anyone else if I have my way."

Cecily now felt foolish for jumping to conclusions and for making her allegation so rudely and publicly. She had fallen into the trap that she often warned others of, 'judging books by their covers'. By allowing a stereotypical image of how she believed a rap star would behave, she fell well short of her own standards. Zeno had been charming and gracious, and she now realised that she had insulted him with her unfounded prejudices. She hoped that not too many people had *overheard* her and now wished the ground would swallow her up.

Seeing her extreme discomfort, Zeno leaned across the table and took her hand before beginning to improvise a rap. Very slowly and quietly he rhymed her name into a lyric which soon had the whole table captivated. Someone further down the table began to beat out a rhythm on the tabletop with their hands and Zeno raised his vocal volume.

By the time it ended with the words, "Cecily so silly that you're quick to judge me. Looks can be deceiving but you seem so lovely. There's motion in the ocean and it ain't the ruff sea. She snubbed me but look now she's gunna love me. Seen it in the stars say they call that astronomy. . ." Zeno's voice was drowned out by the cheering and clapping from the table.

"Zeno, you are a very gracious young man for letting me off the hook like that. I was rude and I apologise. I hope you will forgive me and that we might become friends. Before you leave Menton, you must come on board for drinks or dinner, or both."

"Sure. That'd be cool," Zeno replied, looking to his girlfriend for confirmation only to find her already nodding vigorously because the model knew exactly who Cecily was and all about her famous cosmetics brands.

Cecily thought she should move on while she still had some dignity remaining and squeezed in between Andrea and Roman. She wanted to warn Roman that she had met the rapper whose boat had nearly hit them, in case her husband bumped into him before she had a chance to explain. She didn't want Roman's Sicilian knifeman unleashed again.

"He a sweetheart. It was a hired-in delivery crew in charge of his boat that night off San Remo. Zeno was on tour in the USA and not even onboard. He is now mortified with embarrassment about what I told him and promises to see that those irresponsible idiots are never hired again."

Andrea added, "Yes, Zeno is not at all what you might expect, is he. All that macho posturing when he performs is just an act. He's an intelligent, sensitive guy when you get to know him. Did you know that his boat is designed to be upcycled?"

Roman and Cecily shook their heads in unison, apparently mystified by this concept. "Upcycled?" Cecily questioned.

"That is how I met him. The boat's designers contacted me to explain the idea that, at the end of its useful life, its double-skinned hull can be taken apart and upturned to make insulated portable buildings. They are strong but lightweight and can be easily transported to disaster areas or third world famine-struck places. The upper deck superstructure was demountable as another accommodation unit. All the interior fittings are reusable. It's the first boat of its type. An Italian innovation.

That's why I agreed to attend the launch."

Ben arrived, and Cecily stood to let him sit in her place at the table.

"Sit here, Ben. I want to go and chat to Alessandra and Renata."

"Ah, Ben, good, we have a chance to catch up on what's been happening," was Andrea's warm greeting.

Ben told the prime minister about the private investment he had raised through the crowd-farming scheme for the winery, and that his Rossese had won a bronze medal at a tasting in Monaco.

"Congratulations on both. I saw the label on the bottles that we have been drinking from. A richly deserved acknowledgement. It's a delicious wine."

"How are our eco-experiments going? Do we have any obvious winners or losers yet?" Andrea asked Ben.

"People are a little reticent to try the electric cars. I think they feel that there are just too many uncertainties for many older people. They harbour concerns about driving an electric car for the first time, insurance, running out of power and so on. It will take time."

Andrea thought for a while and suggested, "We need an early adopter. A trailblazer from the traditional community. What about Vincenzo? If people see him using them, they will feel it is Ok."

Ben said that he thought this was an excellent idea.

"Alessandra has been trying to be highly visible in buying the plastic-free loose products from the store. That has encouraged a few other villagers to try them, but there has been reluctance from many to giving up the well-advertised big brands."

"After seeing Alessandra's fabulous hair today, they should be queuing up to buy that loose shampoo," Andrea said.

Ben smiled and continued, "The school plastic survey that you visited has helped raise awareness in every home. Children are excellent at pestering parents when they become enthused about a subject."

Ben told the PM that he had spotted one unexpected phenomenon.

"French day-trippers have seen the price saving to be had and are driving over with their bottles to be refilled, staying to have lunch. They seem to have a keener eye for a bargain that our own citizens and are making it a reason for day out."

Andrea seemed sure things would turn around, saying, "The more people see others using it, the sooner they will be converted. We will get there."

Andrea acknowledged that he was aware that several of the other environmental initiatives would take longer to evaluate. However, he thought the early signs were very encouraging. He revealed that he was already beginning to think about a national roll-out of reduced tax on plastic-free packaged goods. In a recent government brainstorming session, his advisors had pointed out that such a policy also offered an advantage to many Italian producers over imported brands.

"In just a few short months, we have made more actual progress here in Seborga than the previous government did in years of just talking about it. You and Alessandra should be proud, Ben."

The handsome young prime minister was riding high on a tide of popularity. The polls suggested that if he held a snap election, he would considerably increase his existing majority, a situation almost unprecedented in a generation of Italian politics. Since the Second World War, Italy had seen sixty-six prime ministers come and go. Andrea had already beaten the average term served by them and showed no signs of losing his job just yet. Feeling full of good food and goodwill, helped by a slight buzz from Ben's Rossese, Andrea leaned back on his chair enjoying a rare moment of relaxation with people who had become his friends.

"So how does it feel to be married again, Roman?" he asked.

"It feels good, Andrea. Maybe you should try it?" he replied, casting a nod in the direction of Selene, who was deep in conversation with Alessandra and the two new brides.

Andrea looked over his shoulder and saw Selene, who looked radiant, and was reminded of his good fortune. Selene had splashed out some of the advance from her book to buy an expensive black silk, plunging neckline dress from a young Italian designer. It was split at each side and held together with straps, and the hem stopped just above the knee. Andrea had helped her choose it, saying, 'it was sexy yet sophisticated.' With her blonde hair and fair skin, it had undoubtedly gained many compliments from the men around the piazza.

"For what it's worth, you have my blessing, Andrea," Ben chipped in.

"Roman, there's nothing that would make me happier than to have Selene as my wife. I have been on the brink of proposing several times during the last year but with this crazy job, the relentless media attention, plus my son to think of. . .there never seems to be a good time."

34. TORTA NUZIALE MILLE-FEUILLE

It was time for the wedding speeches. Tom and Marius were ushering everyone back to their original seats. Despite the minor chaos caused by Andrea's suggestion of seat switching, during the lunch some unfounded prejudices had been debunked, a few stereotypes dismantled, and many new friends made.

The band had quietly slipped onto the stage to check their instruments and tap microphones in preparation for the first dance. The chefs, cooks and their student helpers were taking a much-needed break. They huddled together, smoking, like comrades moulded together by having survived the heat of battle. They discretely pointed out guests who they thought were sporting the best and worst fashions. The soldiers of the Alpini sweltered in the mid-afternoon heat but did not dare relax with their prime minister present.

Selene squeezed back onto the bench next to Andrea, just as Cecily was also taking her seat opposite. One of the bridesmaids brought Cecily's small bouquet over and placed it in front of her. As she did so, the young girl knocked over a glass of prosecco. It fell towards Selene's side of the table but did not break. Most of the liquid stayed on the surface of the table, but a little tipped over the edge onto Selene's lap. She stood quickly to shake off the droplets from her precious new dress.

Instinctively, Roman reached into his pocket for the handkerchief he always kept there and handed the cloth to Andrea. He patted the front of Selene's dress with it and then mopped up the remaining small patch on the table.

"No harm was done," Selene assured everyone as she sat back down.

Vincenzo was now on his feet about to give his speech. He looked more like a prisoner facing a firing squad, thought Ben. It was short and to the point, as everyone had expected. Fortunately, Roman's oratory skills were more refined, and he had some well-chosen words in praise of his new wife and their relatively new friends. Only Cecily noticed the merest hint of sadness in his words, momentarily speculating as to the likely cause.

Although he had tried to resist because he was tired of making speeches, Andrea had finally agreed to say a few words on behalf of all the guests. When the applause following Roman's speech died down, the prime minister pushed away the plate from which he had been eating wedding cake and got to his feet.

A hush settled as he did so. Andrea used the white cloth that Roman gave him to wipe the crumbs from his lips. As he did so, a small, shiny object fell from the unfolded napkin. As if in slow motion, the white gold band tumbled a couple of times in mid-air before it fell upright into Selene's as yet untouched dessert. There it sat, its single diamond sparkling in the bright sunshine, sending out shards of light like a beacon to those around.

Cecily saw the ring fall, as did Patsy, and Tom, who was sitting by his sister's side. Just as he looked like he was about to say something, Patsy kicked him under the table and his mouth closed again. When Tom looked across at her for an explanation she was gently shaking her head and mouthing 'no.' It was Cecily who spoke, leaving those who could not see in no doubt, spontaneously announcing, "An engagement ring. How fabulously clever."

First Selene, and then Andrea, followed her stare to the ring now sitting glinting in the whipped-cream-topped mille-feuille slice. Roman, who also had no idea where the ring had come from, looked at Andrea, raised his eyes to the heavens, shrugged his shoulders and offered,

"Now seems to be that good time you've been waiting for, hey Andrea?"

THE END

RECIPES FOR DISHES FEATURED IN THIS BOOK

BY ENRICA MONZANI

Enrica Monzani is a born and bred Ligurian food writer, photographer and cooking instructor. She is the lady behind the bilingual food blog www.asmallkitcheningenoa.com where she tells recipes and food stories from the Italian Riviera. She organises regional cooking classes for foreigners in her home kitchen in Genoa and online. In 2020 she launched a virtual Italian Riviera cooking course on the e-learning platform Udemy. She is currently working on her first Liguria cookbook.

LINGUINI WITH MUSSEL RAGÙ

Serves 4

Ingredients
2 kg of mussels
2 salted anchovies
1 clove of garlic
1 bunch of Italian flat parsley
30 g of pine nuts
8 tablespoons of extra virgin olive oil
Salt
350 g of linguini or spaghetti

Method
Put the mussels, shells cleaned, in a saucepan with high edges, cover with a lid and cook on a low heat until they are all open (about 5 minutes).

Set aside the broth they have released.

Remove the shellfish from the shells (keeping some whole aside to decorate) and chop them finely with a knife or with the mixer without reducing them in cream.

Chop garlic, anchovies and parsley together (keep a little parsley, chopped, aside to garnish the dish) and sauté in a shallow pan with the oil for a couple of minutes.

In the meantime, pound the pine nuts in the mortar, or chop them in a until you get a raw paste, and dilute with a ½ cup of cold water.

Add the pine nut milk to your soffritto and cook for 5 minutes.

Then, pour in the mussel broth set aside and the chopped muscles. Leave to simmer for 5 minutes or until the sauce has reached the right density. Add salt if necessary.

Cook the linguini in a big pan with plenty of salted water and drain al dente. Pour directly into the shallow pan with the sauce and sauté for a couple of minutes.

Serve pasta with a drizzle of raw extra-virgin olive oil, a handful of fresh chopped parsley, a grate of black pepper and garnish with a couple of whole mussels each.

PICAGGE VERDI
Serves 4

Ingredients:
1 cup of semolina flour
1 cup of all-purpose flour
2 eggs
2 cups of fresh spinach
A small pinch of salt
Water to taste
Clean and dry spinach, blanch for 2-3 minutes, squeeze very hard and blend.

Method:
Pour the flours on a flat surface in a mound and make a well. Crack the eggs and pour spinach puree in the centre and sprinkle the salt over.

Beat eggs and veg with a fork. Then start adding flour to the mix, gently digging the side of the mixture with the fork tips.

When the dough commences to "stay together," start kneading and pressing it with the lower part of your palm many times.

If it remains too dry and it flakes, add a small quantity of water by just wetting your palms. Repeat if needed until you get a dough that's soft and elastic.
Let it rest under a cup or covered in plastic wrap at least for 30 minutes.

Roll out the dough on a well-floured working surface with a pasta machine or rolling pin at about 2 mm thickness (like a credit card) and then cut in strips ½ inch wide.

Boil in a big pan full of salty water for 7-8 minutes. Drain and season.

Remember always to save a cup of pasta water to add to the seasoning in order to avoid your pasta drying out.

TURLE
Serves 4

Ingredients:

<u>For fresh pasta</u>
300 g 00 flour
1 egg
100 ml water

<u>For the stuffing</u>
450 g potatoes
200 g of toma cheese (or substitute mild cheddar)
2 egg yolks
3 tablespoons of grated Parmesan cheese
4-5 fresh mint leaves

<u>For the dressing</u>
50 g of butter
Grated Parmesan cheese to taste
4-5 fresh mint leaves
Pepper

For the stuffing
Wash potatoes and boil in abundant water. Drain, peel and mash with a potato masher.
When still hot, add toma cheese cut into small pieces, Parmesan cheese, 2 yolks and 4-5 finely chopped mint leaves. Season with salt and pepper and let cool.

For the fresh pasta
Place the flour on a working surface and make a well in the centre. Crack eggs inside and pour in water. Start working

the liquids with a fork, adding the flour little by little, making it fall from the outer edges. When all the flour has been mixed and the pasta starts to stick together, work it with your hands for 5-10 minutes until a smooth and elastic dough is obtained.
Make a ball, cover with a cup and let it rest for 30 minutes.

For shaping turle and serving them
Roll out the dough with a rolling pin until about 2 millimetres thick (leave the other half covered).
With an 8 cm diameter pasta cutter or with a glass, cut discs in the dough, and in the centre of each disc place a nut of filling. Fold the pasta in half and sealthe edges with your fingers. With the tips of a fork, further seal the edges, creating a decorative motif. Arrange the turle on a well-floured surface. Repeat with the remaining dough and filling.

Bring a big pan of salted water to boil and cook turle for about 8 minutes.

Meanwhile, in a shallow pan melt butter, add chopped mint and let it flavour for 5 minutes.

Drain turle with a skimmer and lay them in the pan with the butter, mix very gently and add the Parmesan cheese.
Before serving, sprinkle with some more Parmesan cheese, some pepper, and decorate with few fresh mint leaves.

SCIUMETTE

Serves 4

Ingredients:

5 eggs
1 litre of whole milk
100 g of caster sugar
60 g of pistachios, chopped
1 tablespoon of flour
A pinch of powdered cinnamon

Prepare the floating islands first. Pour the milk in a saucepan, keeping half a glass aside, place it on the stove and bring to a light boil.

Meanwhile, separate the egg yolks from the whites and whip the whites until stiff, adding 50 grams of sugar. They should be pretty firm and shiny.

Pour the mixture into tablespoons (4/5 at a time) in the simmering milk. The floating island will swell slightly. Turn them gently with a spoon. Cook them for about 1 minute or until they are firm.

Remove with the skimmer and lay on absorbent kitchen paper. Repeat the operation until all the whites have been cooked.

Prepare the cream: remove the saucepan with the milk from the heat, add the remaining sugar and the beaten egg yolks and put aside. In a pan, heat the half glass of milk left aside, add the chopped pistachios (keep aside a couple of teaspoons to garnish the dish), cook for 2-3 minutes, stirring from time to time, remove from the heat, strain and add to the cream.

Put the cream back on the stove and on a very low heat let it cook, always stirring until the cream veils the spoon.

Pour the cream into the serving cups, place on top a couple of floating islands and sprinkle with cinnamon and chopped pistachios.

CASTAGNACCIO
(Chestnut pie)
Serves 4

Ingredients:
3 ¾ cups (400 grams) of chestnut flour
3 tablespoons (45 grams) of sugar
A pinch of salt
2 ½ cups (625 millilitres) of cold water
3 tablespoons of extra virgin olive oil
½ cup (100 grams) of golden raisins
¼ cup (35 grams) of pine nuts
1 teaspoon of fennel seeds

Method:
Soak the raisins in warm water for 15 minutes.

Combine chestnut flour, sugar, and salt in a bowl. Add water, little by little, stirring to avoid lumps. The batter should look like pancake batter. Depending on the quality of the flour, you may need a little more or a little less water than called for to obtain this consistency.
In the meantime, preheat the oven to 350° F (180° C) and drain raisins.

Pour extra virgin olive oil in a round baking pan of approx. 8-inch (20 cm) diameter. Pour the batter inside. It should be no more than 1/3-inch-thick (about 1 centimetre). Evenly scatter over the drained raisins and pine nuts and finish with fennel seeds and the rest of the olive oil.

Bake for about 30 minutes or until you see little cracks appear all over the top. Do not overbake or it will become very dry. Let cool in the pan then slice and serve.

CAVAGNETTI
Serves 4

Ingredients:
700 g of all-purpose flour
200 g of granulated sugar
8 eggs (preferably white)
3 egg whites
200 g of butter
30 g of baking powder
1 untreated lemon
½ glass of whole milk

Method:
White or coloured dragee (coloured sugar sprinkles) to decorate.
Sift the flour together with the yeast in a large bowl or in the mixer. Separately, beat 2 whole eggs with the sugar and the butter previously melted. Beat 2 egg whites until stiff and add them to the eggs and sugar, stirring gently. Pour into the bowl with flour and baking powder. Add grated lemon peel. Mix gently adding, if necessary, some warm milk until a soft and smooth dough is obtained.

Roll out part of the dough with a rolling pin up to a thickness of about 1/3 inch and cut out (with the help of a cookie cutter or a cup) 6 disks of 8 cm (about 3 inches) in diameter. Place one egg in the centre of each disc. With the remaining dough, shape very thin rolls that you will place cross-shaped on the eggs until they touch the disc of pasta. Then prepare other thicker rolls, about a finger in diameter, and weave them two at a time to create a braid that you will place around the egg after brushing the surface of the disc of pasta with a little water to help it adhere well.

Preheat the oven to 190°C (375°F–Gas Mark 5)
Whisk the remaining egg white and spread it on your Cavagnetti with a cake brush.

Place the Cavagnetti on a baking tray covered with parchment paper and cook for about 20 minutes or until golden. If you see that the surface darkens too quickly, cover them with a sheet of parchment paper. Once baked, sprinkle them with white or coloured baking candies or dragee, making them adhere, if necessary, with a little sugar syrup.

RECIPES RELATING TO THE FORAGING SCENE IN CHAPTER 18
(from various sources)

Navelwort Omelette
(Umbilicus Rupestris or Navel of Venus)
Serves 2

Ingredients:
Navelwort leaves
4 eggs
Potatoes
1 white onion
4 tablespoons of plain yogurt
Extra virgin olive oil
Butter

Boil some potatoes for about 15 minutes, or until slightly soft but still retaining their shape.

Beat four eggs with four tablespoons of yogurt and let it rest.
In a pan, fry a chopped onion with butter and extra virgin olive oil, add the Navelwort leaves, cover it and cook for a few minutes.

At the end, add a boiled potato cut into thin discs.
Pour the beaten egg with yogurt and fry all together. Serve with other boiled roots as you like.

Sorrel Soup
(Rumex Acetosa)
Serves 2

Ingredients:
200g of young Sorrel leaves
50g of butter
1 spoon of flour
2 spoons of finely chopped flat leaf parsley
2 leaves of rosemary
200cl vegetable broth
2 egg yolks
100g cream or milk

Wash, dry and roughly cut the Sorrel, and put that in a pan with already melted butter.
Cook slowly for 5 minutes. Add the flour, parsley and rosemary and mix gently.

In another pan, heat the broth, add the egg yolk and mix with a fork until you get a smooth consistency. Add the Sorrel, mix and serve hot without boiling.

Mallow Macaroni
(Malva Silvestris)

Ingredients:
20 Mallow leaves (available dry online from Amazon)
30 g of cream cheese
2 tablespoons of parmesan cheese
Macaroni pasta

Choose 20 mallow leaves, wash them well, blanch them in hot water and dry them keeping them warm.

In a pan, heat 30g of fresh creamy cheese, add two spoons of grated Parmesan cheese and mix until the cheese is completely melted. Add the mallow leaves and mix until a homogeneous cream is obtained.

Add this cream to macaroni and decorate the plates with mallow flowers.

The same sauce can also be used together with boiled potatoes.

Apricale
(village above Doceaqua)
Walnut Pasta Sauce

Ingredients:
125 grams of unshelled walnuts
125 grams of cream
parsley, basil
1 clove of garlic

Remove shells from the walnuts and place in boiling water for a few minutes and then peel them. Put them in a mortar, adding the garlic, basil and parsley and cream. Smash and mix it till you get a creamy sauce. If this is too dense, it can be diluted with a drizzle of extra virgin olive oil.

Ideal for dressing macaroni or simply on toasted bread.

Salsa di Badalucco
(town between Taggia and Triora)
Pasta Sauce

Ingredients:
40g of pine nuts
15g of crushed capers
75g breadcrumbs
Red wine vinegar
1 hard-boiled egg yolk
A pinch of parsley
3 olives in brine
Half a clove of garlic
Extra virgin olive oil
1 lemon

Pound the pine nuts in a mortar with the capers, the breadcrumbs soaked in vinegar, the yolk, the parsley, the pulp of the olives and the garlic in a mortar. Add the extra virgin olive oil and the juice of one lemon.

Perfect with pasta or boiled vegetables.

ACKNOWLEDGEMENTS

Although my eclectic career did include a decade of content creation and curating, I am a relative newcomer to creative writing. Therefore, *Recipe For A Nation*, and my two proceeding novels, have only been made possible because of the seemingly inexhaustible (I hope) generosity of people like the following. To any others, whose brains and/or pockets have been picked in assembling my stories, but who have been omitted from this list, I offer my apologies and thanks.

Linda Bulloch, Diane Kane, James Butterfield,

Valerio Dogliotti, Chris Noble, David Penman, Fabio Mazzon,

Gillian McNally, Scott Penman, Mike Brough,

Enrica Monzani–A Small Kitchen In Genoa

Alysia Sutcliffe–The Yorkshire Forager

BIOGRAPHY

Photo courtesy: Kaidi-Katariin Knox

A former magazine editor and university lecturer, James is now an author dividing his time between Northumberland in England and Liguria in Italy. It was his discovery of the ancient Italian village of Seborga, its historical connection to the Knights Templar, its unique culture and the traditional cuisine that was the inspiration for his first book, Cooking up a Country. A follow-up, Unlikely Pairings arrived in 2020. A third book, Recipe For A Nation, in what has become the Seborga Series was published in 2021. Keen interest in artisan food and wine, as well as environmental issues, are reflected in Vasey's writing.

Special thanks to Stelios Haji-Ioannou, founder of EasyJet.

At a point in my life when times were hard, the advent of low-cost airlines still made it possible for me to explore Italy. Since that first Easyjet flight, over twenty years ago, barely a year has passed without visiting this beautiful part of the world. These experiences have broadened the horizons of our children and now our grandchildren. It is serendipitous that my discovery of Liguria has also led to my writing three novels set in the area and that one of these has found its way into the hands of Stelios Haji-Ioannou (pictured), the man who made it all possible.

Thank you
for reading about
Ben and Alessandra's
adventures in,
Recipe For A Nation,

If you enjoy
please write a review on
Amazon or Goodreads.

I urge you to read the two preceding books
in the Seborga Series
Cooking Up A Country
and
Unlikely Pairings

Both available on Amazon
Hardcover, Paperback and Ebook

Follow us on

www.facebook.com/jamesvaseyauthor
to view a video and photographs
of Seborga
as well as regular news about
the culture, food and wine of the region.

Sign-up for our mailing list
to receive updates on the story,
free tasters of more to come and
exclusive invitations to related events.
Enter your email at
www.jamesvasey.co.uk

PRIVACY: If you provide us with your email address by subscribing to this service, we will only use to periodically send the type of information described above. We will not share your details with any third party unless you expressly give us permission to do so. You will be able to unsubscribe from this mailing list at any time.

Printed in Great Britain
by Amazon